The Only Heart That Matters

Only in Goose Hollow
Book 2

Lisa Shelby

Lisa Shelby Books, LLC

THE ONLY HEART THAT MATTERS

BY

LISA SHELBY

The Only Heart That Matters Playlist

Ain't She ~ Adam Doleac
Unfair ~ jnr.
Shivers ~ Ed Sheeran
Closer ~ SIX60
Thicc As Thieves ~ Lauren Alaina & Lainey Wilson
Yeah! ~ Usher feat. Lil' Jon & Ludacris
Just the Way ~ Blanco Brown & Parmalee
Dissolve ~ Abosfacto
Every Side of You ~ Vance Joy
You Should Probably Leave ~ Chris Stapleton
One and Only ~ Adele
High ~ Stephen Sanchez
"Slut!" ~ Taylor Swift
Adore You ~ Harry Styles
Tiptoeing ~ Hope Tala
Crash My Party ~ Luke Bryan
My My My! ~ Troye Sivan
Lights Out ~ Ryan Hurd
Cry ~ Zak Abel
The One ~ Taking Back Sunday
Light On In the Kitchen ~ Ashley McBryde
I Can Do It with A Broken Heart ~ Taylor Swift
Take Forever (Hally's Song) ~ Cooper Alan
Palladium ~ Greyson Chance
Life With You ~ Kelsey Hart

Listen on Spotify while you read:
https://spoti.fi/4bnq2oF

*For all of you who so often sacrifice yourselves for those you love.
I hope you know you are worthy of the same love and sacrifice in return.*

Reader Note

This book contains explicit sexy times, profanity, a flashback to military combat and the discussion of familial loss.

Chapter One

Angus

Something's off.

It's in the way she twists her granny's silver band around her finger four times and then takes it off and switches it to her ring finger on her left hand. Four more twists, and then she moves it back to her right hand.

The birthday boy has opened his presents. He's shoveled handfuls of cake into his face; I say face and not mouth because he's two and messy, and as per usual is the cutest damn kid I've ever seen. The house is drowning in balloons and truck decorations, because trucks are Sawyer's current obsession.

It's been a hell of a party.

A joyous occasion.

So why is his mom faking it?

I've known Mia Powell since the day she was born. Our moms are best friends and I was two, just like the aforementioned birthday boy, when she was born. I'm pretty sure I've been watching her ever since.

Always from the sidelines, but nonetheless watching.

I've seen her happy.

This isn't it.

The usual light in her bright blue eyes is non-existent. The rosy under glow that spreads across her fair complexion when she's experiencing joy is nowhere to be found.

These things may go unnoticed by everyone else. Heck, she's a single mom, after all, and likely exhausted. But the ring gives her away. Her fidgeting tells me she's upset, or maybe nervous about something.

It feels all too familiar.

The last time I saw her like this was two and a half years ago. The day she announced at family dinner she was pregnant. That late spring night on my parents' deck is a memory that will stay with me forever.

The soft orange of the setting sun painted the sky, acting as her backdrop as she sat at my parents' outdoor dinner table. She was wearing a white cotton summer dress with a chunky blue sweater draped over her shoulders. Breathtaking, as always, but the light in her eyes was missing, her porcelain skin a ghostly white. She hadn't touched her food and couldn't leave her shoulder-length raven hair alone. She pushed it behind her ears, then pulled it back in a low bun, then let it loose around her shoulders again. And that ring of hers moved from one hand to the other more times than I could count.

But when my sister, Daisy, cleared her throat to get everyone's attention, Mia sat up straight with the posture of a soldier and grabbed my baby sister's hand so hard her knuckles turned white.

Daisy said that Mia had something to tell us, warning every person at the table with the venom in her eyes that if we didn't take whatever news Mia was about to share the right way, there would be hell to pay.

I worried she might be sick as peaked as she looked and as serious as Daisy was behaving. But she wasn't ill.

She was pregnant.

The moment she shared her news, something shifted in her. An iron-willed, protective nature settled over her as she explained she was only a few months along, but already the mama bear in her was strong.

She defiantly refused to tell us who the father was and insisted she would be fine having and raising the baby on her own. She made it clear she was a willing participant, claiming nobody had hurt her. The father simply wasn't interested.

The news hit me harder than it should have. Some asshole had left her to raise their child alone. It lit a burning rage inside me to find out who he was.

My anger was all-consuming.

I couldn't flee from my parents' property fast enough. The need to escape sent me spiraling. My desperation to know his identity, suffocating. But it was the sinking feeling that her news solidified something I already knew.

She would never be mine.

Coward that I was, I lied and said they needed me at the bar. I was gone before dessert was served.

I drove my truck down the highway faster than was safe and within twenty minutes of walking through the bar door, I had a blonde twenty-something bent over the leather chair in my apartment above the bar.

That night, I wasn't ready to acknowledge the reason my best friend's sister, my mother's goddaughter, and my little sister's best friend being pregnant elicited such a powerful reaction from me.

After my angry drive and fast fuck were over the monster inside me was still at large. He was on the warpath. For a solid week I drank, I worked out, and I fucked, trying to get her and the reason I was so upset out of my head and my heart.

It didn't work.

The truth of the matter is, I've been out of my mind in love with Mia Powell for most of my life.

The problem is she's off-limits.

Not to mention, she doesn't see me that way.

After all these years, I've gotten good at keeping my feelings at bay, but that night they all rushed to the surface. A blind rage different from any I had experienced before, and trust me, I had felt rage many times before, took control.

Thinking back to that night makes me wonder if that's what's gotten under her skin. Is the asshole deadbeat who'd knocked her up here today? Is she nervous and looking as uncomfortable as she is because he's right here in plain sight? Would he have the balls to show up?

I'll never understand how a man could be such a prick he won't acknowledge his own child.

It's a small town. There's no reason to keep him a secret if he isn't someone we all know.

Scouring the room for someone out of place, I come up empty. Most of the men here, other than my brother, Callen, and his best friend, Owen, have been old enough for AARP magazine subscriptions for years now.

Nobody fits the bill.

Shifting my focus back to Mia, I note how different she looks today than she did making her announcement at my parents' table. It's not because her hair now hangs down the middle of her back and is littered with caramel highlights. It's that the indignant defiance she used as a protective shell back then is no longer needed. Her insecurity, which she did her best to hide from those who knew her so well, is no longer present. She is a spectacular mother, and she has nothing to prove to anyone. It looks good on her.

She has this sexy indifference about her that fucking calls to me. It's a call I can't answer but is always buzzing in the atmosphere when she's nearby. But right now, I want to know what has her so on edge. The need to take away her worries so intense it's building pressure in my chest.

"Can we get all the Powells and McKinnons in the living room for a quick picture, please?" her mom, Joy, yells over the crowd.

Mia lifts Sawyer from his spot on the floor, where he had been playing with a pile of toys, and I follow her to the other room.

Grace, who owns the cafe that Mia works at, squishes us all together so we fit on her phone's camera screen and says, "Okay, everyone say *family!*"

Everyone shouts "Family!" through their smiles.

However, I can't quite get the word out, but I do plaster a fake smile to my face because I am glad to be here celebrating my favorite two-year-old on his birthday, but I refuse to think of his mom as family.

We aren't blood relatives, but I would do anything for her just like I would for my mom, brothers, and sister. But she isn't like a sister to me.

She never will be.

Chapter Two

Mia

The biting cold air burns my lungs, but I relish the life it brings to my body. Anything is better than the numbness I've had to enlist today to push away my feelings. The crowd inside the house is overwhelming, and now is not the time to let myself break down.

Leaning on the railing of my parents' deck, I look over their acre of land and Goose Hollow Lake. Lifting my face to the sky, I let the near-freezing air cool my heated face. Sure, it means I'll need to apply a healthy dose of moisturizer tonight, but it's worth it to escape the facade going on inside.

"I wish you were here, big brother. Not only would Sawyer be your favorite person, but man, do I need you right now," I say to the gray winter clouds above missing my brother, Chris, more today than I have in a while.

My baby boy is two years old today. It should be a joyous occasion, but everything about this party feels like a farce.

My parents made sure of that.

I don't even know who they are anymore. I get that they're entering the next season of their lives, and they deserve to live it to the fullest, however, and wherever that may be. But Florida? And by the end of the month?

Looking out over the lake, childhood memories filled with laughter fill my head. "Chris, they're selling our home. A few weeks from now, it will all be gone. Can you even imagine life without this place?"

They've turned Sawyer's birthday party into a going away party, only nobody knows that's what this really is. They sent separate invitations once they decided they were moving without even telling me. I didn't find out until a customer at the restaurant said they couldn't wait for the party. The party I hadn't invited them to. Half the people here have never even met Sawyer.

One of those people being Rhen Mitchell. How that man wiggles his way into everyone's life, I'll never know. He doesn't deserve to share the same air as my son. Every time I see Angus or Callen talking to him, it makes me nauseous. Why are Daisy and I the only people who see the real him?

The whoosh of the back sliding glass door opening and closing means my momentary peace and quiet is coming to an end, but when Daisy and Angus place themselves on either side of me, mimicking the way I'm leaning on the railing, relief finds me.

Next to Sawyer, these are my two favorite people.

"Aren't you cold, Goof?" Angus asks, calling me by my childhood nickname.

What can I say? I did a mean Goofy impression when I was five, and it stuck. But to be honest, only the McKinnon brothers, mostly Angus, still call me by that name. We're all in our thirties. You would think he would have let it go by now, but no such luck. So, I've learned to accept it. There are worse things in life than a childhood nickname sticking for a lifetime.

"Nah, it feels good out here. There are too many people inside. I needed to cool off."

"Okay, I'm glad it's not just me," Daisy says on a puff of white air. "I mean, who are all those people and why are they at Sawyer's birthday party?"

"Today is a mess, isn't it?"

Angus leans his shoulder against mine, giving me a nudge. "It's not a mess, but something is clearly up. Everything okay with you?"

I look over my shoulder to make sure it's just the three of us before turning my attention back to Angus to answer his question, but he's so close I forget what he asked for a heartbeat. His light brown eyes are piercing me with genuine concern, and his pillowy lower lip is near enough to kiss. But this is Angus McKinnon, and to him, I will always be Goof.

Nothing more. Nothing less.

I pushed my unrequited love for him aside years ago, but every now and then, when he's this close, well, my heart forgets I don't feel those things for him anymore.

Hoping to find my bearings, I look straight ahead over the acre of snow-covered grass that leads to the rocky shoreline of the lake I've been fortunate enough to live on for most of my life. How the ducks and geese float along the surface in this weather still amazes me even after three decades of feeding them from our dock.

But this won't be my view for long.

"My parents sold the property and they're moving to Florida. They have to be out by the end of the month."

"I'm sorry, what?" Daisy asks shocked, her mouth agape.

"Yep, they said they didn't want to overshadow Sawyer's birthday, so they aren't telling anyone yet, but you'd think this was their going away party with all the people they invited."

"When did they decide they were moving to Florida? This is news to me." Daisy straightens, settling her hands on her hips. "Does our mom know?"

Their mom, Sharon, and my mom have been best friends since they were kids and raised us all as one big, happy family.

"I don't think so. They met with a realtor just to get an idea of what the property was worth for when the time came, but a few weeks later their agent called and said she had a buyer who was offering well over what they would likely put the property up for. She said it was the offer of a lifetime. The only catch... they have to be out by the end of the year." I look at the nonexistent watch on my wrist. "And since it's nearly the middle of December, the end of the year is just two and a half weeks away. Still, they couldn't pass it up." My voice is shaking now, the cold finally settling in.

Angus shrugs off his dark gray Carhart jacket and drapes it over my shoulders without a word. The clean smell of soap and whatever it is that is uniquely Angus, along with the warmth of his body still inside the jacket, wraps around me like a warm blanket.

"Oh, sweetie. I'm so sorry," Daisy says, putting an arm around me.

"I don't know what we're going to do. I seriously doubt the new owners are going to let us stay in the barndominium. And my shifts at the restaurant sure won't cover rent anywhere around town."

This isn't who I am. Being a thirty-three-year-old living in a barndominium on her parents' property is not what I dreamed of. I've taken care of myself and lived on my own since the day I left for college. Right out of school, I took a job as a medical assistant for several years. While working full time as an MA, I applied to nursing school, got in, and did well. After graduation, I was lucky enough to score a paid internship with a clinic in San Francisco. It was my dream job, and I felt like I had taken life by the balls. I'd been on top of the world.

A week later, a positive pregnancy test changed everything. I became a single mom who needed the support of my family. Instead of staying in California, I moved home. My parents have been wonderful but finding employment in my field in a small town isn't easy, so I've been working shifts as a server at a local cafe to make ends meet.

"We'll figure it out," Daisy says as if my problem is her problem. I'm not sure what I would do without her. "You can crash at my place if you need to. It's small, but we can make it work for a bit."

"Well, there is an opportunity, but it's too good to be true," I say, the new shake to my voice because of the excitement I'm trying to tamp down.

"Do tell," my best friend, says blowing in her hands before rubbing them together to warm up.

"A couple of doctors from San Francisco are opening a new clinic in Bend and they need medical assistants and nurses. They provide paid insurance and free day care on-site."

"Mia, that sounds perfect!" Daisy says, excited.

"Right? But that's not even all of it. *They* reached out to *me*. Apparently, one of my professors put them in touch with the doctor I did my internship with who gave me rave reviews. They asked me to apply for one of the nursing positions and I did."

"Goof, this is great news! So, why do you sound so down?" Angus asks, still so close, his breath tickles my cheek. I don't dare turn to look at him.

"Well, it's too good to be true, isn't it? A job in my field of study, health insurance, and day care. There's just no way it will work out. Have you met me? Does this sound like something that would happen to me? Besides, the interview is a week from Monday. And of course, my car took a shit yesterday and needs a new driveshaft and who knows what else. The parts won't be here until later next week. My parents will be in Portland for Dad's doctor's appointment, and I can't borrow either of their cars because they are monsters who only drive stick shifts. And as we all know I don't. So, I'll take that as a sign from the universe that this job's not meant to be."

Daisy pulls her phone out of her pocket, searching the calendar on her phone. "Shoot, I'll be in Pendleton with meetings starting at 8am, otherwise you know I would take you or let you borrow my car."

My high from their excitement at this opportunity

crashes and burns. "Don't worry—" I start, but Angus interrupts me.

"I'll take you."

"What?"

"I'll take you. Just tell me what time to pick you up."

"Seriously?" I ask, thinking I must have heard him incorrectly.

"Seriously," he confirms.

I squeal and pull him into a hug, too excited to take the time to think about how good he feels pressed against my body.

"Thank you so much! I'll figure out a sitter for Sawyer and then I guess I'll be interviewing for my dream job!"

Angus's big coat bounces around me, the snow crunching under my boots as I jump up and down in excitement.

"Don't worry about a sitter. I'll hang out with him while you do your thing."

Wait. What?

"You're going to babysit Sawyer?" Daisy asks, sounding skeptical her brother is up to the task, while I stare at him with my mouth hanging open.

"Nah, we're gonna hang out. There's a difference."

"Are you sure?" I whisper on a cloud of winter air.

"Yep."

My voice is still small when I accept his offer. "Thank you."

He puts his arm around my shoulders. "I got you, Goof."

Chapter Three

Angus

Threatening my manhood if I didn't comply, my older brother, Callen, made me promise to take the night off. I'm not allowed to step behind the bar tonight. A promise is a promise, even if all I want to do is hurdle the damn thing to put a barrier between myself and the dark-haired beauty standing across from me.

Mia's dark hair hangs in long curls down her back. A second ago, someone yelled her name and when she turned, her hair whipped around and fell over one of her shoulders. Something about the sight has my pants suddenly feeling too small. Throw in the way her bright blue eyes sparkle with amusement, mixed with her killer smile, and you've got one toxic combination, even if it's not aimed at me.

I'm a goner.

Every time she smiles, she does me in.

As the owner of The House, an old fire station I purchased after leaving the military and transformed into a bar and restaurant downstairs and an apartment upstairs—though the women in my life insist I call it a *loft* with its open one-room floor plan—I can usually hide out behind the bar and pour drinks to distract myself when Mia's in the building. I've become an expert at finding reasons to keep my distance when she's here.

Before Sawyer was born, I ended many a night screwing some random woman whose name I would never remember to rid myself of the built-up tension from watching Mia dance with one too many cowboys for my liking. Since Sawyer, she's only been in a handful of times, making my life a hell of a lot easier.

Thankfully, the sound of beer bottles loudly clinking together steals my attention. I gladly take the opening to stop torturing myself by watching Mia. Turning, I'm not surprised to see my brother's best friend, Owen, standing on a chair, bottles in hand.

"Ladies and gentlemen, and I use those terms loosely, can I please have your attention?"

Our group of friends and family stop talking and throwing darts to hear what the best man has to say.

"Tonight, we are here to celebrate our friends Callen and Charlotte, *or* as her friends call her, Charlie, as they have one of their last nights of freedom before they join themselves together for eternity. Usually, they would each have their own parties and go to their respective strip clubs, but not these two. It will come as no surprise to any of you that they just can't get enough of each other. So here they are together as they say goodbye to the carefree life of singledom." He rolls his eyes in fake exasperation. "We get it. You're in looove. But you could have had one night apart." He winks in the ridiculously happy couple's direction as they laugh along with the rest of us.

As usual, Owen soaks up the attention of the crowd and they all laugh at him, including Mia. So much for giving myself a break. I can't help but watch her when she's beaming like she has been tonight. I haven't seen her smile this much in a long time. It feels good to see her happy, and I know she isn't into Owen, so more smiles aimed at someone other than me doesn't bother me. As long as she's having a good time, all is right in my world.

"Charlie, you do know the sexy is gonna wear off in a couple of months, right? He'll be belching and rubbing his bare belly after a night of beer and sausage in no time. That sex appeal of his is gonna fade into oblivion. Mark my words."

Owen is an idiot in the best possible way. He even has me laughing. And that's something I don't do often these days.

"But before things go south, let's all lift a glass to the happy couple and their current state of blissful love." We all raise our glasses as instructed. "In all seriousness, we love you two and we all wish you the best. Now, let's drink and dance and drink some more! Oh, and ladies, I'll be giving lap dances in the back booth at 9pm. Please form a line to the left and no fighting!"

My sister and Mia roll their eyes at his antics but can't help but laugh at the nonsense that is Owen Swift.

While my brother and his fiancée accept hugs and hand-shakes from friends, the volume of the music goes up as the house lights go down. The first song is a line dance that has the crowd gathering in the open space, usually filled with tables and chairs, that's converted to a dance floor after 8pm. That's when the fun begins.

"Gus, thanks for letting us use your fine establishment for this evening's festivities. It's been a while since you've been on this side of the bar. It looks good on you," Owen yells over the music, clamping his hand on my shoulder.

"Of course. I wouldn't want them to go anywhere else. This was where they got back together, after all. Seems full circle."

"That was what? Five or six months ago, they sure aren't wasting any time."

I shrug. "I guess when you know, you know."

"I guess so." His tone changes, like he knows exactly what I'm talking about, except he hasn't been as fortunate as Cal.

Interesting.

We watch the crowd dancing in sync and my eyes drift to Mia as her ass sways side to side, making it impossible not to watch her. Nobody else on the floor moves like her. She's always been impossible not to watch when she's dancing. She looks free and happy. It's a nice change from the sadness and stress she had last Sunday at Sawyer's birthday party.

As she told me and Daisy about her parents selling the house, her voice shook. I wasn't sure if it was from the cold or her nerves, but I had to do something. So I offered her my jacket and wasn't that a colossal mistake? Not only did seeing her in it give me a semi, but I swear I can still smell her on it. I may just buy a new one, because I'm never washing this one again.

The song ends and the bride and groom's requested playlist continues to play and everyone, who hadn't been line dancing, including me, join in to sing along and shake our asses to the party song we all know by heart. Yes, even me. Soon Garth Brooks croons about his friends in low places, we all throw our arms around each other and sing along.

This. This right here is why I love being from a small town.

There's nothing like the camaraderie and comfort that comes with knowing pretty much everyone in the room. I fucking love it. I can't lie, though. There are times the town feels a little too small. More times than I can count, I've wished everyone wasn't in my business, or that I could have a moment of peace, but right now is not one of those times. Nights like tonight are why I came back home after my enlistment was over.

Back then, everything had fallen into place. When I was little, I dressed up as a fireman for Halloween for three years running. I had always been obsessed with fire trucks and fire houses growing up, so when the old county fire station came up for sale, the idea of buying it and turning it into The House was a no-brainer.

The loft upstairs that I use as a second home was a bonus. I could have made it a two-story business, but it was nice to have a place to stay while I built my house at the ranch. With help from Cal and some buddies, I remodeled the bar, updated the electrical and plumbing, and changed the upstairs from barracks style living to an open concept loft. Next on the to-do list is to upgrade the electrical and plumbing upstairs and maybe rent it out one day when I'm ready to move to the ranch full-time. The bar is doing well, but a little extra income never hurt anybody.

Many have asked why I didn't become a firefighter after my enlistment, but being a part of the fire department is like being a part of another extended family. The men and women of a firehouse form bonds that can't be explained. Just like the bonds I had in the military.

I lost a lot of that family in the Corps.

The pain of that loss is something that continues to weigh on my soul.

I can't lose another person on my watch.

Losing my dad a year ago was almost more than I could take. Another hurt that still hasn't gone away. I'm not sure it ever will. My immediate family, that includes Mia, her little boy and her parents, and my remaining military family are all I need. Throw in the town of Goose Hollow and that's more than enough.

A slow two-step comes on, the crowd thins, and Rhen Mitchell taps Mia on the shoulder to ask her to dance. He's met with a look of disgust.

Humor dances over Rhen's face, as though her reaction comes as no surprise to him, but she doesn't budge.

Whoa.

What is that all about?

My body moves of its own accord and before I know it, Mia's hand is in mine and I'm pulling her to the middle of the dance floor. My eyes lock with Rhen's. "Sorry, she promised the first two-step to me."

"Whatever," he says. "Maybe next time." He chuckles as though the last twenty seconds were nothing if not entertaining for him. Seemingly unbothered, he walks away.

The moment we're out of earshot she releases a heavy sigh. "Thanks for the save, but you don't have to dance with me."

She turns to walk away, but I'll be damned if I'm

letting her go now. I'm not passing up a rare opportunity like this. Not only to be this close to her, but the chance to be there for her if she needs me. Her parents are moving and she's a single mom with all the complications that brings. If Rhen is pissing her off, I'm more than happy to intervene.

I spin her back around to face me, not missing the surprise in her eyes.

"Why not?" I ask, my other hand settling on her shoulder as I start to move us around the floor. She flawlessly falls into step with me. "You don't want to dance with me, Goof?"

I use her nickname as a reminder to myself that she is my sister's best friend and completely off-limits, because damn, she feels nice in my arms.

"Well, no, it's not that." Her cheeks pink. "I just didn't want you to feel like you had to."

"It's my pleasure, besides I wanted to talk to you about Monday. Are you excited about your big interview?" It's not the first question I want to ask, but I can tell she doesn't want to talk about Rhen.

"Oh, uh, yeah." She stammers a bit. It seems I've taken her by surprise. "I'm more nervous than I am excited. We don't get opportunities like this around here, you know? I don't want to mess it up."

"You aren't gonna mess it up. You're gonna do great. Besides, it sounds like they already know they want you. This interview is just a formality. I have all the faith in the world in you."

"Thanks." She blushes, and it is stunning. "If only you were the one interviewing me."

"What is it they say to do? Picture them naked?" I offer.

She laughs. "I think that's for public speaking. It may make a one-on-one interview a little awkward."

"Fair point." I swing her out in front of me and keep us moving around the wood floor as I bring her back to me. I'm not sure we've ever been this close, for this long. It's fucking exhilarating.

"Thanks again for offering to take me Monday, Angus."

"No thanks needed. We're family. It's what we do."

Her cheeks pink again, her voice shy when she says, "Right."

Unable to hold back my curiosity any longer, I ask, "What's with you and Rhen? You seemed pretty pissed at him."

"I just don't like him." She wrinkles her nose. "I don't get what everyone sees in him."

He's a good-looking guy. I imagine most women would describe him as tall, dark, and handsome. I'm not hating that she wants nothing to do with him, but it worries me all the same. We've known him our whole lives. "Tell me what I'm missing?"

"Listen, you wouldn't get it."

"Get what?"

"Gus, come on. I don't want to talk about Rhen. He's just an asshole."

There's more to this story, but I don't push her.

"Fine. We won't talk about Rhen, but if he bothers you, let me know. I'll take care of him."

"I'm a big girl. I don't need you to come to my rescue. It's not like that."

The song ends, and she drops my hand. "Thanks for the dance. I'm gonna go get a drink."

I follow her off the floor but take my time so I don't look like a stalker, even though I kind of am, only taking my eyes off her when I see Rhen in my peripheral. He's already distracted by a blonde out of towner.

Why does she hate him so much?

I catch myself examining his features to see if there's any resemblance to a certain two-year-old, and I curse under my breath.

What the hell is my problem?

How am I not over this by now?

I've spent the last two years scanning the faces of every man in Goose Hollow, wondering if they could be Sawyer's father. It's a real shitty pastime. One I'm not proud of. But when I think back to the night she told us she was pregnant—the desolate expression on her face and the humiliation in her eyes only visible for a brief moment—I can't help myself.

The need to shatter the skull and rip out the heart of the man who made her feel less than. Unworthy. Well, that need still hasn't left me. The man who isn't here helping her emotionally or financially. The same man who isn't giving Sawyer the father figure he needs and deserves in his life.

Whoever he is, he better hope I never find out.

Chapter Four

Mia

"Woo hoo!" Daisy yells as the song ends.

It must be the twentieth song in a row we've danced to. The sweet country songs didn't last long and party music has been fueling the energy for the last hour. We're both out of breath and sweaty. And I'm happy! So happy! I can't remember the last time I had this much fun! However, the last time I was out at a bar I wasn't a mom. In my previous life, dancing and jumping around with three beers in my belly wouldn't have affected me the way they have tonight.

"Daisy, I am gonna pee my pants! Be right back!"

"Okay, make it quick!"

Maneuvering through the crowd of people, I round the end of the bar to the hallway that leads to the restrooms and stumble as I run into a line of women who got here before me.

Shit!

Bouncing from one foot to another, I glare at the back of a guy who walks by and right into the men's room, because, of course, they don't have a line.

When the same guy walks back out and our line has only moved a few inches, I'm seriously contemplating sneaking into the guys' bathroom when I feel a warm body behind me. I nearly melt when warm fingers gently wrap around my elbow and a deep voice whispers in my ear.

"Come with me before you pee on my floor."

Okay, not the sexiest thing ever said to me, but it is the first time Angus has ever whispered in my ear. Feeling his breath in my hair does things to me that leave me wet for all the right reasons.

"What?" I ask, tossing my hair over my shoulder like I'm in a shampoo commercial.

What is with me tonight? I'm just so extra.

One side of his mouth lifts, because I'm ridiculous, but he can laugh at me all night if it brings the light to his eyes that we so rarely see since he came home.

"Come on, Goof. This way."

He turns and I follow him behind the bar and through the kitchen. I watch him unlock a door at the back and after I'm over the threshold, he shuts it and locks it behind him. The sound of the music is gone and his proximity in the dark space is overwhelming. But with the flip of a switch, the darkness vanishes. An overhead light illuminates a set of stairs he's taking two at a time.

Holy shit.

He's taking me to his loft.

I've heard many tales of ladies who have had the night of their lives in Angus McKinnon's loft. But that's all they usually get, one night.

"You can use the bathroom in my place. Trust me, it's a lot cleaner than the ladies' room downstairs. I don't know what you all do in there, but by the end of the night, it's fucking disgusting."

"Right?" I carefully take one step at a time. "I will never understand it."

Once we reach his loft, he spins on his booted heels and opens his arms up wide. "Well, here we are. Home sweet home."

He picks up his Carhart jacket lying on the table and drapes it over the back of a chair. Stealing it crosses my mind, but I push the thought aside. Other than that one item, his place is spotless. I expected dirty clothes on the floor, and pizza boxes and beer cans littering the countertops. I couldn't have been more wrong. It's perfect.

"Angus, it's beautiful."

I know my mouth is hanging open, but it really is gorgeous. And huge. One big open room with shiny hardwood floors, brick walls, a very well-made king-size bed, and an area with weights that includes a workout bench, dumbbells, and a punching bag.

"The bathroom is over there. I'll turn on some music so you don't get stage fright."

"Thanks," I whisper, letting his stupid comment go by, still shocked at the lack of neon beer signs and the neatness of the space.

In the far corner, the door to the bathroom is open, and

before I've entered, NSYNC's "Bye Bye Bye" starts playing through the surround sound speakers.

Oh, he thinks he's cute, playing the song that Daisy and I know every word to. We know every dance move from the video, too. Angus watched us do it at least a hundred times.

"Hilarious!!" I yell over the music as I shut the door behind me.

The bathroom isn't as nice as the rest of the place. It's clean, but looks decades old. As if he remodeled everything but forgot this part. There's a small shower, a sink, and a toilet. The walls are dark gray and one lone towel on the rack hangs from the wall. It's simple and in need of some sprucing up.

I take care of my business and while I wash and dry my hands, my reflection stares back at me. There's a smile on my face. It's been a good night, and it's nice to have these small silly moments with Gus. And, of course, everyone else. But mostly with Gus.

I've never truly been alone with him. He's always around. I mean, always. But I can't recall many moments between just the two of us. I know there are times we've been alone in a room, but they don't really stand out. Not like tonight. He may have been saving me from Rhen and asking about my interview, like a good friend does, but being in his arms made it hard to breathe.

Who knew the man could dance like that? I've seen him dance with other women, but I do my best to look the other way. So, tonight his two-step took me by surprise. As did his whispered words in my ear. They may not have been the sentiment I dreamed of hearing as a lovestruck teen, but they did the trick. Sure, I convinced myself there would be no more pining for Angus when I got pregnant. In fact, the night I announced my pregnancy, I also shut down that part of me. The part who desired men. Especially one particular man. For a while, it worked. I was a little too busy worrying about being knocked up and then trying to figure out life as a single parent to worry about childhood crushes.

Not sure who I thought I was kidding, though, because I am far from over Angus McKinnon.

He's standing in the kitchen looking at his phone when I come out. The music is so loud he doesn't notice me at first, allowing me the briefest of moments to take him in, here in his own space.

You could say his short buzzed hair lacks style, but with his perfectly shaped head, it works for him. As always, his T-shirt strains against the muscles of his broad chest and tattooed arms, but it's the way his thick thighs and that ass of his threaten the denim of his jeans that mesmerize me more often than I'm proud to admit.

"Everything come out okay?"

"Dork," I say, walking in the opposite direction of him.

Now that I've finally made it into his bachelor pad, I need to explore. I feel him watching me as I read the spines of the books on his shelf. Lots of history and military books, but there is also *The Count of Monte Cristo* and *Wuthering Heights*.

He turns the music down before he asks, "You've never been up here before?"

"Nope. I'm your sister's best friend and your mom's goddaughter. I don't really fit the description of most of the women who have visited Angus McKinnon's lair."

"Whatever, Goof."

"Have you really read *Wuthering Heights*?" I ask, looking at him over my shoulder.

"What? You don't think I can read?"

"Shut up. It's just so... I don't know.... depressing."

"Why? Because it doesn't have a sweet little happily ever after?"

"Forgive me if I prefer not to be in a deep depression for days after reading a book."

"Well, it's good to have realistic books out there, don't you think? Nobody is perfect, and love can be selfish and cruel. It's not all roses and chocolates."

Leaving his books behind, I meet him in the middle of the room, where he continues watching me with his hands in his front pockets.

I've had a million conversations with him over the years, but never alone in his loft and the topic has never been happily ever afters and the truth about love.

He still surprises me after a lifetime spent in his orbit.

"The chocolates I can get behind. But I've never understood spending money on flowers that are going to die in a few days. Don't get me started on how expensive they are! People could do so much more than buy flowers with that much money."

"Like what?"

"I don't really know. Unlike some women, I don't need a man to spend money on me. They don't even have to take me to dinner. I'd be happy with a home-cooked meal that wasn't made by me."

"So, food is your love language?" His head tilts to the side in question.

Hmm... is it?

"Strange, I never really thought about it, but I guess it is. Just feed me and I'm happy." I chuckle at how true the notion is.

He stares at me.

No smile.

No eye roll.

Is he having a seizure?

His adorable head tilt is about to do me in. I need to make a break for it before I say something stupid and make a fool of myself.

"Well, thanks for letting me use your spotless and line-free bathroom," I say, hoping to break the awkward moment. Walking backward toward the stairs, I lift a hand waving goodbye. "I appreciate it."

"Anytime," he says, snapping out of his stupor.

He follows me down the stairs, locking the door behind us. I see a basket of tots on the counter and can't help but steal one as we make our way back through the kitchen.

"I saw that."

Once again, the deep timbre of his voice only inches behind me sends a bolt of electricity through me.

"Put it on my tab," I reply.

"Like I'd let you spend a penny in my bar. Your money's no good here, Mia."

"Family discount?" I joke.

"Sure. Family discount, Goof," he says cooly. But I don't have time to think about the sudden shift in his attitude because Daisy is waiting for us on the other side of the bar.

"There you are! I've been looking all over for you."

"Sorry, the line was long and your brother let me use the upstairs bathroom."

"Score! Bet it was a lot clearer than the mess down here."

Now on the other side of the bar, she grabs my hand and pulls me toward the dance floor. "Come on, mamma. We need to get you on the dance floor before you turn into a pumpkin."

She's right, my nights out are few and far between. Until tonight, I hadn't realized how much I needed a break to let go and have fun. But it will be over before I know it. I don't need to spend what little time I have in lofts talking about books with a cute boy. Especially a cute boy who is completely off-limits.

Chapter Five

Angus

Every song on the radio reminds me of her.

I can't walk past my bookshelves and not see her dragging her finger over each book as she studied the titles.

Strangely, I wanted her to look at my things.

To see me.

Not Daisy's brother.

Just me.

If I'd had my way, we would have stayed upstairs talking about books the rest of the night. I would have been happy to never have rejoined the others downstairs. She brought a light to my space that had never been there before. With her in the room, everything felt smaller. There was no escaping her.

And I didn't want to.

But downstairs we went. Daisy stole her away, and they partied until the bar closed. It was paramount that I kept her out of touching distance for the rest of the night. I watched her. And I watched Rhen, just in case. But there were no more dances. No more touching.

The dreams I've had with her as the main character the last two nights confirmed what I already knew was true.

I'm used to this attraction being one-sided… but lately… I swear, it's not just me wanting more. We've been more casual around each other. Touching more than usual. Even if those touches have been innocent.

I've always been aware of her when she's in the room, but there's some sort of new thread pulling me toward her. It's a thread I need to sever, because I cannot go there with Mia.

Forget about the connection between our moms and my sister. That's the smallest thing keeping me away from her.

If she knew the real me, well, it wouldn't take a woman as intelligent as her to realize I'm not worthy to breathe the same air as her. If she knew the things I keep buried deep inside, she wouldn't want anything to do with me. She wouldn't want me anywhere near her son.

I've lost too many people. I refuse to lose her, too. If friendship is all I'll ever get, it's enough. I have internal demons I have yet to slay, but I'm working on it. Every Tuesday at 11am. With my therapist.

Putting the truck in park in front of the barndominium she and Sawyer call home, I roll my neck and take a deep breath.

You are just her friend. You're driving her to an appoint-

ment and hanging out with her kid. You'd do it for any of your friends. Because that's all she is. Your. Friend.

Leaving the truck running so the cab stays warm, I make my way to her front door. It's been snowing for days and it's colder than a witch's tit out here. The last thing she needs before her big interview is a case of the shakes because she's freezing.

I knock on the door and hear what I think is a *come in,* so I let myself in.

"Gus, Gus!" Sawyer yells as he tries to run to me, but his dark blue snowsuit slows him down.

He is the cutest kid I've ever seen. No surprise since his mommy, well, she's the prettiest damn woman I've ever known.

There isn't a day that goes by that she doesn't look good. Hell, Mia with her hair in a messy bun and no make-up is a dream, but this morning she's not my sister's teenage best friend. She's a grown woman and it's all I can do not to stare.

Her long waves are straight, with the sides pulled away from her face and her minimal make-up is just right. Her black blazer, white silk blouse, and matching black pants fit her like a glove. The jacket curves in at her waist before flaring just right at her hips. Her pants are fitted, but not too tight, and the look is complete with what seem to be two or three-inch heels.

She is spectacular.

"Sawyer, did you tell your mommy how nice she looks?" I say, picking him up as his mom's cheeks turn my favorite color of pink from my roundabout compliment.

His little arms squeeze around my neck and it feels

fantastic. There's something about a child's unconditional love.

"Do I look okay?" she asks as she frantically spins for me and scoops up a pair of snow boots. "Professional enough?"

"Very professional," I assure her.

I'm not lying. I would hire her in a minute. However, she also looks delectable, but it's safer to keep that part to myself.

"Okay, good."

She kicks off her heels and slips the snow boots on, shoving her shoes in a bag she slings over her shoulder.

"I think I have everything Sawyer might need in here." She pats the bag now also carrying her heels and looks at the clock on the wall. "Shit, we still have to put his car seat in your truck."

"Don't forget your coat," I say, trying to be helpful.

"I'm too nervous to be cold."

I see a puffer jacket lying over the back of the couch. "Is this your coat?"

"Yes, but seriously, leave it."

I grab her coat and the car seat sitting on the floor next to the door with my free hand. "You might want it later. Sawyer and I will meet you at the truck."

The Powells must pay a service to shovel their driveway and Mia's because from her front door to my truck is snow free. Looking around the always immaculate property, a pang of sadness hits me square in the chest at the thought of no longer making memories here.

Our families have spent countless summers camping out, water skiing, grilling, and throwing some of the best 4th of July parties around. Easter egg hunts, Christmas Eve dinners, birthdays, anniversaries, we'd shared them all between this place and my parents' ranch. Daisy and Mia learned how to ride bikes together, right here in this very driveway. This property is so much more than a house or piece of land. It would be like selling the ranch. Like selling a piece of your soul. If it means this much to me, I can't imagine how hard it must be for Mia.

I open the door to the back cab of the truck and set the car seat, her coat, and Sawyer on the bench seat, hopping in behind him. He immediately stands up and jumps with excitement where he had been sitting. Keeping a hand on him at all times, I look at the car seat as beads of sweat tickle my neck. How am I supposed to keep him from hitting his head or falling while fastening this seat into place?

Luckily Mia opens the door and an adult who knows what they're doing enters the picture. "It goes in the middle."

"Really?"

"Yep, scoot over and I'll lock it in real quick."

I slide across to the other side of the cab, bringing the safety seat to the middle. She climbs in and I'm struck dumb as vanilla infiltrates the air. There is no escaping her or the scent that has always reminded me of her. Any time I smell vanilla I think of her, but today she's so damn close it's like I'm high on her.

Our proximity doesn't seem to have the same impact on her as she wastes no time getting to work without even a glance in my direction. When she pulls the seat belt through the designated spot, she finally looks up at me, only inches away.

"Can you clip this in, please?" She hands me the belt.

"Sure," I mutter. It takes me three tries to click it into

place because she's leaning over the seat to watch, putting her head only an inch away from mine.

She smells too damn good. I'm not sure what has changed over the past couple of years, but being around her feels different. What I always tossed aside as a childhood crush has morphed into something I have a hard time controlling.

"There we go." Her breath glides over my face as she looks up and beams me a smile. Seemingly unfazed, she moves away to grab her little man, plopping him in his seat.

"Let's get you settled, munchkin. You're a little puffier than usual, aren't you?" She adjusts the straps so he fits and clicks them together at his chest before running her finger over his cheek.

Bam!

That's when it smacks me upside the head. It's seeing her as a mom. Her love for her son, who she's raising on her own, unlocked something inside me I didn't know existed.

I haven't been the same since that Sunday dinner when she told us she was pregnant. It was her indignant defiance warning all of us not to push her for answers or to shame her. She wouldn't take our pity and insisted her child was not a mistake.

We all agreed it was a happy situation. But a situation, all the same.

I had a nameless fuck in my loft that night and have been trying to fuck her and the thought of someone else getting her pregnant out of my head ever since. But it hasn't worked. In fact, having the privilege of watching her become the mother she is has changed everything. I've resigned myself to the one-night stands that parade through my loft. There's no need for anything serious, because anyone else would mean I had settled when I know a woman like Mia Powell exists.

I've spent a lifetime watching her from the sidelines, telling myself I was fine with that. It took her becoming a mom for my feelings for her to burn too hot to be safe.

And it took until this very moment to realize exactly why.

Ain't that some shit?

Chapter Six

Mia

"Here you go," Angus says, as soon as my seat belt is on. There's no hiding the surprise on my face when he hands me a warm cup of coffee with a peppermint candy sitting on top of the lid.

"Ooh, you went to Becks. Thank you. You didn't have to do that." I take a sip, thinking it's just a black coffee, and am surprised to find it's my exact order. Cue the teenage giddiness doing cartwheels in my belly.

"No biggie, I was stopping for myself anyway."

He holds up his cup.

"How in the world did you know my order?"

"Goof, you've been drinking nonfat white chocolate mochas since high school." He taps his temple. "Besides, you know this is a steel trap."

Goof. That's all it takes to send the butterflies that had

come to life from his kind gesture, back into the winter hibernation I've relegated them to since my trip to his loft. I don't have the space in my life for unrequited love.

"Did you already eat your mint?"

"Nope, that's just for you. You're the only person I know who loves coffee but hates the smell of it. Didn't want you stressing about coffee breath during your interview."

Who in the world is this man and when did he become so observant? Attentive? He's always been thoughtful and kind, but this is different. It's not generic thoughtfulness he dishes out to everyone. Things seem more personal than before. Or maybe I'm imagining the change.

I'm sure it's my lack of sleep causing delusions. I'm feeling more than I'm sure he intended me to?

He isn't doing anything for me he wouldn't for his sister.

I will forever be Goof to him.

Nothing more.

"Gus, Gus!" Sawyer squeals from the back seat.

"Hey buddy, you ready to hang out with me while your mommy kicks some interview butt?"

"Gus, Gus!" my sweet boy yells again, his legs kicking in his seat.

Hey, I get it. There was a time when I used to get just as excited in the back of his truck as a teen. Only I had to bottle it up and keep it all to myself, not wanting Daisy, who was always sitting right next to me, to catch on.

Holy crap. Until today, I've never been in a truck with Angus when his sister wasn't in it, too.

"Thanks again for doing this. I really appreciate it."

"Not a problem. You know I love the little guy. We'll go

throw some snowballs at the park and if it gets too cold, we'll warm up inside the truck."

"Hopefully, I won't be gone long enough for him to need a diaper change, but should something happen, everything you need is in the bag. There are snacks and a sippy cup and…"

"We'll be fine, Mom. Right now, you need to focus on getting yourself into interview mode. You feeling ready?"

"It's not like you spend a lot of time with two-year-olds."

"Yes, but Sawyer and I have a gentlemen's agreement."

"Really? And what kind of agreement would that be?"

"That is between the two of us gentlemen, but rest assured, it is one of trust and understanding. That is all you need to know. Isn't that right, buddy?"

"Gus, Gus!"

Well, would you look at that? My own son is Team McKinnon. Typical.

* * *

"So, that's the clinic."

"It's fantastic."

"Thanks, we're pretty happy with it," Dr. Gibbons says as we head back to her office.

My interview went well. So well, that as she gave me the tour of the facility, she spoke as if me getting the job was a forgone conclusion. So far, so good.

"Have a seat." She gestures to the tan leather chair I sat in while she and her colleagues interviewed me. I'd stumbled over two of the typical questions—more from nerves than anything—but recovered quickly. I think I did well, but who really knows?

And just like during my interview, I can't help but turn my granny's ring round and round my finger. It's a simple silver band with small gemstones embedded into the polished silver. I never leave the house without it. It's how I keep her close. When my nerves get the best of me, I tend to move it from hand to hand or spin it around my finger. It's basically my own version of a fidget spinner.

Something catches her attention out the window behind me and her face beams with a smile. "Your husband and son are adorable together."

"Excuse me?" I asked, confused.

Husband?

"I saw them drop you off, and it looks like they're entertaining themselves rather well."

Turning to see what in the world she is talking about, my heart melts when I take in the sight.

In the park that butts up to the new medical building, Angus has Sawyer on his shoulders, and they're both laughing hysterically. Sawyer yells something and Angus jogs a few paces and when Sawyer yells what looks like, "Stop!" Angus freezes in place. My baby boy is beside himself with laughter. By all appearances, the two of them are having the time of their lives.

"They're clearly close. It's so nice to see the family bond between them."

Her eyes flash to the ring that I only now realize is on *that* finger, and my heart drops.

"Oh--"

"It was so sweet to see them send you off with well wishes when you got here."

"Yes, they are sweet, but--"

"Family is one of our core values here," she interrupts me again. "It's why we plan to have day care on-site. Children shouldn't be away from their parents and parents are more productive if they know their children are nearby and well taken care of. You should feel as comfortable at work with your little boy in our care as you do with him playing in the snow with your husband."

"That's wonderful and one of the many reasons I would love to work here for you and *your* husband, but--"

"We still have a few more interviews to do and with it being the holiday season, we'll make our decision just after the new year. If we hire you, when do you think you could start?"

"Well, I'd like to give my current employer two weeks' notice if possible?"

"Of course." She stands from her chair on the other side of her desk and I follow her lead standing as well. "I really do think you and your family will be the perfect fit."

I cannot let her hire me believing I'm married. There is a lot that comes with being a single mom. If Sawyer is sick, I'm the only one who can stay home with him. If he has doctor appointments, I'm the only person who can take him.

"Dr. Gibbons--"

"Oh, dear. You better get out there. Looks like your little one is upset," she says just as she takes her hand in mine.

Sure enough, a glance out the window and I see tears streaming down Sawyer's face. Fear grips my heart.

"Go, we'll be in touch."

I rush out of the room, down the hall and push out of the clinic without changing out of my heels and into my boots. The need to get to my son is all-consuming.

Just as I take my first step into the frigid foot-deep snow-covered park, I hear my favorite laugh in the entire world. The tension leaves my body, making me far too aware of my wet feet. The snow is now inside my heels and covering my pants.

"Mama!" the sweetest little voice yells when he sees me.

"Hey, buddy," I yell, taking a step back onto the snow free concrete.

"Goof, what were you thinking? Your feet are getting soaked."

"I know, but I saw him crying. I was rushing to see if he was okay. I wasn't thinking."

The smallest smile tugs at his lips. "He's fine. We were playing and a bunch of snow fell off a branch and landed right on him. Went down his face and a little into his coat. It shocked him is all. He's good now, aren't ya, Sawyer?"

"Yer, all good, Mama," he says, from atop Angus's shoulders.

He can't quite get his full name out, so Yer it is for now. We're working on it.

"You didn't leave your interview early, did you?"

"No, it was pretty much over, anyway."

My body shakes from the cold as we walk toward the truck. He holds on to Sawyer's legs with one hand and pulls his key fob out of his pocket with the other. He presses a button, and the truck comes to life.

"How'd it go?" he asks, opening the truck door. Reaching inside, he grabs my coat and holds it open for me while I slip it on. With Sawyer still beaming from his shoulders, Angus bends his knees and zips my coat up like it's the most normal thing in the world.

"Uh, it went great." I nearly forgot he had asked me about my interview after his chivalrous gesture.

"Told you it would. Now hop in and get warmed up. I'll strap this little monster into his seat."

Sawyer roars like a monster and we both laugh.

"Get in," he whispers, opening the door. His face is relaxed. Happy. He hasn't looked like this since we were kids. All it took was forty-five minutes with Sawyer.

Oh, my heart.

After hopping in the passenger seat, I turn around to see if he needs help with the car seat, but he's a quick study, because he's almost done, whereas I don't even have my seat belt on yet.

Getting settled, I try to think of how to tell him what Dr. Gibbons assumed and how she hadn't let me correct her. I feel so incredibly stupid. And a small, self-conscious part of me wonders if the doctor would have treated me differently if she knew I was a single mom. I need this job and I don't want her to think less of me. But I don't want to accept it under false pretenses, either. Besides, I have to come clean. What if she or my coworkers run into him in town or something? He is a business owner, it could happen.

He jumps into the driver's seat and turns up the heat, rubbing his hands together and holding them in front of the heater vents.

"Thanks for *hanging out* with him. I owe you one." I'm gonna owe him a lot when he finds out what just happened during my interview.

"You don't owe me a thing. I had a blast." He looks at me with a soft smile that reaches his eyes. "You're a wonderful mom, Mia. He's a great kid."

My eyes instantly water. His compliment about my parenting hitting me right in the feels. There's no way he'll ever know how much his kind words mean to me.

"Thanks." I glance over my shoulder and notice that Sawyer's face is rosy from the cold, but he's grinning and content as can be. "I did hit the lottery with him, didn't I?"

"I'd say you both hit the jackpot. Now, tell me everything."

"Well, it went great. After the interview, they showed me around and it's beautiful. Everything is brand new and all the tools are the latest and greatest. It's a phenomenal clinic. It would be a dream to work there."

"And could you tell if they were into you?" He wags his eyebrows.

"Yes, I think so. I mean, she did say..." Mia, just rip the band-aid off! "That she thought my family would be a perfect fit."

My cheeks burn with embarrassment.

"Your family?"

"This is so embarrassing, but she thought you were my husband and Sawyer's dad."

Chapter Seven

Angus

"I'm sorry, say that again."

"I am so sorry, Gus. She saw you drop me off, then she saw the two of you playing in the snow. She assumed and never really gave me the chance to correct her."

Mia's talking a mile a minute, but I let her go. Savoring the moment because it's fucking adorable.

"She went on and on about how important family was to them. And how a strong family unit was key to raising children and right when I finally got the chance to correct her, she noticed Sawyer crying and all other thoughts fled from my brain. I am so sorry. I promise I'll set her straight. I'll call her as soon as I get home."

Fuck if hearing that someone thinks I could be the father to this amazing little boy and the husband to someone like

Mia doesn't fill me with pride. I wish I were half the man I'd need to be to be worthy of the two of them.

"No. Don't," I blurt out, surprising myself with my reaction. Working in a bar, I've overheard people talking about single moms. Granted, nobody has ever said shit about Mia in front of me, but I've heard other assumptions and judgments.

Her eyebrows shoot up. "What?"

"Goof, this job is exactly what you need right now. If letting them think we're together helps get you the job, then so be it."

"Gus, you can't mean that."

If she only knew how wrong she was.

"We've already established that I don't do things I don't want to do," I remind her as I fight a smile. "Besides, they likely live in Bend and don't really have a reason to visit Goose Hollow. Let them think what they need to get the job and then eventually you'll leave my sorry ass. Just let me know when you file for divorce."

Her mouth falls open. "Gus, come on. You can't be serious?"

Serious as a damn heart attack.

"Listen, I've been thinking about something and this seems like the perfect time to bring it up."

She squints her eyes, wondering what I'm up to.

"You and Sawyer need a place to live and, well, I think the two of you should move into my place at the ranch. Using my address seems like a perfect solution."

Silence is her reply. Her eyes are still on me, but her cute little eyebrows furrow in confusion. Her mouth drops open, as if she wants to speak, but nothing comes out. Finally, she clears her throat. "You... you want me...," she shakes her head, "I mean us to move in with you?"

Shit, I forgot the second part of the setup and she's understandably freaking out. "I've been staying in my loft at The House half the time anyway, so it's no big deal. I'll just move in full time. There's three bedrooms at the ranch so the kiddo can have his own room."

Her shoulders, that were up to her ears, drop in relief and understanding. I know it would be odd for me to ask her to cohabitate, but her reaction to the possibility of being roommates still causes a tight twisting pain in the center of my chest.

"Angus, no way. We are not moving into your house."

"But you are."

I'm not giving her a choice. She'll be homeless in a week and a half and that will not happen on my watch.

"No, I will not kick you out of your home."

"Fine, I won't move out. We'll be roommates."

Her face goes white as a ghost again and that chest pain twists a bit more.

"I'm kidding. I wouldn't do that to you."

"It's not that, I just... well... I just can't. You've already done enough."

"I gave you a ride to an interview. I wouldn't say I've done much."

"Uh, you just agreed to be my fake husband!"

There's no stopping the shit-eating grin that spreads across my face. "That's right I did." I wag my brows at her again.

"See? That's plenty!"

"But didn't you say you owed me one?"

"Like you said, all you did was give me a ride." She huffs back in her seat, playing with the band currently on her ring finger. No wonder they thought she was married.

"Well, I changed my mind. You do owe me one, and what I want is for you to move into the house."

"Gus, I can't afford to cover the mortgage."

"Sweetheart, that property has been in my family for years and I paid for it as I built it. There is no mortgage."

She can't say anything to that, now, can she?

Her teeth sink into her bottom lip as she thinks about my offer. Fuck, I really wish it were me biting that lip.

"I can't. It's too much."

"Says who? I get to decide what to do with my house. This is how you pay me back. Besides, I'll know you're safe on the ranch. It'll ease my mind."

Her ring spins around her finger for several heartbeats before she speaks again.

"I would have to pay you something."

Ah, ha. She's coming around.

Relief that she might change her mind lessens the pain in my chest.

"Nope. That doesn't work for me." She protests, but I talk over her. "You don't have to stay forever, Mia. But while you're there, you can save money and have a nice down payment to buy your own place once you're ready. No rush. You can take as long as you need."

She says no more while we drive down the long road that leads to the Powells' lake property. Doing my best to give her time to process and think my offer through, I stay quiet as a mouse. I'll go along with letting her think she has a choice in the matter a little longer, but the reality is they're moving in and that's all there is to it. It's a chance to change her circum-stances.

To change her life.

I park the truck in front of her kick-ass barndominium and just as I reach to open the door, she says the one word I needed to hear.

"Okay."

Thank God!

"But I'm paying the utility bills."

And just like that, all is right in my world.

Chapter Eight

Angus

It's moving day.

The past forty-eight hours have gone by in a blur. I may have gotten eight hours' sleep total over the last couple of days, but it will all be worth it to see Sawyer's reaction. I've spent day and night preparing the house and cleaning out my clothes and essentials. Since the loft is fully furnished, and half my things are there anyway, all my stuff fit in the cab of my truck yesterday when I moved everything. The house is ready for them, but I can't shake the nervous energy I woke up with. It probably didn't help that I downed several much-needed cups of coffee before heading out to pick Mia and Sawyer up.

Mia is putting what little furniture she has in storage for now. I think she's bringing more kitchen supplies than anything. Between Daisy's car, Callen's truck, and my truck, one trip is all we need.

As soon as our caravan pulls up to the house, I get out of the truck like my ass is on fire, throwing open the back door to get Sawyer out of his car seat. I feel the smile I can't suppress stretching across my face when he grins at me. This kid in his car seat in the back seat of my truck is better than any after-market accessory I could have paid for.

"I have a little surprise for you," I say, ruffling his blond hair before freeing him from the straps of his seat.

When I come around the truck with Sawyer in my arms, Mia is waiting on the other side, arms open to take him from me. The tears she was silently crying when we drove away from her parents' place are gone, replaced by a lightheartedness I know she's faking.

"What kind of surprise?" She's trying her best to seem wary, but her eyes are full of trust and excitement.

"Come on, I'll show you."

I hand her boy over and her ocean eyes look up at me. The world around us ceases to exist. She holds her son, while I gently rub his back, and our gazes lock as something passes between us. I'm not searching for anything, and I don't think she is either. This is different. I see her. Her heart hurts, and she fears what the future holds for her and her little boy. I see exactly how hard she's trying to hold herself together and I appreciate the hell out of her strength. My rambunctious nerves relax. The only thing I hear is my heartbeat's slow thud in my ears. Sawyer breaks the spell we were under, trying to wiggle out of Mia's arms.

Clearing my throat, I step away from them and walk

toward the front porch. They follow, leaving my siblings to start the unloading process. They're adults, they don't need me to tell them what to do next. And I'd like the next minute or two to ourselves.

When we step into the family room, Mia gasps. "Angus, it's beautiful." Her hand covers her mouth for a beat, before worry takes over her face. "I can't believe you are letting us hijack your Christmas. Look at your tree. It's huge."

My face burns, and for the first time in years, I feel myself blushing. Damn, this is unexpected. So, I did something nice for them. It's no big deal. There's no need to be embarrassed, but I am. It may just be a tree, albeit a big ten-foot tree that draws your attention to the wood beams that run along the vaulted ceiling, but it feels like my holiday gesture is much more than that. It's like I'm telling her how I feel about her without really saying a thing.

"It's yours. You're moving in on Christmas Eve. Santa comes tonight. We had to make sure there was a tree for him to leave gifts under."

She moves to the fireplace. "And stockings. With our names on them. Angus, you've done way too much."

"No... um... I... Well..." *Pull yourself together, McKinnon!* "I just wasn't sure if you'd have time to unpack all your Christmas gear. Figured better safe than sorry. Besides, the tree only has lights and the star on it. I didn't have time to decorate it, but feel free to add whatever you want to it. It's yours."

She faces me again. "Angus, I don't—"

I cut her off, knowing the others will walk through the door with boxes any second. "Look at him." My gaze drops to a beaming Sawyer who is leaning to get out of her arms as he reaches for the lights on the tree that sparkle in his eye. "This is why I did it." I didn't mean to say that last part out loud, but Sawyer's joy is fucking contagious. He deserves a good Christmas. So does she.

Her mouth snaps closed. She turns back to the tree and her eyes turn a little watery. "Thank you. It's beautiful."

Time to change the subject. "So, I figured you want him to have the room closest to yours. I hope that's okay?"

"Of course."

"Okay, well, you also said you were going to move him to a toddler bed and, well, it is Christmas Eve."

"Angus, what did you do?"

"Well... I sort of..." Opening the door so they can see for themselves, I step out of the way. "Merry Christmas, Sawyer."

"Vroom truck! Vroom Truck!" Sawyer yells with excitement, squirming to get out of his mom's arms.

She takes a couple of steps into the room, then sets him down, keeping her back to me. I can't read her expression, but when her hands go to her face, I worry I may have overstepped.

In addition to a fire truck toddler bed, I've decked the room out with everything trucks and dinosaurs that I could find in two days' time. There is a rug in the center of the room that looks like a small town with roads he can drive his trucks and cars on. A big stuffed dinosaur takes up one corner next to a little table and chair. A small dresser and a toy storage bin set that may or may not already be filled with toys.

"Listen, if you don't like it, just let me know. It's no problem. I can return whatever you don't like."

With her back still to me, her head slowly moves back and forth.

I start to panic. "If he isn't ready for the big boy bed just yet, there is still plenty of room for his crib."

"Vroom," Sawyer says from the floor, still in his winter coat, where he's playing with the fire truck he found next to the dinosaur.

His mom still hasn't said a word.

"Hey," I say, taking a step into the room behind her, doing my best to ignore the awkward tension. "Did I mess up?"

She finally turns in my direction and there are tears streaming down her face. "No."

"Why..." My gaze drops to her wet cheeks. I shove my hands in my pockets to quell the urge to wipe the tears from her face. I'm already pushing the limits of our friendship, and I don't want to fuck this up. "What's wrong, then?"

"Angus, you didn't have to do this. First, the tree and the stockings. Now this. It's too much."

"It's not. Look at him." I point to the floor where he's playing, having the time of his life. "Besides, it's Christmas."

"You've already moved out of your house. I'd say you've already done plenty. This must have cost you a fortune. How much do I owe you?"

The mere idea of her thinking she has to pay me back pisses me off.

Sawyer climbs into his fire truck bed and makes his version of a siren sound. "That right there is all I want in return. Seeing him happy."

"Thank you, Angus. Thank you so much."

Unexpectedly, she throws her arms around my middle and rests her cheek against my chest. My arms naturally wrap around her, my chin resting on her head. Even though this isn't an intimate moment for her, like it is for me, I do my best to imprint it on my soul. The feel of her body pressed against mine, the dampness of her tears on my T-shirt. The smell of her fruity shampoo and her signature vanilla. I'm taking it all in while I can. The house is quiet except for the sound of Sawyer playing and Mia's sniffles. Nothing else matters.

I pat her back, not knowing what else to do. "No thanks needed. It was fun."

To my disappointment, she releases me and wipes her face dry with her hands. Even with a red nose and bloodshot eyes, she is breathtaking.

"How did you do this so fast?"

"Monday morning after I dropped you off, I took a trip to Portland. Hit a specialty shop for the bed and then Ikea. Built everything yesterday. I swear I could have built it from scratch faster. You may need to smudge this room after all the cursing I did putting that Swedish stuff together. But it was fun at the same time."

"Whoa. What do we have here?" my brother asks from the doorway.

"Isn't it great?" Mia says, her smile big and her hands clamped together in front of her chest in excitement. "Did you see the tree?"

Yep. It was worth every hour of missed sleep.

I'll be damned if today doesn't feel better than I know it should. I love knowing they're living in my space. Even if it's only temporary. Even if I won't be living here with them, I know I've made the right decision.

"Uh, the tree was hard to miss," Cal says, but I don't look in his direction. "You did good, little brother."

"Oh, my goodness!" Daisy exclaims, bursting into the room. "Gus, did you do all this?"

Clearing my throat and feeling a little uncomfortable with everyone scrutinizing me in the small space, I say, "Guilty as charged."

"Aw, aren't you just a big cinnamon roll of a man?"

"Cinnamon roll?" Cal and I ask at the same time, me rubbing my belly against her possible accusation that it's suddenly grown big and soft.

"It means tough on the outside, but all soft and sweet on the inside."

"Whatever," I huff as everyone else laughs at my expense. "I like fire trucks, and Sawyer and I are buddies. What can I say?" I clap my hands together and take a deep breath. "Now, let's unload some boxes."

Scrambling out of the now crowded room, I rush outside to my truck, where the cool December air feels good against my heated skin. The excuse of unloading the truck helps to not only escape everyone in the house, but also the way it felt to hold her in my arms.

For the next thirty minutes, I carry in boxes and help set things up, enjoying every second. Until I tried to help in the kitchen. Mia was already in there, and no matter how big the space might be, we were way too close for comfort, and her proximity was enough to make me lose my mind. Every moment that passed left me feeling more off-balance than the next. When I was unloading a box of Sawyer's unbreakable cups and plates meant for toddlers her fingers would graze mine when I handed them to her to put in the dishwasher. The same happened when we reorganized the countertop space, so her mixer and blender found homes. There was no escaping Mia. No way not to bump into her as we worked together. When her perfect ass brushed against me, in those tight yoga pants she was wearing, I had to retreat. So, now, here I stand. Outside in the cold, taking a much-needed moment.

The crunch of snow under feet gets my attention a moment before Charlotte sidles up to me. At her request everyone but Callen calls her Charlie, but in my head she's still Charlotte.

"That's a pretty cool room."

"It turned out okay."

"Lucky kid."

Is he though? When his father isn't interested in being a part of his life.

She bumps my shoulder with hers. "You okay?"

"Yep. You? You're only a week away from the big day."

"Things are getting crazy, but I've never been better. I can't wait to marry your brother."

I wrap my arm around her shoulders, pulling her against my side. "We can't wait to have another sister. Thanks for making Cal so happy."

"Well, when you find the one, the happy thing is a lovely little side-effect."

"That's what I hear."

"Are you really trying to tell me you haven't found her yet?"

Sure, I could lie, but it's not as easy anymore. Because, I do know without a shadow of a doubt, that I have met the one.

"I may have, but it doesn't mean I'm the one for her."

"And why is that?"

"The list is long, and it's Christmas Eve. We don't have time to get through it before dinner."

"If it's meant to be, that list doesn't mean a thing. There's no stopping love once you find it."

"Says the blushing bride. We aren't all as lucky as you and Cal."

She opens her mouth to reply but her fiancé interrupts before she gets the chance.

"Hands off," Callen growls and pushes my arm from Charlotte's shoulder.

Charlotte and I roll our eyes, but she loves his antics.

"You're a Neanderthal, you know that?" she says, beaming at him.

"Sure do. Now get that fine ass of yours in the truck. We have some business to take care of before dinner."

"Gross," Daisy says, following behind them. "It's the holidays, for Santa's sake. Let your gift to us be that you keep your sex life to yourselves for the rest of the Christmas season."

"You're the one who went there. If that is what you call business, then that's on you, little sis. I can neither confirm nor deny what said business is."

Charlotte mouths, "Sorry," as they get in the truck.

"Got to go. I'll see you at Mom's in a couple hours." Daisy lifts onto her tiptoes to give me a hug. "Thanks again for everything you're doing for Mia. You're a lifesaver."

"I'm happy to help."

As much as this whole thing feels like some sort of self-induced torture, it settles me. I need to know that the two of them are safe and taken care of more than I need my next breath.

Once the holidays and the wedding are over, I'll need to put some distance between us. I'll be fresh out of excuses to be around her.

Well, there is that whole fake husband thing.

Chapter Nine

Mia

"You know, I'll never be able to thank Angus enough for letting you two stay here. Not only is it a beautiful home, but I'll sleep better at night knowing you're on the McKinnon ranch," my mom gushes for the umpteenth time, while she helps me handwash my cookware, and Dad plays with Sawyer in the family room.

Angus has gone from war hero to walking on water status in my mother's eyes. She's right about the house, though. It's not a simple one-bedroom cottage he's giving up for us. It's a beautiful custom-made home, big enough for a family of four or even five if you turn the office into a bedroom. The high ceilings with exposed beams are straight out of an architecture magazine and the kitchen is a dream. It's huge, but somehow when Angus and I were in here together this morning, there wasn't room for the both of us. We kept bumping into one another. Even just a slight graze from him as he passed by sent shivers all over my body.

It was way too close for comfort.

When I saw the tree, and then Sawyer's room, I was beside myself with emotion. He really is kind. He's a great friend.

"It's only temporary, but I agree. He's gone above and beyond. I still can't believe he offered us his home."

When she doesn't continue raving about St. Angus, I turn to find her standing at the sink, where she had been handwashing a mixing bowl, letting the water run as she stares out the window.

"Mom? Are you okay?"

When again, she says nothing, I follow her gaze out the window, but there's nothing there. Reaching in front of her, I turn the water off and put my hand on top of hers. "Mom, what is it?"

As if snapping out of a spell, she squeezes my hand, planting a fake smile on her face. "Sorry about that. There is just so much going on my mind wanders off from time to time." The small shake she gives her head doesn't hide the glossiness in her eyes.

"Are you sure everything's okay?"

"Of course." She pats my hand and turns the water back on.

I'm not convinced, but I don't push. They do have a lot going on with the holidays and their big move. They've lived here their entire lives. Everyone they know and love is here. They're packing up a lifetime of memories and shipping it across the country to live somewhere new where they don't know anyone. But it's their dream. A dream they kept close to the vest, because I never knew Florida was where they had one day hoped to land. None of it makes sense to me, but it's not my life.

Wrapping an arm around her shoulders, I pull her against me, leaning my head on her shoulder. "I'm gonna miss you, but I am so happy your dream is coming true. You and Dad deserve a life in the sun."

"Oh, Mia," she sobs, turning to embrace me. "I love you so much."

"Mom, I love you too." I pull her tighter to me. "Hey, we're gonna be okay. You said it yourself. We're safe and sound here, and we have the entire McKinnon clan to look after us. And we'll visit whenever we get the chance."

"I know. I just love you both so much." She pulls back, looking me in the eye. "Please tell me you don't hate us. That you don't think we're abandoning you."

Well, you are. But I'm a grown woman who put myself in the position I'm in and my parents deserve to live their life. I get it, but it still sucks.

"Of course not. Why shouldn't you follow your dream because your adult daughter got knocked up? I can take care of myself. We're gonna be fine. I promise."

Stepping out of my arms, she dries her cheeks with a paper towel and takes several deep breaths. "You're a wonderful mama to that grandson of ours. I hope you know that. You've sacrificed so much for him and one day he'll be just as proud of you as we are."

Willing my tears not to fall, I tip my head to the ceiling and blink rapidly, but one rogue tear falls when I look back at the best mom in the world. "Thanks, Mom."

Devastated. That's how I felt the night they told me they

were selling the house and moving to Florida. The first thing that came to mind was, *what about Sawyer?* What about all the milestones they're going to miss? They won't be a part of his day-to-day life, and that absolutely breaks my heart. For me. For him. For all of us.

Then the anger set in.

Yes, it was selfish. And childish. But they had blindsided me. No warning, no time for us to find another place to live. Essentially, they were evicting me with less than the standard thirty days' notice a stranger would get. My own parents!

And what about Chris?

How could they leave our memories of my brother behind? They weren't just selling a piece of land with a boat dock and a five-bedroom home. They were selling our childhood. The place that held all our family traditions. Our secrets, big and small. It's where we celebrated birthdays and graduations. Fourth of July parties and slumber parties outside in tents. It's where me, Chris and the McKinnons would meet before prom so we could get pictures with the view of the lake behind us. It was the last place I saw my brother and where my son took his first steps.

Except for losing Chris and Aiden, Daisy's dad, this was going to be the biggest loss of my life.

My rage blinded me for several days. I called in sick to work and if it wasn't for Sawyer, I wouldn't have gotten out of bed. It was Daisy who talked sense into me. Reminding me that Chris would always be with me and that nobody could take my memories away from me. Honestly, I would be lost without her.

Once I was over the anger, I was sad again. Only this time, fear accompanied the heartbreak. Fear of how I was going to take care of my child and where we were going to live. Goose Hollow is a small place. There aren't any apartment complexes or many rental houses and the neighboring resort towns were out of my budget.

Everything in my world flipped upside down with one conversation at my parents' kitchen table.

I was drowning.

Then a kind man offered us his home.

Mom looks at her watch. "Well, shoot. We need to be at Sharon's in an hour. Time to skedaddle. You gonna be okay if we head out?"

"Sorry Joy, not sure that's possible," Dad yells from the family room. "I've got a dinosaur attached to my back!"

Sawyer roars then yells, "Pop-Pop!"

He roars again just as he comes into view and Mom and I burst into a fit of laughter, which throws Sawyer into hysterics. Dad is on his hands and knees, scurrying around the ottoman, yelling for help from the big scary dinosaur. Sawyer's cheeks are bright pink from laughing so hard. No sound comes out as his eyes dance with delight. He has the hood of Dad's sweatshirt in his hands and is riding him like a horse. My eyes are still damp from our moment in the kitchen, but my baby boy with his grandpa brings on an entirely new set of tears, only this time I don't even bother trying to hold them in.

"Thank goodness your father had that knee surgery." Mom pulls her phone out of her back pocket to take a video. Like me, she hasn't taken her eyes off them, so she hasn't noticed my tears.

Adding to the scene, Mom takes on an Australian accent as she narrates what she's seeing. We're all laughing at

Sawyer acting up for the camera. He loves being recorded and watching himself back later. You could say Sawyer is his own number one fan.

Exhausted, Dad finally collapses face-first onto the area rug.

Sawyer crawls off him, then puts his little face next to Dad's. "Pop-pop?" He gently pats Dad's cheek with his hand. "Pop-pop?"

"Rawrrrrrr!" Dad roars, coming back to life, surprising him as he rolls to his back. Dad scoops Sawyer up, holding him over his head, eliciting giggles. It's the sweetest sound I've ever heard.

Dad settles Sawyer on his back, lifts his shirt, and blows raspberries onto his tummy.

More giggles only mean more tears for me.

You can't replace these priceless memories with a video-call. All four of us are going to miss out on so much. Visits a few times a year won't continue the bond Sawyer already has with them.

"Oh, honey. No," Mom says, noticing me. She puts her phone away and places a hand on each of my cheeks. "No tears. It's gonna be okay. We've still got Christmas, New Year's, and the wedding. Let's enjoy every second and save our sadness for the first."

Dad joins us, with Sawyer in his arms. "Hey, now. What's going on over here?"

"I'm just missing you already, but I'm fine."

The somber look on his face surprises me. Stepping closer, he rests his free hand on my shoulder. The three of us put our heads together, Sawyer still roaring under his breath. It's adorable, but I don't have any laughter left to muster.

Dad, looking as heartbroken as I feel, has turned our silly moment into a much deeper one.

"I'm so sorry, Mia."

"Don't be sorry, Dad. I want you to be happy. We're gonna be fine."

Pulling me into a one-armed hug, he chokes on his words. "You'll always have a room waiting for you. Both of you. If you need anything at all..." His voice trails off and when I pull back to look at him, I'm met with a pair of watery blue eyes that match my own.

"Oh, Dad." We embrace again.

Mom takes Sawyer, leaving Dad to wrap me up in one of his famous bear hugs. We stay connected, both shedding tears, but neither of us saying a word. I've never seen my dad like this. The only time I recall him crying was the day we found out Chris wasn't coming home. Then, it was still just the one time. Even at the memorial, he remained stoic, acting as the rock Mom so desperately needed.

"Okay, okay," Mom says gently. "We still have a lot of memories to make in the next week. Starting with Christmas Eve with the McKinnons. C'mon Earl, let's hit the road or we'll be late."

With that, he releases me and leaves without another word.

"Is he okay?" I ask Mom.

"He will be, honey. He will be."

Chapter Ten

Mia

Christmas Eve with the McKinnons is one of my favorite days of the year. But tonight is different. Seeing Dad so emotional has sort of tipped things on its side for me. I had been so certain this was *their* dream, but now I'm not so sure if maybe it's Mom's dream, not Dad's. All I know is I plan on soaking up every moment I have left with them. Even if I am mentally and physically exhausted.

I miss them already.

There was no hiding my tears from Gus as he drove us to his family's ranch, but he didn't say a word. Didn't try to make it better. He simply slid his hand onto my shoulder, letting me know he was there, while I cried. Without saying a word, he told me it was okay to feel everything I was feeling.

And there was, and still is so much to feel.

To top it off, I have no idea how to feel about moving into Gus's place.

My sixteen-year-old self would never have believed that one day I would be living in Angus McKinnon's house. That he decked out my son's bedroom into a little boy's heaven, and put up a tree and stockings so Santa didn't forget to show up. That he did all of this, but we're not together and he's not the father of my child. We're just friends. I would have told my thirty-three-year-old self how lame that was.

But also, how very cool.

There's been a lot of change in a matter of weeks, so it's nice to have the tradition a night like tonight brings. Although, as much as our traditions stay the same, they are always changing.

My parents have lost a child but gained a grandchild. Charlotte is now a part of the family, but it's our first Christmas without Aiden, the McKinnon patriarch.

We're all doing our best to pretend things are normal, but from time-to-time Sharon, Daisy, or one of her brothers have all had moments. We've shed tears, but for the most part things have stayed festive. Now we're all sitting around Sharon's tree and passing around Secret Santa gifts, just like we do every year.

Angus, Daisy, Charlie, Sawyer, and I sit on the floor while my parents take their place on the love seat, Sharon in her favorite chair, and Cal and Knox on the couch, each taking up the space of two or three. It used to be all of us kids on the floor, but Cal and Knox, the old men of the group, have graduated to the couch this year.

"Mia, you're next!" Daisy hands me a gift. Her up-to-no-good smile tells me all I need to know.

"You're my Secret Santa, aren't you?"

She bounces with glee. "I am. Now open, open, open!"

Her excitement is infectious, so I tear the paper off the thin box like a savage. "An e-reader! Daisy, thank you so much. I love it."

I really do love it. Reading is the only thing I do solely for myself these days. It's my one luxury when Sawyer goes to bed at night.

"I know you're old school, but trust me when I tell you, this is gonna change your life. Oh, and you won't need your library card for a while. I've already loaded it with all my favorites." She gives me a wink and I know what that means. It's full of naughty romances she knows I'm too embarrassed to check out at the local library. I know everyone that works there, and this is a small town. People talk!

"Pirate porn!" Callen coughs into his hand.

"What in the world are you talking about? On Christmas no less," Sharon yells at her son, but there's a smile on her face.

"That's what Daisy put on Mia's e-reader, Mom. Pirate porn. Alien porn. You know, all that mommy porn stuff. Apparently, the kinkier the better."

Charlie gasps. "You are such a jerk!" She smacks him on the leg. "I am never telling you anything ever again."

"Hey!" he balks. "You're marrying this jerk!"

"She's got a week to change her mind, you know. You better mind your p's and q's until you get her down the aisle," Knox chimes in. Yes, even Knox, the elusive eldest McKinnon sibling, is home.

Knox is always here for Christmas, but this year he'll be staying longer than the usual float in and out of town for two nights max. He gets itchy if he's home for too long. It's a shame, because their family is incredibly close, and they miss him.

Charlotte was a big-time entertainment lawyer before moving to Goose Hollow to be with Callen and start a business with Daisy, and Knox and his band were her biggest clients. This year, he's home for not just the holidays, but for all the wedding festivities culminating in the wedding on New Year's Eve. Sharon has been beside herself with joy to have him here for so long.

The whole family is here.

Chris and Aiden may not be here physically, but they're always with us. I refuse to believe otherwise. We lost my brother in combat eight years ago. The first couple of holiday seasons felt impossible to get through without him. I still miss him every day. We all do. But Angus... he hasn't been the same since. He was with Chris the day he died. They were best friends, as close as brothers, and coming home without Chris changed something deep inside him.

"Listen to your big brother. I haven't said *I do* just yet!"

"Don't even joke about that, baby. I can't help it if my sister is a perv." Callen leans forward to kiss his fiancée from where she sits on the floor between his legs. Their Spiderman kiss is so dang sweet.

The whole room moans, and Cal smirks, loving every second of the teasing.

"Daisy, I am so sorry."

"There's no reason to be sorry, Charlie. I'm not embarrassed. Mom, let me know if you want to borrow any of my books."

"Daisy Brianna McKinnon, there is a child present. That

is something you can talk to me about in private after everyone leaves."

The room bursts out in laughter. Well, not everyone laughs.

"Mom, no!" Knox yells while Cal pretends to vomit. The rest of us laugh and I hold my hand up to Sharon for a high five.

This crazy cast of characters is what I hold most dear to my heart. I love the family I was born into, but the family my parents chose for us is also amazing. You need to have tough skin around this group, but that's what makes life fun.

Angus isn't chiming in, though. He chuckled to himself during the mommy porn conversation, but most of his attention has been on my little boy. Sawyer has already used Agnus as a jungle gym. Now, he sits in front of him as they drive different toddler-safe fire trucks, tow trucks, and even dinosaur trucks around the floor. They quietly play as if they're the only two people in the room. Angus makes truck noises and cute little siren sounds. Sawyer crashes his bestie's vehicle, pretending it flies through the sky while his audience of one looks like he's never had this much fun.

Angus McKinnon is a serious man. He doesn't smile or laugh nearly enough, but something changes when he and Sawyer are together. He turns into a kid, playing and laughing with abandon. They are like whipped cream and hot cocoa, the perfect combo.

He looks up and catches me watching them. My cheeks heat, but I don't look away and neither does he. He gives me a small smile. My belly somersaults, as per usual, but I swear he's looking at me differently. In my exhaustion, I must be imagining the change I sense in him because I will always and forever be Goof to him.

It's easy to take his kindness for more than it is when I've wanted his attention for as long as I can remember. Not to mention, we've had more one-on-one time together in the past week than we ever have. That's all it is. I'm tired and loopy from the stress of my parents leaving, the move, and the anxiety waiting to hear about the job.

I'm emotionally spent.

He has never and will never see me romantically.

But what about our moment at the house earlier today? It felt like something more. It felt so real. More intense than things usually feel with Angus.

Lately, nothing feels normal.

Daisy examines the tag on another gift. "Okay, enough of this nonsense. Let's see. The next present is for Angus. Looks like Mia drew your name this year."

He plucks Sawyer from the floor beside him and sets him in his lap. "Wanna help me open this, buddy?"

They unwrap the gift and when he sees the dark blue copy of *Pride and Prejudice*, he smiles a knowing smile before turning his grin to me.

"I thought I would give you a classic with a happy ending. Your book collection is way too emo."

"You got Angus a book?" Knox asks in mock confusion. His long dark hair is pushed behind his ears, and one of his tattooed arms is thrown across the back of the couch like nothing in the world could phase him.

What I wouldn't give for an ounce of that confidence.

"Gus can read?" Cal teases next.

"Sweetie, did you put the tag on the wrong gift?" Daisy asks, the multi-colored lights of the tree dancing in her eyes.

Ignoring his siblings, his eyes lock with mine and there is nothing but joy and sincerity shining back at me. "Thank you. I love it." And he means it. His eyes always give him away, but right now there is no lie to reveal. He really does love the gift.

The embarrassment warming my cheeks a moment ago bursts into a searing heat because he looks at me a little longer than he should. Once again, my stomach flips and my heartbeat accelerates.

Charlie leans over and whispers, "I'd say he likes his gift."

"It's an inside joke," I assure her.

He continues to watch me from across the room as my little boy sleepily cuddles against him.

"I bet it is."

Hearing the innuendo in her voice, I hurry to explain, "It's not like that."

Sawyer takes Gus's attention away when he snuggles against his chest. I miss his eyes on me the instant they're gone, but watching my baby boy cuddle into him has tears threatening to fall. Not only because of how much I love the sight, but because it's obvious Sawyer is missing out by not having a daddy in his life. It breaks my heart.

"Whatever you need to tell yourself," Charlie says, continuing to stir the pot.

"No, really. He doesn't see me that way. We're just friends," I whisper to her.

"If you say so."

Chapter Eleven

Angus

"So? What do you think?" Callen asks as we wait for our drinks at the bar. We're at The House, where we've closed for the night to host the rehearsal dinner.

I'm surprised they didn't ask to have the wedding here instead of the barn. I know the space is free, but you'd think they would want to change it up a bit. First the combined bachelor and bachelorette party, and now the rehearsal dinner.

"About what?" I play stupid, even though I know exactly what he's asking. Callen, Charlotte, and Daisy seem to think there could be a possible love connection between me and Karissa, Charlie's best friend, but I have zero interest. It's not that she isn't attractive, because she is. She's funny and I do like her, but when Mia is in the room, no other women exist.

The day has been a blissful torment for me. I'm walking Mia down the aisle at Callen and Charlotte's New Year's Eve wedding tomorrow night, which means I've spent a lot of time not only near her but touching her. Like a pubescent kid who feels each innocent grazing of her fingers like it's some sort of foreplay, I have savored each brush of her skin against mine, likely inconsequential to her but they're everything to me.

Earlier today, she slid her arm through mine as we practiced our pace down the makeshift aisle in the enormous barn usually used for storage, but has been transformed into the perfect wedding venue. Her breast kept brushing my bicep as we walked, making me curse under my breath.

For fun, Callen and Charlotte made each of the paired-up couples pose for photos like we were going to prom. It was supposed to be funny, and I suppose it was, but having Mia in my arms, my hands on her hips. It was no laughing matter.

There was nothing funny about it at all.

As if the fleeting touches weren't blissfully painful enough, considering they'll never be the real thing, that was just the beginning. I've had to watch her make conversation with Mark all night. Just like Callen and Daisy are trying to set me up with Karissa, they think Mark is a perfect match for Mia. I used to think my brother and sister were smart people, but they don't have a clue what they're doing because there is no way Mark is the man for her.

"Karissa," Callen says, bringing me back to the present. "What do you think?"

"She's nice enough, but I don't think she's my type."

"Since when do you have a type?"

"What the hell is that supposed to mean?"

"Well, the parade of women going in and out of your apartment would lead me to believe your only type is female."

"Whatever. It's not a crime to not want to get tied down. Besides, what's wrong with trying out the sample pack life throws at you?"

I'm making light of the truth that he's slinging my way, but only because he's right. I bury myself in one-night stands because there's only one woman I want the real deal with. But big brother doesn't need to know that.

"Nothing wrong with it. Just saying I didn't know you had a type."

"Well, now you know."

She's five foot three, with the brightest blue eyes you'll ever see. Her long dark waves are striking against her pale skin and the formfitting navy dress she's wearing tonight makes it hard for me to breathe. She and my sister have matching tattoos of a tiny star constellation on the inside of their left wrists and her laugh, when aimed at you... well, it will fill even the coldest, darkest soul with a peaceful light that warms you from the inside out.

And right now, that laugh is being aimed at someone else and it's eating away at my cold, dark soul instead of lighting it up like it usually does.

Mark, the lawyer from L.A., whose bank account balance likely has seven or more digits in it and who even I can admit is moderately attractive, has said something that has genuinely made her laugh. Not a courtesy laugh, but an honest-to-goodness hold on to your sides laugh. And doesn't that fucking suck?

"C'mon, man. Just talk to her. She's great."

"I have talked to her. How could I not, when you sat her right next to me at dinner?"

"You haven't had a serious relationship since you came home. It's been ten years, Gus. I'm sorry if I want to see you happy."

Giving my brother's shoulder a squeeze, I take a deep breath and sling him more bullshit. "I know you do. And I appreciate it, but for now, I'm happy with the way my life is going. Besides, tonight is all about you and your blushing bride."

I point to where Charlotte is talking to Knox. When they see us looking, they hold up their glasses from across the room.

"Is it me, or is it strange to see him back home?" Callen asks.

I think about what he's saying, and he's right. Knox, being one of the biggest rock stars in the world, doesn't come home often. His life is either on the road, in Los Angeles or in New York. He had outgrown our little town before he ever left it. He wanted more. And he sure as hell got what he was looking for.

Always the tallest, most handsome guy in the room. He was the only one of us boys who grew his hair out and went through that angry, rebellious teenage phase. He's the king of his own little universe, but whenever we need our big brother, he never fails us.

"It is. But, thanks to you, he didn't just fly in and fly out for the holiday. It's got to be killing him to be here for a week straight. Christmas, the wedding, and New Year's all in one trip. You know he's itching to get on that private jet of his as soon as he can. I've never understood why he wanted out of this town so badly. You couldn't pay me to trade small town living for his life of fame and lack of privacy."

"Yeah, but that's him," Callen shrugs. "He feeds off the chaos."

And I avoid it at all costs.

There was enough chaos during my six and a half years in the military. Enough to last me a lifetime.

Originally enlisting for four years, I extended for two more when Chris did. There was no way I'd leave him behind. Our six years were up, and it was finally time to come home, we were in so deep the brass basically forced us to stay six months past our contract. It was safer to stay than try to leave. Or so they said. What it really meant was six more months watching families torn apart by war and seeing more people than I like to remember lose their lives. I may have made it out alive, but a piece of me is still over there with my brothers. With Chris.

Owning a bar and all that comes with it is as much drama as I need, and trust me, it comes with plenty.

"Here you go, boss."

I thank Laurie, taking the beers she slides in my direction and hand one to Cal as we both push off the bar and head toward our big brother and the bride. They've known each other for years since she was his entertainment lawyer before she gave it all up to move to our sleepy little town. Now, she's gone into business with my sister flipping houses and building furniture.

"He says he's on his farewell tour. Do you think he'll come back when it's all over?" I ask Cal before we reach them.

"I don't think we'll ever get that lucky. I'm not sure what

it is about this place that sends him running, but whatever it is, seems like he can't get far enough away."

"I'm not sure if it's something he's running from or something he's trying to run to," I say. "He's more of a free spirit than the rest of us. At least, that's what I tell myself. Feels better than wondering if he doesn't want to be around us."

"Well, he's here now and, for the most part, he shows up for all the big stuff. We'll have to take what we can get."

Callen sneaks up behind the love of his life, wraps his free arm around her waist, and kisses her on the cheek. "Are you two still talking business?"

I don't hear the rest of their conversation because, on instinct, without realizing it, I'm storming across the room. Because the douche canoe from L.A. is touching Mia.

Touching her like he has the right to.

What a delusional fucking prick.

He's holding her upturned hand while his fingers trace over the tattoo on her wrist.

The closer I get to them, the hotter my blood boils. All I can think about is punching the smug look off his pretty boy face.

I mean, what the actual fuck? Doesn't he know she's a mom and not some random wedding hook-up?

Granted, Mia *is* single and maybe she *is* looking for a no-strings-attached roll in the hay. Hell, she fucking deserves one, but not with this guy.

Not on my watch.

When she glances over his shoulder and sees me approaching, the sparkle in her eyes brightens, nearly blinding me.

Now, *that* feels fucking fantastic.

"Hey, Goof. I brought you a fresh beer," I say, handing her my barely touched beer. Anything to occupy at least one of her hands.

Luckily, she pulls her hand from his and the fuckwad gets to keep his face intact.

"Thanks. You didn't need to do that."

"Well, got to keep you hydrated."

Smooth, McKinnon. Real smooth.

"Oookay, I appreciate it."

She sounds as confused as I am pissed.

Setting my feet firmly at her side, I plant my flag and have no intention of leaving.

Mia takes a drink and licks a drop of foam from her lips. God damn her and her sexy mouth.

"This is a great place you've got here," Mark says.

"Thanks."

"It is great, isn't it?" Mia beams. "You should have seen it before. It was just an old, rundown firehouse that had been sitting for years. Angus worked his magic and transformed it into the local hot spot."

Her gaze drifts back to me and I'll be damned if she doesn't look at me like I'm worthy of her praise. I'm not, but she doesn't know that. Thank Christ she doesn't, because the way she's smiling at me warms up the coldest corners of my frost covered heart.

"Impressive," fuckwad replies and I lose the warmth of her eyes and her smile when she turns back to him.

The after effects of her words linger, though, leaving me to think I may have done something right in life after all.

"He sure is. Did you know--"

"Sorry to interrupt." Daisy scoots in, putting her arm through Mia's. "But the ladies are heading out. We have to gossip about boys and get our beauty sleep."

Did he know what? What the hell was she going to say?

"Well, it was nice meeting you, Mark. I'll see you tomorrow." She reaches out to shake his hand while I envision ripping his arm off his body and shoving it up his ass.

"I can't wait," he says, reverently taking her hand in his. I'm surprised he doesn't lean down and kiss it as slick as he's acting.

"Bye, Mark. See you in the morning, Gus," Daisy says.

The moment she drops his hand I move to follow them before he can. "I'll walk you out."

"Uh, I think we'll be okay."

Ignoring my sister, I keep pace behind them. I am not letting Mia out of my sight until she's belted into my mom's SUV. If Mark thinks he's gonna come in here like some single mom slayer, he can think again.

With my mom behind the wheel, the rest of the ladies load up and buckle their seatbelt's. I say goodnight and go to shut the door, but before it closes, big sapphire eyes lock on mine. There's a question in her gaze, but I'm clueless as to what she's trying to ask.

When she doesn't say anything, I close the door. Finally, I can breathe again. It's been a long damn day. All the close contact has brought up the fake husband scenario, making it impossible to separate fact from fiction. It's not like we've had to pretend to be a couple in front of anyone, but the possibility is always in the back of my mind.

Once they drive away, the worry over her attraction

toward the hotshot Hollywood lawyer fades and my body relaxes. Walking back inside the bar, I let her words about how impressed she is with what I've done with the place lighten my mood and contemplate what in the world was going through her mind as she drove away.

Chapter Twelve

Mia

"I can't believe you're getting married in a barn. If you had asked me to plan Charlotte Carruthers' dream wedding, it never would have been on New Year's Eve. And certainly not in a barn," Karissa, who was born and raised in Los Angeles, says from her spot on the couch where the bride's feet rest in her lap.

The four of us are wearing matching pajamas and drinking hot toddies, huddled around the gorgeous stone fireplace in the living room of Callen's ranch house. It's a shame Cal refuses to live here. What he and his family built is beautiful, but his ex-wife wiped away all the beauty for him when he found her in bed with his cousin, Wyatt. Assholes, the both of them.

"That makes two of us. But I never really dreamed of my

wedding day growing up. It was never on my to-do list," Charlie replies.

"Well, I think it's dreamy."

Karissa's right, it is all quite dreamy.

Knox's gift to the beautiful couple was to send his party planner to do all the decorating, and the barn looks like a fairytale dream. White lights cover the wooden walls, and an enormous ornate chandelier hangs over the dance floor. It may only be family and their closest friends in attendance, but Knox's planner spared no expense. Flower arrangements, candles, gold-trimmed dishes, the finest cutlery, and crystal glasses.

Dreamy is an understatement.

Daisy nods. "I've told my mom more than once to use the spare barn as an event space. It's perfect for weddings and she could use the income, but as per usual, nobody ever listens to me."

She's right. It's a great idea. After seeing what they can do with the place, it's almost a no-brainer.

"Speaking of spare buildings. This house is beautiful. I can't believe Callen lets it sit here empty," Karissa says what we all think. "He built it from scratch and it's freaking beautiful."

"I know," Charlie replies wistfully. "I'm working on it. The moment I walked through the front door, I was in love, but it reminds him of his failed marriage. He didn't even want the four of us staying here tonight, but it makes too much sense for him to refuse. There's plenty of space and we each have our own room. And it's on the same property as the wedding. Eventually, I broke him down."

"Are you excited about tomorrow?" I ask. "You feel like everything is ready to go?"

"As ready as we'll ever be. Knox sending his team in was the best gift he could have given us. We didn't exactly give ourselves a lot of time to plan, did we?" She chuckles. "Thank you all for giving up your New Year's plans. We just figured it would be easier since Knox would be in town for the holidays."

"It's not like I had plans. I would have been having a private house party, with just me and the kid, so thanks for the invite." I hold up my drink in salute.

"Speaking of you and plans," Daisy says, pointing her fuzzy socked foot in my direction from her spot on the love seat. "You make any wedding hook-up plans with that hottie, Mark?"

"Ha," I bark. "Uh, no. I don't think he sees me that way."

"Honey, please. You are one hot piece of ass and don't you forget it! Besides, I saw him using your tattoo as an excuse to touch you tonight. Well played, Mark. Well played."

"Don't be ridiculous."

"She's not the only one who noticed him touching you." Charlie gives me a knowing look I don't quite understand.

"See! Charlie saw it too! He was totally into you!"

Charlie arches an eyebrow at me. "Wasn't that right before Angus brought you your beer?"

What the hell? Is she implying Gus interrupted us on purpose?

It's not like I didn't think it was odd that Gus brought me a beer I didn't ask for or that he didn't walk away after doing so. In fact, he didn't leave my side until I was safely in

Sharon's car. His actions brought my old crush to the surface and for the briefest moment, before he closed the door, that naive girl I keep tucked away poked her head out and thought, does Angus McKinnon like me?

No.

That's just ridiculous.

Isn't it?

"Uh, was it? I'm not sure."

"C'mon, how can you not be interested in Mark?" Daisy pleads, thankfully shifting the conversation away from Gus.

"Why even bother? He lives in California and has a big life. I'm a single mom in Central Oregon, living in her best friend's brother's house."

"First, don't act like you aren't fabulous. You know you are," Daisy counters. "Second, we aren't suggesting a long-distance relationship. We're talking about a wedding hook-up!"

"Maybe she's into someone else?" Charlie says, with no humor in her voice. Just that all-knowing raised eyebrow of hers.

But what does she think she knows?

"No way. Who else could there be?" Daisy counters. "We know everyone in town and trust me, there isn't anyone noteworthy."

Feeling like a caged animal, not wanting to talk about my love life, or lack thereof, my heartbeat increases and my face heats. How does Charlie know how I feel about Angus? Because she knows. But how, when I won't even admit it to myself?

She must see the panic in my eyes because she comes to my rescue and moves the spotlight from me to her best friend.

"What about you, K? What do you think of Angus?" she asks Karissa, keeping her damned knowing look aimed at me.

Never mind. She isn't coming to my rescue. She's slowly torturing me while she studies my reaction.

"He's hot, in that brooding, self-assured way."

"Gross," Daisy gags.

"But, as much as I'd like to take him for a ride, he's not interested."

"Oh, he's interested. He's always interested. I'm sure you'll make it up to his loft before you catch your flight home," Daisy assures her.

Now I'm the one gagging. Just the thought of them together has my stomach rolling. Not that I have any right to feel any kind of way about it. Nevertheless, I do.

Charlie continues to watch me, only this time compassion flickers in her eyes. She finally changes the subject, taking pity on me. "What about you, Daisy? You looking for a wedding hook-up?"

"Nah."

"You can have Mark," I say and mean it. "There's no spark there."

"What about Owen and those dimples?" Karissa asks.

"Uh, his goal in life is to make my life miserable. He is nothing but a thorn in my side."

Charlie, Karissa, and I share a knowing look, and then burst out into a fit of giggles.

"What? What is so damn funny?" Daisy screeches.

"Thou doust protest too much," Charlie says through her giggles.

"Oh, whatever!"

"What do you mean, whatever?" Karissa howls with

laughter. "He's hot. You're hot. You would make pretty babies with pretty dimples!"

I'm a bit taken aback when sorrow flashes in Daisy's eyes. "He's my brother's best friend. It could never happen."

And just like that, I know there's something between them I've somehow missed. But most of all, she confirms what I've always known.

What I feel for Angus doesn't matter, because even if he felt the same, which there isn't a snowball's chance in hell that he does, he's off-limits.

Chapter Thirteen

Angus

Hall and Oates sing about dreams coming true while Charlotte and Callen dance their first dance as a married couple. It may not be your typical cheesy slow dance, but it's them and it's perfect.

The whole day has been a perfect, masochistic whirlwind.

Knowing my excuses will be gone after the clock strikes twelve, I've been using the wedding as an excuse to touch Mia in ways that aren't usually acceptable. We walked down the aisle together, stood side by side during the wedding photos, and sat next to each other at dinner.

Her red velvet wrap dress fits her like a glove flaring slightly at her hips to hang loose all the way to the ground. But that split up her left leg goes nearly to her hip and every time I glimpse her bare skin, I fight off images of my hands gliding up her thighs to part her legs so I can taste her.

And let's just say, today of all days, surrounded by family, is not the most opportune time for those kinds of R-rated thoughts.

My fantasies may be just that. Fantasies. But that didn't stop me from relishing every time the photographer asked me to move closer. Close enough to smell her shampoo. Or Charlotte insisting my hand rest on Mia's hip or low back when we posed for pictures. Once again, the bride asked for several shots of the two of us together, posing like prom dates. All I could think was, *finally*. And what is up with Charlie? Why isn't she asking the rest of the wedding party to take the same kind of photos.

Thankfully, Owen was the best man, and I had nothing to do but stare at her while my brother and his now-wife exchanged vows. The crazy thing is, Mia watched me right back.

Maybe it's our proximity to one another or all the casual touching, because I've let my guard down, not giving a shit if I'm acting out of character or who might notice. The electricity I feel every time I touch her is worth whatever fallout may come from my boldness.

She doesn't seem to give a shit, either, because she hasn't pulled away once. In fact, she's leaned into me on more than one occasion.

Like she is right now. We're standing on the edge of the dance floor watching the first dance. My arm is draped over her shoulders and hers is around my waist, her head resting on my shoulder like it's something we do every day.

There's something here.

There always has been, but the fight to resist it is no longer as strong. It's the opposite. My need to give into this palpable. We have an inescapable chemistry that is all-consuming.

The song ends and Usher and Little Jon start singing about their night in the club. In two seconds flat we're all on the dance floor shouting, "Yeah!"

Even I'm shaking my ass. It's impossible not to when *this* song comes on with *this* group of people. This is our party song and my eyes, as always, are on Mia. Her hands are up in the air, her ass sways, and she sings along, holding nothing back and it's fucking gorgeous.

We all know to stand back when Ludacris comes on because it's time for Knox to shine. In preparation for his big moment, we form a small circle. Using my big brother as a distraction I gently grab Mia by the hips, so her back is pressed against me.

She doesn't miss a beat, keeping pace with the song and my hips. I love every purposeful sway of her ass against my cock. She doesn't falter when Knox takes his long flowing locks out of his man bun and lip syncs, bending to touch his toes, just like the lyrics say the girl in the club does. We scream for him, like we always do, and then the circle disperses. Mia continues to dance in front of me, and I don't give her an inch of space.

We're both being reckless and honestly, I've never been happier or more turned on.

Mia's parents along with Sawyer join us when the next song begins, and I take a few cautious steps away from them. Mia picks Sawyer up and holds one of his pudgy little hands out as she dances with him in a small circle. Her eyes lock on mine for the first time since our dirty dancing began while she kisses Sawyer on the cheek.

The organ pumping life through my body thunders in my ears, the sight of them filling my lungs with life and my heart full of something foreign.

Something warm and powerful.

Something that feels a whole lot like a word I'm not sure I should acknowledge, even though it's obvious.

At the end of their dance, Mia excuses herself to change his diaper. Her mom follows her off the dance floor, and because I am a moth to her flame, I follow, too, unable to be more than a few feet away from her.

Mia's mom insists on changing Sawyer, so Mia hands him over. When she turns and finds me standing directly behind her, she gasps, her eyes wide with surprise. They quickly go all soft and sparkly like they do when she's happy, and fuck if the warmth pulsating in my chest doesn't speed up.

She's about to say something when a blonde woman I've never seen before interrupts her. "Excuse me, but you're Mia Powell, right?"

"Yes, I'm Mia." At first, she seems as confused as I am, but then recognition dawns on her face. "Oh, you're Hailey from the clinic, right?"

"Yes, it's so good to see you again. You must be the husband I've heard so much about? Your little boy is just adorable."

Mia stills, her face crimson red, fear setting in.

Wrapping my arm around her waist, I pull her against my side, basking in the sound of someone calling me her husband. Calling her mine. But I don't linger in the glory because Mia needs a lifeline, and I'm happy to jump in and save the day. "He is pretty dang cute, isn't he?" I ask the stranger. "How do you know the bride and groom?"

"Oh, I'm Owen's date."

Of course she is. I've been so singularly focused on the woman currently clinging to me in desperation, I hadn't even noticed he'd brought a plus one.

"So, have you heard about the job yet?" she asks Mia.

"No, not yet. They said it won't be until after the new year, so I should hear soon."

"Well, you didn't hear it from me, but I think you'll be getting a very nice start to your new year."

Mia's face lights up with hope. "Really?" Her voice is full of happiness.

"I mean, it's not up to me, but I think they knew once they met you. They can't stop talking about what a cute little family you have. To be honest, the other interviews seem like a formality."

"I sure hope you're right."

Owen saunters up and if he notices my hold on Mia, he doesn't show it. "Excuse me, but I'd like to dance with my date, if you don't mind?"

"She's all yours," I say.

My thumb rubs circles on Mia's hip and I'd give my left nut for Hailey to ditch Owen and stay here and chat with *my wife* a little longer. I'd do just about anything to keep touching her.

"It was great to see you, Mia, and nice to meet you, uh, Angus, right?"

"That's right. Nice to meet you too, Hailey," I reply, dreading the moment she walks away and Mia drops the facade.

Owen leads her to the middle of the room and onto the hardwood floor where they slow dance with other couples.

"Holy shit," Mia says, putting space between us.

I miss her body against mine the instant she pulls away, but she's panicking.

How do I know?

Her granny's ring is getting more action than I am.

"We didn't lie about anything. We did not confirm or deny that I was your husband," I say, trying to calm her.

"But what if she says something to Owen?"

I look over my shoulder and chuckle when I see Owen and Hailey making out on the dance floor. "I don't think he's much into chit-chat."

"But, what if?"

"You can't live your life worrying about all the what-ifs."

I know I'm a hypocrite, but this is about her, not me.

Her gaze drops to the floor as she continues to fidget with her ring.

"It's gonna be fine, wifey," I joke.

Her head pops up, her eyes wide, but the lift to one side of her mouth makes me think she liked the sound of it almost as much as I did.

In fact, I liked it a little too much because it's taking a herculean effort to ignore the semi in my pants.

"Shut up," she whispers shyly, but her smile widens. "You are so stupid."

"I think you like my kind of stupid."

She rolls her eyes but doesn't deny it. "Seriously, though. This could get messy."

"Why don't you tell the family, then? You know they'll go along with it if it means you get the job, the insurance, and the day care."

"It's too embarrassing."

"You don't have to say anything tonight, but it might be wise to let them in on the secret soon. It's not like they never leave town. One of them is bound to run into someone from the clinic at some point."

"I'll think about it," she says. The ring still moving from hand to hand says she's stressed, and I miss the carefree woman from the dance floor.

"Come on, Goof. Let's go have some fun. It'll be midnight before you know it."

On instinct, I reach for her hand, but she pulls her fingers away as we touch, reminding me of the cold, hard truth. She's not mine and therefore I don't get to hold her hand tonight.

But I've seen that look in her eyes. I've seen the sexy-assin smile lighting up her face, and I think she wants to be mine. Even if we are only pretending.

She pulled away, but I don't let that sucker punch me like it could have. It's then I decide I'm giving myself the rest of the night to keep my give a shit guards down and let go of all the chaos constantly running through my head.

Of course, I know I'm not good enough for her, but it's a wedding. The champagne is flowing, the music is thumping, and I'm gonna make the most of it.

"Dance with me," I yell over the current banger everyone else is already dancing to.

This time, when I take her hand and walk us toward the

party, she doesn't pull away. She laces her fingers through mine.

And we dance.

And we sing.

And we laugh.

And it's almost perfect.

If it were real… Now that would be perfect.

Near the end of the night, her parents appear with Sawyer to say their goodbyes.

Holding my hands out to Erin, I say, "Here, let me take him so you can make your rounds."

"You sure? He's getting cranky."

"We'll be fine, won't we, buddy?"

He rubs his eyes and gives me an exhausted, "Gus, Gus."

"I got him." I take the worn-out kid from his grandma, and he lays his head on my shoulder. His arms wrap around my neck, his body heavy with sleep. "Go."

Mia spots us from across the room and makes her way to us, her eyes never leaving mine.

"You want me to take him?" she asks, rubbing his back.

"No, we're good."

And we are. The feeling of him completely relaxed in my arms grounds me. Gives my pathetic existence some sort of meaning. It's ridiculous to feel that much over something so small, but this little boy in my arms and his mama looking up at me like I hung the moon feels like everything.

My everything.

"Well, if you really are okay, I'm gonna run to the little girls' room, and then make sure all his stuff is together for my parents. I'll be back in a few minutes."

"We'll be here."

She walks away, and Knox fills the space. "Uh, Gus. You got a little something... right... there..." He points to Sawyer. "It's a kid. Brother, it's all over you."

I roll my eyes, but before I can reply, something catches my attention. Mia's ring. Rolling across the floor.

"Shit. Here, hold him for a sec." I quickly peel Sawyer off me and hand him to my brother to go running after Mia's most prized possession.

It's moving fast across the dance floor, between high heels and boots, but I snag it before anyone steps on it.

When I get back to Knox, he's holding a sleeping Sawyer out in front of him like the kid is bug-infested or something. Sawyer's poor little limp body hangs so heavy his chin is practically touching his chest.

"He doesn't have cooties, you idiot."

"How can you be so sure?"

"You are an ass. That I know for sure. He's a sweet kid. It might do you some good to get his germs all over you."

His face contorts in disgust. "Here. Take him back."

Slipping Mia's ring in my pants pocket, I accept the sleeping angel, cradling him in my arms.

Knox is wiping imaginary germs from his body and pretending to have the shakes. But after a second, he gives me a wink that says he's only messing around and the real him is in there somewhere.

"You aren't getting any younger, big brother. When are you gonna find someone to settle down with and start a family?"

"Oh, no, no, no. You've got the wrong sibling. Cal's the settling-down type. You," he points at me and then himself, "me, we don't have that domesticated side." He tilts his head, examining me. "Well, I know, I don't." He waves his hand in front of me and Sawyer. "But you... I'm not so sure anymore." He tilts his head to the other side. "Shit, I think this might just look good on you."

That's what I'm afraid of.

Chapter Fourteen

Mia

I've been standing in the shadows by the abandoned cake table for two songs now, unable to bring myself to end the beautiful scene before me. Everyone I love in the world is in one place, and at the center, Gus sways to the music with Sawyer fast asleep in his arms.

When I ducked back into the barn, Angus was walking them toward the dance floor with Knox. Angus rubbed Sawyer's back as he gently bounced them along to "We Are Family," and there was no way I could interrupt the moment. When the song ended, I started to close the distance, but then Sawyer snuggled deeper into Gus and the tattooed cinnamon roll of a man gave him a kiss on the head.

That's when the first tear fell.

My little boy deserves someone like Angus in his life.

He deserves to be loved.

Wanted.

Cared for.

Sometimes I wonder if I'm doing anything right. Should I have handled things differently with his father? Not that he has any desire to be a parent. He sure as hell doesn't deserve that title, but biologically, that's what he is.

If I could go back in time, I wouldn't change anything. I couldn't, because then I wouldn't be lucky enough to be the mother of my sweet, smart child. But will Sawyer feel as fortunate to have only me when he's older? Because the day will come when we finally have the talk about who and where his daddy is.

Will he hate me? Will he ever forgive me?

Watching him with Angus breaks my heart. What I wouldn't give for him to have a man as special as Angus McKinnon as his father.

The same Angus McKinnon who hasn't left my side all night.

My head is all spun up and confused from our constant touching. Dancing. Laughing. Having my back when Hailey introduced herself. Calling me *wifey*. And now this.

We've always been close. How could we not be? Our families are practically one and the same. He was my brother's best friend. I'm his sister's best friend. We've spent so much of our lives around each other. But something has changed, hasn't it? Or is my sad little heart feeling things that aren't there?

My parents have finally said all their goodbyes and Angus is gently handing Sawyer to my dad. Which means, sadly, my time in the shadows is over.

Wiping my face to ensure there's no remaining trace of

tears, I take a deep breath and meet them as they're walking toward the table where I left Sawyer's packed bag.

"Hey, you two sure you want to go? I can take him home," I offer as Angus lingers off to the side, watching us.

Watching me.

What I wouldn't give for them to take me up on my offer to take him home, because the thought of being here without someone to kiss at midnight is depressing. Especially with the only person I want to kiss staring at me in an unfamiliar but not unwanted way.

"Nonsense. Stay," my mom insists.

"Sweetheart," my dad says, holding his grandson in one arm while pulling me close with his other. "We're going to miss our time with him, honey. It's as much for us as it is for you."

"I'm gonna miss you two. And not just for the free babysitting," I giggle through the sorrow of missing them already, refusing to let the tears start again.

"Tomorrow, sweet pea." Mom takes me by the hand. "Save all that for tomorrow."

Angus is still standing to the side of the table, waiting. Is he waiting for me?

Am I imagining things?

Have I completely lost my mind?

I glance at him, feeling my eyebrows pinch together in confusion. He replies with a sexy little wink and the tiniest lift to one side of his mouth. Still unsure what to make of him, I follow my parents out to the car, leaving Angus inside.

The distraction of getting my sleeping baby boy strapped into his seat only lasts a moment. I hug my parents, holding each of them a little longer than usual, then back up to stand alone, waving as they pull away.

Alone.

I've never felt so alone.

With Mom and Dad leaving, it will be just the two of us from here on out. I know I can handle it, but it was nice to have the support of my parents. Sure, I have Daisy and the entire McKinnon clan, but it's not quite the same.

What I wouldn't give to have my big brother back right about now.

Even though there's snow covering the ground, and I'm certainly not dressed for the frigid weather, I'd rather be out here than inside as the clock strikes twelve. Not having anyone to kiss at midnight only adds to the loneliness sitting like a weight on my chest.

Following the snow-cleared path with the moonlight as my guide, I sneak around the corner of the barn where I find more shadows to hide in as the cold air burns my lungs and, hopefully, clears these ridiculous thoughts of Angus from my mind.

But I'll be damned if his reaction to seeing me in my bridesmaid dress this afternoon didn't make me feel like the most beautiful woman in the room.

He had come over to Cal's house to deliver a gift to Charlotte from Callen. When I answered the door, he didn't speak. And he didn't hide the hungry way he took me in from head to toe. When he was done with his appraisal, his heated gaze met mine for a beat before he said, "Mia, you are the prettiest damn woman I have ever laid my eyes on, you know that? It's gonna be a long ass day."

After his compliment, I was the one left speechless. He

walked past me, in his suit jacket and tie, dark denim jeans and cowboy boots, as I stood there, letting the freezing air in as I held the door open in shock.

His subsequent looks and gentle touches have frankly had me feeling a little horny all day.

Sexy. For the first time since becoming a mother, I've felt confident about my body. I've added a little extra swing to my hips tonight. And I may or may not have been purposely posing to maximize the slit of my dress, displaying more of my leg than is respectable for a single small-town mother. If only my self-confidence hadn't brought with it even more confusion.

Exhaling several fortifying breaths, my emotions finally settle for the first time in two days when something in the air shifts. Holding my breath, hoping I'm not found, I still at the sound of boots on snow.

"Hey, wifey. Whatcha doin' out here in the cold without your coat?"

And just like that... All calm flees from my body. The person I was hiding from has found me. Still, I refuse to look in his direction, hoping maybe I'm hearing things.

But then he steps in my line of sight, holding my coat open for me. "Put this on before you freeze to death."

"Thanks." One word is all I give him, not trusting myself enough to say more.

Being alone with Angus at midnight was not the plan.

Stepping closer to him so he can wrap the coat around me, I slip my arms inside and he pulls the front together but doesn't zip it.

Doesn't step away.

Instead, he moves closer.

My body buzzes from his nearness, as though every nerve is on high alert. I wait to see where he takes this, because his unwavering gaze hints at what I never dreamed could be true.

He wants me.

God, how I want him to want me.

Inside the barn, the countdown to the new year begins. This is my moment. My chance to take what I've always wanted and not let another what-if pass by unanswered. When the clock strikes midnight, I can either kiss him or forever wonder what it would feel like to have his lips on mine.

Adrenaline races through my body as I lift a foot to step into him, but before I get the chance to take what I've always wanted, he reaches inside my coat, resting his powerful hands on my hips. His eyes search mine, asking for permission.

Any other night, I would have stopped him, afraid to let this thing building between us ruin our friendship.

But not tonight.

When the countdown gets to three, one of his hands blazes a path up the side of my body, along the side of my breast, and up my neck. By the time the crowd yells, "Happy New Year," that same hand tangles in my hair. His lips ever so gently press against mine. Once, twice, three times. Nothing has ever felt more natural. So right. On the fourth kiss, he traces the seam of my lips with his tongue, and I open to him.

He pins me against the ice-cold barn, his warm body pressing into me as if he can't get close enough. My hands wrap around his back, exploring his expansive muscles.

"God, Mia." One of his hands grabs my ass, connecting us even more. "You're everything. Do you know that?"

Did someone spike my drink? Am I on some sort of trip right now?

"Angus..." I breathe out a puff of white air as he trails kisses down my neck.

Is this really happening?

"I've wanted you for so long."

He what?

Another kiss on the neck.

"You. Are. All. I. Think. About." His lips trail across my exposed collarbone.

"What?"

Chapter Fifteen

Angus

"What?"

The champagne may have helped me find the courage to follow her out here, but the intoxication flowing through my veins is all Mia. To finally have her in my arms. My lips on hers. It's like a damn dream come true.

I know she's confused, and as wrong as this may be, I can't hold back anymore. I want her to know how I feel, even if I know it won't change anything, and in the end, we can never be.

Placing a kiss over her heart, I pull back, so I have her full attention and fuck me if her parted lips, swollen from our kisses and the rise and fall of her chest aren't the sexiest fucking thing.

"Mia, you've been in my head since I was eighteen,

watching you and my sister leave for prom. I've known since that day nobody would ever compare to you and they haven't. But shit, that was before this. Before I had tasted you. Now, there's no saving me."

My lips collide with hers again, craving another taste, because I'll never get enough.

Never.

"I know I don't deserve you," I say against her lips. "But it doesn't stop me from wanting you."

Her eyes grow wide, like she's about to flee just before she says, "I can't."

Cupping her exquisite ass with both of my hands, I pull her against me so she can feel what she's doing to me. "Why? Why can't we have one night together?"

"Angus, you don't know what you're asking for. There are things you don't know."

Her head hangs, and she looks down in what looks like shame. And that just won't do.

I lift her chin with my finger. "Do you want me even half as bad as I want you, Mia?"

From the moment my question is out on the icy air, the wait for her answer is excruciating.

When she nods her head up and down, the stranglehold my ribs had on my lungs eases and I can breathe again.

"There is nothing you could tell me that would ever change the way I feel about you. Trust me, I have my own demons, Mia. Demons that would have you running. But I'm a selfish man."

A snowflake lands on her eyelash, and I lean forward to kiss it away. Her eyes stay closed for a heartbeat before she opens them again. Unfortunately, her uncertainty remains.

"I know we can never be because if you knew the real me, you wouldn't want anything to do with me. But, god dammit if I don't still need to have you this one time. You can keep your secrets and I'll keep mine, but let's give each other what we both want."

"What about Daisy? Our families?"

"What about us? You and me? Don't you think we deserve to know just how bright we might burn together?"

Her body answers for her when her hands wrap around my neck, fingernails gently gliding over my head. Like she wants this.

Wants us.

Like she wants to know just how bright we might burn.

My hands move up and down her back before sliding over her ass. My need for her is so intense, so distracting, it takes a moment for me to realize she's freezing. Her entire body is shaking, and it isn't simply a result of the off-the-charts chemistry between us. She may have her coat on, but her dress is thin, and she's in heels.

Adjusting my hold, I wrap an arm around her waist and bend so I can position my other behind her legs, lifting her into my arms. She doesn't protest. Instead, she wraps her arms around me and buries her face in my neck.

As I walk us through the snow to the horse barn, she kisses my neck and nibbles at my ear, keeping the flame burning as we trek through the snowy night. And if I didn't care about her so damn much, I would lay her down in the snow and take her right here and now. But somehow, I make it to the barn and into the tack room.

It's not where I imagined it would happen, but it's the best I've got.

Luckily, Knox upgraded the room a few years back, installing hardwood floors, a large island with a marble countertop, and a sink in the middle of the room. There's a heater, a mini fridge, and a leather chair in the corner. I send a silent thank you in my brother's direction. His intention may have been to make the space nicer for all of us to hang out while we worked, but I plan to make good use of it for a completely different reason tonight.

I set her on the counter and she gasps when her ass comes in contact with the cold marble. I do my best to distract her with a kiss on her lips. "Let me turn the heater on." Another kiss. "Be right back."

The sound of her feet on the floor has my heart sinking into the deepest part of my stomach. It only takes me a few seconds to turn on the heater, but it's enough time for her wariness to creep back in.

Has she come to her senses? Is she trying to flee?

When I turn back, she's dropped her gaze to the floor and shyness reddens her cheeks. A moment ago she couldn't get enough of me, and I want more of that.

I need her to be on the same page.

With her nerves getting the best of her, she reaches for her ring, and panic flashes in her eyes when she notices it's missing.

I tug it from my pocket and hold it up. "Looking for this?"

She exhales with relief, but I don't give it back to her.

Not yet.

Chapter Sixteen

Mia

The room is dark, except for the orange glow of the heater, but as Gus comes closer, there's no escaping the passion in his eyes. It's an intense version of him I've never seen before. As if after confessing his feelings, he doesn't have to hide them anymore. Like a weight has been lifted. He seems so sure of what he's feeling whereas I'm not sure how I even got here.

I'm scared to death of what this all means, but also absolutely terrified of never feeling his lips on mine again.

Nothing has ever felt so right.

"Mia, I've wanted you for years, but if you don't want this, tell me now."

When I don't reply, he shuffles closer, reaching out and brushing his knuckles over my cheek.

"I know I don't deserve you. But I'm not sure I can keep

fumbling through my days without knowing what it feels like to have you in my arms." He lazily drags his thumb over my bottom lip, and I do my best not to whimper under his touch. "To be inside you. To hear you say my name when you come."

My core clinches with desire as my head spins and my heart swells.

Of course, I know we shouldn't do this. He's my best friend's brother and if he knew my secrets, he would hate me. Because they're unforgivable. But his words. His touch. It's all so intoxicating, and I don't have the self-preservation to stop him or to speak, so he carries on.

"I've already said it, but to make sure things are crystal clear, I'll say it again. You consume every one of my thoughts. Every. Single. Day. I'm tired of wondering what it would be like to be with you. I need to know."

Still stunned silent, I lean into his touch and his hands reach inside my coat and roam over my hips to the top of my ass as he pulls me against him.

"Just once, Mia. No expectations. Just this one moment between the two of us. Nobody ever has to know. It will be something just for us."

Deep down, I know this is a mistake. Look what happened the last time someone said similar words to me.

But this is different.

Angus is different.

I have had feelings for this man for as long as I can remember, and he's making it nearly impossible to reject his offer when I want nothing more than to have this with him.

Not only do I want Angus, but since the day I found out I was pregnant, I had turned off the part of me that allowed myself to feel wanted. I have done nothing for myself since and even though this goes against my better judgment, I don't want to let this chance slip through my fingers. Who knows if a night like tonight will ever come my way again?

If he can be brave, maybe I can too.

He deserves to know his feelings are reciprocated.

"Angus, I want you. I've always wanted you."

He curses under his breath, and his body relaxes. His head angles as he leans in for a kiss, but I pull back.

"If we do this, it has to be a one-time thing. Nobody can ever know. Especially Daisy. Are you sure one night is all this is?"

"One night."

It's the answer I need to hear, even if it's not the one I want. A zap of pain goes straight to my heart, and he must see it in my expression, because he has more to say.

"But this isn't a one-night stand, Mia. *You* are far more than that, and you deserve better than me. But I'm a selfish bastard and I'm asking you to give yourself to me anyway."

It's like he's in my head and knows exactly what I need to hear to ease the pain in my chest. Although he has it backwards, he's the one who deserves better than me.

"I'm a little rusty," I confess.

"Yeah?"

"I haven't really, well, you know, since Sawyer."

As if I've just returned the favor and said exactly what *he* needed to hear, his lips crash into mine. It appears he's done talking.

He lifts me back up onto the island and pushes my coat off my shoulders. The slit in my dress is so high that when he gently pulls my legs apart, my dress falls open, leaving me exposed to him. He steps between my thighs, running his hands up and down my legs.

When I first saw it, I thought my dress was too much. Too sexy for a wedding, but the way Angus watched me all day... has touched me all night... I'd say it was just right.

I feel beautiful.

Kind of hot, if I'm being honest.

Not like a mom.

The material is thin, allowing me to feel every touch Gus has placed on my body.

His eyes dart back and forth between mine as if searching each one to make sure this is really happening. Like he finds it hard to believe this is what I want, and he's looking for the faintest hint of reluctance.

To see this self-assured man second-guess whether I want him as much as he wants me astounds me. How could *he* be the one feeling doubtful when he's all I've ever wanted?

Assuring him with a nod, I pull on his tie to bring him closer, hating to have his lips so far away now that they've been on mine. Needing him to know just how wanted he is.

"Kiss me."

It's not a request.

He follows my order. His hands only leave my body when I push his suit jacket off him. Before it hits the ground, his hands are back on me, rubbing up my thighs and around to my ass. He grips me tightly, bringing me to the edge of the counter.

Needing more, I tug his shirt out of his pants. My fingers fumble over the buttons. Pulling back so I can see what I'm doing, I say, "I need to touch you."

While I loosen his tie and work on the buttons at the top of his shirt, he starts from the bottom up.

"Say it again," he whispers.

My hands reach under the material and glide across his pecs. His shirt opens and I place a kiss over his heart, gently pushing his shirt off his shoulders. "I need to touch you. I want you, Angus."

The faint smell of champagne tickles my senses as his breath comes out in a heated rush. His relief is palpable. The pressure of his fingertips intensifies against my thighs, but he doesn't move them from where they hang onto me for dear life.

His reaction to my words, my touch, sends a powerful sensation through my system. It awakens something that has been buried deep inside me.

He removes his hands from my legs holding them up in front of him. "Show me what you want, Mia."

Angus may not know it but him letting me, no, wanting me to show him what I want, letting me control how I take just that, is fueling a power I can't remember feeling in a long time, if ever.

We've been hiding from each other for a lifetime. It's dark, but there's no hiding from one another now.

Not anymore.

Knowing this is my one chance to explore him, I might as well make all my naughty dreams about Angus McKinnon come true while I can. My fingers explore down his neck, where the pounding of his heart thrums beneath my touch. Lowering my mouth, I follow the trail left behind by my fingers, and his heartbeat against my lips. They trail his tattooed sternum, while my hand takes its time caressing his pecs and the rigid lines of his abdomen until I reach the muscles that form the V disappearing into his waistband.

"You're beautiful," I say. My breathing picks up its pace when I wrap my fingers around his thick length, but the denim of his jeans is a barrier that simply must go.

My fingers work the metal on his belt buckle and with newfound confidence, I pull the belt from his pants. The sound of it hitting the floor sends a shiver down my spine.

"You're freezing. Let's grab a blanket and move to the chair."

He's mistaken my shiver of excitement to mean I'm cold, but when he pulls me into his arms and sets me on the ground, how can I protest?

He steps away to get the blanket, and I miss him immediately. He pulls a Pendleton throw off a rack made especially to hold the beautiful wool blankets but when he reaches for the lamp, my confidence retreats.

Panic sets in.

Chapter Seventeen

Angus

"Please don't."

Mia's voice is barely above a whisper. Gone is the confident woman who was just exploring my body with her hands and lips. It hurts my heart to think she doubts I would find her anything but perfect with the lights on or off.

But if leaving the light off brings back her confidence, then, by God, the light stays off. Besides, the glow from the gas fireplace gives me all the light I need.

"Whatever you want, Mia."

She takes the blanket out of my hands, opens it and spreads it over what I'm sure is an ice-cold leather chair.

"Just once and it stays between the two of us, right?" she asks again.

"Right."

It's not the answer I want to give her, but I agree, because the realistic part of me knows tonight is all we can have.

What I want to tell her is that she's mine. That I want to be the last man who ever gets this with her. But the needy look in Mia's eyes as they roam over my body is quite the distraction and the words never leave my mouth.

"Condom?"

"Right here," I assure her, sliding one from my wallet. She takes it out of my hand and slips it into my front pocket.

"Boots."

Without hesitation, her wish is my command, and I toe off my boots faster than ever before.

Closing the space between us, she drags a finger over my abs and then hooks it behind the button of my jeans and leads me to the chair. The clicking of her heels against the hardwood floor the only sound.

She places me in front of the chair facing her. "You said whatever I wanted."

"Anything, Mia. When it comes to me, you can have anything."

Her shoulders are back, her gaze heated. Biting her lip between her teeth, she leisurely tugs down my zipper, as if we have all the time in the world. Then she stops and takes a step away from me.

My pulse quickens, but the way her smile forces her lip free from her teeth, I know she's not changing her mind... she's got an idea.

Her ass is a work of art, swaying as she saunters to the island. I've never seen this side of her and it's sexy as hell. She removes her thick wool coat from the counter and brings it back, dropping it at my feet. My cock flexes in anticipation.

Pressing another kiss above my heart, her hands wrap around my lower back and then find their way under my pants and boxer briefs. Her hands squeeze my ass while her tongue teases one of my nipples.

God, damn. Mia Powell taking what she wants may just be the hottest thing I've ever experienced. Her teases slowly killing me.

I need her sweet lips on mine again.

My hand snakes into her hair at the nape of her neck and her big blue eyes flash up at me. I watch her tongue circle my nipple before she flattens it against my pec.

"Mia," her name is a prayer on my lips.

The grin I feel against my skin says she knows she has the upper hand as she bites and licks her way up my neck.

"Say it again, Angus."

The heat of her words against my ear lights a fucking fire inside me. It's taking every bit of the limited self-control I have left not to take over, but I'll be damned if I'm going to miss this opportunity to find out exactly what it is she wants to do to me.

"God, Mia."

I swear she purrs when I give her what she asked for, but when she takes my bottom lip between her teeth, I growl back.

She kisses me unhurriedly. Seducing me with her tongue as one of her hands finds its way down the front of my pants. Taking my raging cock in her hand, she elicits a hiss from me as she strokes my erection.

"You said whatever I want, and I want this," she says against my lips as she runs her thumb over my tip, rubbing the pre-cum off before bringing it to her mouth for a taste. I nearly come right here and now.

I've dreamed of this woman for years, but not even my fantasies included this heady version of her. Does she not know she's about to bring me to my knees?

Releasing me, her hands slip back under the waistband to push my pants and briefs slowly down my thighs. Her mouth glides down my body as she traces my abs with her tongue.

My pants slide to my ankles, and she drops to her knees. Stunned, because there is no way Mia Powell is on her knees before me. No way this is what she wants. But with one hand on my ass, holding me in place, her other wraps around my shaft. All the while, her sapphire eyes watch my reaction. She leans forward, and the tip of her tongue traces the vein running along the underside of my raging hard length. I hiss out a curse as her tongue swipes over the head before perfect pink lips wrap around me. Her cheeks hollow as she takes me all the way to the back of her throat, her gaze unwavering, fixed on my face.

Her mouth has been on me in scenario after scenario in my fantasies, but reality eclipses fiction. My world tilts on its side. I'm unsure how I'll ever find my balance again.

As good as she feels, I doubt this is how she wants things to start *and* end.

"Sweetheart, if you keep this up much longer, I can't promise not to come down that pretty little throat of yours. I'm hoping you want more than that."

Her responding moan reverberates around me and just when I think I'm going to have to pull her off me, she releases me with a pop.

Before she rises to her feet, she retrieves the condom out of my pocket, tucking it inside the front of her dress.

As she stands, her fingertips spread across my chest, and she gently pushes me back into the chair. She taps her lips with her finger, blatantly looking over every naked inch of my body as if deciding what she wants to do next.

Tugging my jeans the rest of the way off, she tosses them aside, kicking my feet apart so she can step between my legs. She licks her lips while eyeing my hard cock, still wet from her mouth. Her shoes land in the same place she tossed my clothes just before she bends over to shimmy out of her panties. They land on my face, the scent of her arousal eliciting a feral growl from deep in my chest.

"Fuck, Mia." I rub the lace against my nose, inhaling her sweet smell. "You're wet for me, baby."

Her gaze doesn't leave mine, as she lifts her dress up her legs, the moonlight lighting her up like an angel sent from above. I tuck her lace thong between the chair cushion, because she's not getting it back. It's mine now.

Straddling me, she moves her hips back and forth, rubbing her wetness over my cock, her lips and tongue tasting me at a luxurious pace. Her hands brace on my shoulders as she teases me, my hands gripping her ass, encouraging the pace and pressure of her clit against me.

"I need you inside me, Angus."

Her moan against my lips is desperate even though she's the one setting the pace here.

"Then take me, Mia."

Dipping her fingers into her dress, she retrieves the condom from her bra. Tearing open the foil wrapper with her teeth, she rolls the latex down my shaft. With my length in her hand, she lifts herself above me, her incredible tits in my face as she aligns our bodies and slowly lowers herself onto me.

Nothing and no one has ever felt so significant. The way she wraps around me changes my life forever. Her eyes close and her body relaxes as though having me inside her is the salve that takes away all that is wrong in her world.

She opens her eyes and starts grinding up and down, taking me deeper and deeper until she's fully seated in my lap, her lip caught between her teeth again.

So. Fucking. Tight.

My hands are still under her dress, gripping her perfect ass, but I don't dictate the rhythm. Watching her take control of her pleasure is breathtaking. I don't dare do anything she doesn't ask for or take for herself. I happily give up control.

This is a first for me.

I've never done it before in any aspect of my life.

Only in the worst times of my life did I not control my own destiny, and those moments had the worst possible outcomes.

But here.

At this moment.

Mia's confidence and pleasure are paramount.

And to be honest, nothing has ever felt better.

Chapter Eighteen

Mia

The way Gus watches me with unadulterated need spurs me on, giving me the courage to take what I want.

What I've always wanted.

Him.

It takes a few moments to adjust to the size of him, but now that I have, I've set a leisurely pace, not wanting to rush what he has promised is our one time together.

"Fuck, Mia. Look at you riding me. You are fucking exquisite. You feel so damn good."

His words are as intoxicating as I'm sure his tongue would feel if his head were between my legs. The thought threatens to end my slow and steady pace. But when he puts his thumb into his mouth to wet it, I know what's coming. My heart rate picks up, only to soar off the charts when he presses that same thumb against my clit to work me over in a way I never want to end.

"I want to watch you come apart for me, gorgeous. I *need* to feel you come apart for me."

"Not yet," I breathe out with a throaty moan.

"Whatever you want, Mia."

The way he fills me to the point I almost can't take it, the sweet intensity against my clit, and his eyes all but worshiping me collide together to form the most beautiful agony. I hate for it to end, but my world is going black.

"Angus..." I lean forward, my hand on his chest to brace myself, and the new angle intensifies things. His cock hits that sensitive wall inside my core. Stars burst into my vision as my world combusts.

"Don't stop, gorgeous. Don't you dare stop! You're gonna bring me right over that beautiful fucking edge with you."

I yell his name, blacking out for what feels like endless heartbeats. When I open my eyes, I find his brows furrowed, his expression almost angry. I push back from his chest and settle my hands over his that are still on my ass, applying pressure to let him know he can set the pace.

"My turn to watch you come, Gus."

In answer, he grips my flesh and sets a grueling pace, working my body up and down, his eyes never leaving mine.

Then, Angus McKinnon growls *my* name as he comes. The pace and intensity of his thrusts make my body hum as I come right along with him.

I don't know how we got here, but thank God we did.

His features soften, and he makes a request of his own. "Don't move. Not yet."

He reaches for my face and kisses me softly.

Gently.

Our one time is coming to an end, and he seems to be savoring every last moment.

Releasing my lips, he rests his forehead against mine. "Do you know how many times I've dreamed of having you?"

"You've dreamt of me?"

"Mia, you don't have a clue what you've been doing to me all these years. And even if this is a one-time thing, it's something I'll be fantasizing about at night while I touch myself for years to come."

A red-hot blush burns my skin. "You can't be serious."

He flexes inside me, still hard like he can go again. "Feels pretty serious to me."

Kissing him, I let my hands roam freely over his naked torso, not ready to let reality take hold just yet.

"Sweetheart, you're shivering. Let's get you dressed, and as much as it kills me to say it, we need to get back or things are going to get real weird."

I'm so wrapped up in him, I didn't realize I was shaking, but he's right. The cold is seeping in, and as much as I hate to admit it, our time must end.

Rising from his lap, I instantly miss the fullness of having him inside me. I slide to my feet and slip my shoes on as I watch him in all his naked glory. Still hard, his impressive length bounces between muscular thighs as he removes the condom. Chiseled abs ripple as he stands. When he turns and bends to scoop up his pants, I finally get a view of his ass, and oh, what a view it is.

He stands, pulling on his pants with a knowing smile. Why bother hiding my obvious ogling of him now? After what just happened, I'm not sure how to lock my attraction away again.

"Keep looking at me that way, and we'll stay in this room all damn night."

"Sounds good to me."

"Sure does."

He returns to the chair and pulls my lace thong from the cushion, tucking it into his suit jacket pocket.

I don't bother asking for my panties back. If I'm being honest, I want him to keep them. To have a souvenir of this night. Of what we just shared.

While he buttons up his shirt, I pull my coat on. Once he's fully dressed, he turns off the heater and grabs me by the hand, guiding me to the door through the dark room.

He opens the door, but before we cross the threshold, he turns, kissing me long and hard before slipping Granny's ring on my finger. Then he scoops me into his arms, carrying me through the snow to the barn where our family and friends are saying their goodbyes. We're back just in time.

"There you are!" Daisy yells when she spots me. "Where the heck were you? We're gonna get one last group shot."

"Sorry, needed some fresh air."

Her eyes dart back and forth between me and her brother, who may not be holding my hand anymore but is standing much closer than usual.

"With him?"

"Neither one of us had anyone to kiss at midnight, so we thought we would remove ourselves from the awkward situation and chill out somewhere else."

Relief fills her eyes, highlighting the second reason on my list of why I can never be with Angus like a flashing neon sign. My heart drops to the pit of my stomach, guilt washing over me.

What was I thinking?

"Well, that's just silly. You two should have stayed in here with us. You could have kissed me." She winks then, hooking her arm through mine to tug me away from her brother before leading us to the bride and groom.

Daisy releases me and gives Callen a hug. "Congratulations, brother. You did well."

"I did, didn't I?"

I reach for the bride, hugging her tightly, praying she can't smell the sex on me.

"Thank you for including me on your special day. It means the world to me."

It really does. Charlotte surprised me when she asked me to be in their wedding party since we haven't known each other that long.

"We wouldn't have wanted to do it without you. You're family, Mia."

And that's the third reason on my list. No matter how perfect it was, Gus and I cannot happen again.

We all gather on the dance floor for one last group picture before we start to say our goodbyes.

Cal approaches, looking a bit out of sorts, but pulls me to his side. "How are you getting back to your place?" he asks, almost absentmindedly.

"I got her," Angus says from behind me and I freeze worried everyone will know.

Do they know?

"You sure?" Cal counters.

"You just worry about your bride. I've had nothing to

drink in the last two hours and it's not like she lives far from here."

He's focused on his brother, thankfully, and not on me. There's no way I'm ready to meet his gaze in front of his family after what we just did. It would be way too obvious. It already feels like *I just screwed Angus* is stamped onto my forehead. I need to remove myself from his presence.

I hug Cal and give him my best, then rush away to get my bag.

Gus is waiting for me at the barn door. He silently walks me to the truck's passenger side and helps me into the cab, leaning over to buckle me in. I would normally protest, seeing as I am an adult, but something about having him so close feels too good to complain about.

Within minutes, we arrive at his house.

"Don't open that door," he says when he shifts the truck into park.

Running around the vehicle, he opens my door, pausing in front of me before helping me out. It takes everything in me not to close the miniscule space between us and kiss him. But I keep my feet planted firmly in reality.

Our moment is gone.

For the last week, Angus has been driving to the ranch to shovel the walkway from the house to the driveway so the path is walkable, but he still takes me by the hand and escorts me up the porch steps.

He unlocks the door, holding it open, and I thank him as I pass by.

I drop my bag on the couch and slip out of my coat, but before I can turn to say goodbye, the door clicks shut.

He's gone. Just like that. Without so much as a goodbye.

Keeping my back to the door, I take in a deep breath.

Be grateful. You knew it was a one-time thing.

But just as I've released my breath, the floor creaks a beat before two powerful arms wrap around me, and relief I shouldn't feel has me settling against him.

"What are you doing?" I whisper.

"Well, technically, it is my house."

"True."

He brushes my hair off my neck, exposing my skin that he immediately covers in warm kisses.

"I thought we had an agreement?"

I don't care about the agreement. I want more of him. But the guilty part of me forces myself to remind not only him, but the both of us.

"We agreed to one night, and the night is far from over, Mia."

His hands begin to wander. Growing wet and needy for him, I press my legs together only to be reminded my underwear are in his pocket.

God, that's hot.

"Besides, you deserve better than a cold tack room in a barn."

"I do?" I gasp when he cups my breast.

"Damn straight," he whispers in my ear. "Not to mention you're already sleeping in my bed."

Without warning, he scoops me up and carries me in his arms, down the hall to his bedroom as if I were his bride.

He flips the switch on the wall. "Only this time we leave the lights on."

My body stiffens. The control I felt in the barn nowhere

to be found. I've carried a child. Nursed a child. I have stretch marks and cellulite. I can't let him see me.

"Gus, I'm not sure I can." I squirm out of his hold. "I'm a mother. Not a hot cowgirl or twenty-something tourist like the women you usually invite up to your loft. My body has been through, well, a lot in the last two and a half years, and I have the stretch marks to prove it."

"You have always been and still are the most beautiful woman I have ever known."

"Because you haven't seen all of me."

"Trust me."

It's not a request, it's a demand.

He reaches for the silk tied behind my neck and in one move, my halter dress falls to my feet. I'm left standing in front of him in my strapless bra and heels. Scared motionless, I'm frozen to the spot as he examines every inch of my body. Unease churns in my stomach, threatening to make me sick.

"You. Are. Breathtaking."

"Angus, you don't have to--"

"Tell me I'm lying," he says, grabbing my hand and cupping it over the tight denim straining to contain his erection.

Is this really happening?

Is Gus McKinnon planning on taking me for the second time tonight? In his bed, no less? And is he standing in front of me admiring my body as if I am exactly what he says I am?

Breathtaking.

He releases my hand and takes a step away from me. I let it fall to my side, missing the feel of him. Slowly and with purpose, he slips off his jacket and untucks his shirt from his jeans. He tugs on his matching black tie, loosening it enough to pull it over his head before sliding it over mine. The silky fabric tickles my skin as it falls into place.

"I'm not sure how this night keeps getting better, but you standing in front of me looking like a god-damned goddess right now is proof that it can."

He unbuttons his shirt. My stomach twisting with fear and lust, I reach behind my back to unhook the clasp of my strapless bra. His eyes darken and his tongue snakes out to wet his top lip, fire igniting in my lower belly.

When my bra falls to the ground, he all but growls, "Fucking perfect, Mia. *You* are fucking perfect."

He rips his shirt open the rest of the way. Buttons scatter across the hardwood floor.

His shirt hits the floor beside my dress. He yanks his boots off and removes his jeans in the blink of an eye. Tucking his thumbs into the waistband of his boxer briefs, he bends and, in one more swift move, stands before me naked as the day he was born.

It's only been an hour since I saw him without his clothes on, but he's no longer shadowed in darkness. Now, with the lights on, I can really take him in. And he is a masterpiece.

It shouldn't come as a surprise. Over the years, I've seen him shirtless more times than I can count. But this... Well, nothing quite compares to the vision before me, and I doubt anything ever will.

It's clear he uses the weights I saw in his loft. His body screams strength. Thick thighs, a broad chest, and corded muscles beneath intricate tattoos running up his forearms to his broad shoulders fight to steal the focus from his hard length, but his handsome face and the way he's looking at me are what draw my attention.

Standing before him in nothing but my heels and his tie, I twist Granny's ring around my finger, not sure what to do next. In the barn, hidden by the dark of night, I was bold and took what I wanted. Now, here in the blinding light, I feel exposed and uncertain.

He closes the distance between us, covering my hands with his to stop the incessant spinning of my ring.

"Let me show you just how beautiful you are."

Mesmerized by his words and his gentle touch, I simply nod in reply.

Trusting him to take control, although I'm not sure I'll ever understand what he sees when he looks at me, I let him guide me to the bed. He releases one of my hands, and circles one of my nipples with a fingertip before cupping my breast. Dropping my other hand, he moves behind me, the heat of his body setting me on fire when he whispers in my ear.

"You. Are. Magnificent."

Standing in the middle of his bedroom beside his bed, the same one I've been calling my own for the last week, with nothing to cover me, I gasp when I catch my reflection in the wood-framed full-length mirror I've used every morning this week to get ready.

Angus's larger body frames mine from behind as he presses against me. His knuckles glide over the side of my breast and down my side until his arm wraps around my waist.

His gaze is fixed to mine in the mirror when he speaks in a low velvety smooth voice. "I want you to watch me worship you. I want you to see what I see."

Fear creeps in. I'm not sure if I can do this. "Angus, I--"

He steals my words before I can get them out. Releasing

me to turn my face, he kisses me until I'm dripping for him. His tongue caresses mine while his calloused hands explore the curves of my body. I am lost to him. Hands fumbling behind me, I run my fingers over his skin. He is all I feel. No insecurity, no guilt, no fear.

Just Gus.

When he pulls his lips from mine, he moves so he's standing in front of me. Needing to touch him I rest my fingers over his heartbeat. The steady rhythm under his skin calls to me. On instinct, I move my hand to press my lips to his chest.

"I'm going to worship you." He places his finger under my chin tilting my head, so I meet his eyes leaving only a breath of air between us. His tongue flicks out over my top lip. "And you're going to watch."

This time I don't protest, closing my eyes as he kisses down my neck.

"Open your eyes, beautiful."

My fingers run over his short hair, enjoying the feel of his lips on my skin, ignoring his demand.

"Eyes, Mia. If you want me to continue, you will open your eyes."

Hesitantly, I blink them open, not willing to give him up just yet.

"Good girl," he purrs against my throat.

God, the view of him in the mirror as he goes back to kissing my neck is magnificent. His tattooed back, the hard round globes of his ass, and his muscular legs should be illegal.

As his lips move across my collarbone, my attention snags on my face. My lips are swollen from our kisses, my cheeks rosy with intoxicating lust, my eyes full of need. Whatever it is he's doing looks good on me.

Bending lower, he sucks one of my nipples into his mouth, trapping it between his teeth. The sting from his bite sends an electric jolt through my body, waking any nerve endings that weren't already activated. Watching his mouth on one breast, his hand on the other while his tie hangs between them, feels like an out-of-body experience. Like I'm watching a different couple in the mirror. His tanned skin against my pale body is absolutely gorgeous. I burn this into my memory, never wanting to forget a moment.

His mouth drifts to my other breast, giving it the same awakening sting. My back arches, pressing into his mouth, my body begging for more. My red nails scratch over his shoulders and down his tattooed arms. The sight is heady, heating me from the inside out.

"You watchin'?"

"Yes."

"Good." He swings his tie over my shoulder. "Don't take your eyes off that mirror, Mia."

His arms reach around my back and hold me steady as he kisses his way between my breasts and down my stomach. My breasts hang heavy, the tight pink buds of my nipples begging for more attention. He slowly lowers to his knees, his hands dropping to my ample ass.

They don't stay there for long, traveling over my hips and then up and down my thighs. His mouth dips lower and I tense, trying to take a step back, but he holds me firmly in place. His warm lips land on the small silver streaks I was hoping to hide from him, and I want to pull away and hide. As if sensing my reaction, his grip tightens.

Between kisses across my lower stomach, he says, "These gave us Sawyer. What could be more beautiful?"

Warmth settles behind my eyes, and I blink rapidly. A tear escapes, falling down my cheeks at the truth in his words. I wouldn't trade Sawyer for anything in this world, including a flat, smooth stomach. There truly is beauty in our scars and watching this man I've wanted for as long as I can remember, as he worships my body is like some sort of mommy porn, my mind will play on a loop for years to come.

His hands grab my backside as he growls against my pelvic bone. He looks up at me, but I keep my eyes on the mirror like he instructed. "I have always loved your ass in a tight pair of jeans, but I have to tell you, naked, it exceeds all my expectations."

He gives one cheek a gentle slap, and the corners of my mouth lift in the mirror.

His mouth glides back to my pelvic bone and he kisses me right above my clit. "Hold on to the bedpost, sweetheart."

My fingers wrap around the wooden post as he lifts one of my legs and drapes it over his shoulder. What I see in our reflection is by far the hottest thing I have ever witnessed. My alabaster skin against his tan back and my stiletto over his tattoo is enough to make me weak in the knees, but when I simultaneously feel and watch him drag his finger over my clit, down my wet center, and then press it deep inside me my chest rises and falls on heated breaths. My core throbs, needy.

He spreads me open and licks me from my opening to my clit before burying his face in my pussy. The tandem sensation of watching and feeling threatens to take me over the edge. His grip on my ass intensifies as he pulls me closer, feasting on me like a man starved. I'm a quivering mess, ready to combust when he pulls away from me.

Glancing over his shoulder, he catches his first look at the two of us and his eyes roam up and down my body in a way that makes my cheeks heat. "Look at you, Mia. You're fucking perfect. And you taste like fucking heaven." He turns his attention back to me and flattens his tongue against my core, the tip teasing as it presses into me.

My hands run over his head, my body humming with pleasure.

He adjusts moving to the side and taking my leg with him, opening me even more. Bared to him. Vulnerable.

"Look how wet you are for me." He licks his lips as he drags two fingers through my wetness before sliding them inside me. He doesn't have to demand that I watch. I couldn't force my eyes off his hands on my body if I wanted to.

My eyes catch his and his hand stops its divine stroking. Realizing why he stopped, I drop my gaze back to where his fingers had been working their magic. He rewards me for following instructions when his fingers begin moving in and out of me again. He hungrily watches me watching his hand work me into a divine madness. And right there, in nothing but my heels, I come for the second time tonight.

Instinct demands I close my eyes, but I resist because I want to watch. Want to see what it looks like to come apart in his hands. I repeat his name, like a prayer. Just as my world fades to black, he sucks my clit into his mouth, circling it with his tongue over and over until I scream his name. Finally, I close my eyes where I'm met with bright stars as I crash into blissful oblivion.

His mouth releases my clit and the last waves of my

orgasm crest over me. When I finally flutter my eyes open, they find Angus as he continues to watch the slow movement of his fingers, his hand dripping from my release. He strokes his hard length with his other hand, and the sight intensifies my desire once again.

"Fuck."

It's all I get out before I come again, just as hard as the first time. Only this time I keep my eyes open and watch him.

After every last ripple of pleasure has run through me, he pulls his fingers out and then gently rubs his hand and my wetness around my sensitive pussy, not releasing me from my high.

Thank goodness I'm holding on to the bed for dear life when he releases my leg and stands. Otherwise, I would be in a puddle on the floor.

He kisses me hard before pulling the covers back on the bed. Tugging his tie back in front of me, he peels my fingers from the bedpost.

"Baby, we're just getting started."

And he isn't lying. He lowers me to the bed and makes slow, luxurious love to me until the sun comes up. He kisses and caresses every inch of my body from my head to my toes, all while telling me every fantasy he's ever had of the two of us together.

We take advantage of our one night.

He lives out his fantasies while ruining me for all men to come.

I let him brand himself on not just my heart, but my soul.

Chapter Nineteen

Angus

I'd say waking tangled up in Mia was fucking everything, but is it really waking up in someone's arms if you didn't actually sleep?

How could I waste even a minute when this is it?

Our one night together.

We certainly didn't plan what happened between us last night. Sleeping with my sister's best friend was nowhere on my list of groomsman job duties for my brother's wedding. I'd had no agenda other than to bring Mia her coat when I spotted her outside. Yet here we are and I'm not sure I'll ever be the same as I was before the clock struck midnight.

I refused to go to sleep knowing when I opened my eyes again our night would be over. Instead, I've been more than happy to lie here listening to the cadence of her beautiful heartbeat and memorizing the rhythm of the light rise and fall of her chest, etching every detail into my heart.

When I wasn't buried in her, we laughed over stories from our childhood and the many times we had *almost moments*. Like the time we all accidentally went skinny dipping the summer before I left for the military. Mia and I were on a two-person inner-tube and Cal was driving the boat at full speed. We fell off, hitting the water so hard my shorts and her bikini top flew off.

God, how I hated not being able to see anything in the water that day. If only I had known that sixteen years later, I would have much more than a glimpse of her. That we would make love all night long and she would fall asleep with my arms around her, my head on her stomach.

I've screwed my share of women, but I've certainly never felt like this after. Because last night wasn't just some random hook-up.

Last night was Mia.

Last night was more.

More than a man like me deserves.

Mia thinks I'm the same person I was before I enlisted. Everyone does. All anyone sees is the CMH they pinned on me when I came home. I'll admit, it's shiny and garners a lot of attention. It also serves as a reminder of the brothers I lost and the innocents... I do my best to keep those memories packed away with that God-awful medal.

When I first got out, I drank way too much. My days had been occupied with building my house and working with my dad and Callen at the family-owned hardware store. At night, I drank. I drank to forget. To drown out the guilt. I drank because I didn't like the man I had become. But mostly, because Chris hadn't come home with me. After a year of my downward spiral, my brothers and sister sat me down on our annual birthday trip to relay how concerned they were about me.

It was their version of a gentle intervention. And it hurt to see the worry in their eyes.

They insisted I could tell them anything and they would be there for me, but they didn't pry. I couldn't talk to them, but they wanted me to talk to someone.

I will forever be grateful for the way they sat me down and shared their concerns without demanding the reasons I was trying so desperately to escape. How could I ever explain the things I had seen? The things I had inadvertently been a part of? Yes, we're family, all four born in August two years apart. We share the middle name of Brian, well, Brianna for Daisy. My siblings are the people I love the most in this world. We may share almost everything, but I couldn't share that.

So, I reached out to a military friend who recommended their doctor. I've been going to therapy for the last nine years now. Dr. Laughlin helped me get my shit together. Thanks to my siblings and the doc, I'm a business owner. I only drink socially, and for the most part, I'm a pretty happy person. Unfortunately, the shame that came home with me lingers, but buried as deep as it is, it no longer controls my life.

Still, when I'm around Mia, all those memories and shame seem to work their way out of their tightly sealed box to remind me why we can never have more than this night. The thing is, last night felt different. She shoved my demons aside when she looked all the way to the deepest recess of my soul. Made me believe she saw who I was and still wanted me.

If only that were true.

Because even though there isn't anything I wouldn't do for her, there are still secrets she doesn't know. Secrets that would push her away forever. Burying them away for the last 24 hours, I've let myself luxuriate in her. I can say without a shadow of a doubt this has been the best night of my life.

Being wrapped up in her feels like home.

As content as I am, the sun is up, and our time together is over.

"Mia. Baby," I say begrudgingly, placing kisses on her stomach. "I have to go."

Using my mouth to wake her, I leave a trail over her ribs and nibble on each of her nipples on my way to her neck. Her eyes are still closed when she wraps her legs tightly around me, trying to hold me in place as her hands roam over my head.

"Your parents will be here with Sawyer soon. I better get out of here."

"I was hoping the night would never end."

"Me too, Goof. Me too."

Our night may be over, but my cold, dark heart belongs to Mia Powell.

It's hers.

There is nothing left for anyone else.

"Really? We're both lying here naked, and my nipple was just in your mouth and you're gonna call me that?"

I kiss her on the cheek. "One night or a thousand, you'll always be my goof, Mia." I nuzzle her neck. "Always."

"Angus."

If I don't get up right now, I never will, and I promised her one night. So, against everything my body and heart want, I do the right thing and peel my body from hers, our skin sticking together. She scoots to sit against the headboard of my bed, pulling the sheet up to her chest, and watches me dress.

God, seeing her in my bed, my room, my house... it's overwhelming. Her rosy morning cheeks, mussed hair, and exposed skin teases me more than ever now that I've memorized every inch of her body. Seeing her like this messes with my head, because it's all I've ever wanted and the one thing I can never truly have.

I am so fucking fucked.

Leaving her is the last thing I want to do, but her parents don't need to see me making the walk of shame or find her naked in my bed the day they move to the other side of the country.

One night.

That's all this was.

At the bedroom door, I take one last look at her, instantly wishing I hadn't. Because fuck me, if the sight of her teary-eyed in my bed watching me walk away from her doesn't bring years of repressed longing to the surface. Something I've never given myself permission to feel with anyone.

Her tears confirm this can't happen again, because it already hurts too much. I don't know what to say. This isn't goodbye, because I'll see her again. And again. Just never in this capacity.

She whimpers, my name a whisper on her lips. It awakens something deep inside me that lay dormant until my first taste of her. A possessiveness I've never felt for another woman screams at me to go back to her. Dry her tears. Console her. Claim her again.

For both our sakes, I do the opposite, leaving her in my bed crying as the organ beating inside my chest fractures.

Racing out of the house, I climb into my truck, chest heaving as if I just ran a 10k. As I leaned in to kiss her last night, I told myself I'd take this one shot and then shut my heart down for good.

How could I have been so fucking stupid?

Taking that one shot was supposed to get her out of my system, but it only cemented her even deeper into my soul.

We had our moment.

It was beautiful.

She was beautiful.

And even though she has my heart, it's over.

It has to be.

Chapter Twenty

Mia

My head is as much of a jumbled mess as my heart this morning.

After Angus left me crying in his bed, I crumbled. I buried my face in the pillow that smelled like him and sobbed.He left without a word, but he didn't need to say anything. Everything he felt was written on his face.

He was just as conflicted as me, knowing last night shouldn't have happened, but he wouldn't take it back. Neither of us could regret something so beautiful.

Angus McKinnon didn't just want me, he truly saw me.

Flaws and all, he still wanted me.

He worshiped me. Made me feel beautiful. Made me feel comfortable in my own skin, something I wasn't sure I would ever feel again.

Outside the barn, when he touched me, I thought maybe

I was hallucinating. But then his lips met mine, and I have never felt more alive. It felt like existing in a dream state, yet I'd never been more grounded. His kiss, his hands roaming my body, it all felt like we were made for each other.

Nothing had ever felt more right.

Of course, my insecurities had to rear their ugly head, but Angus didn't let them win. Didn't let them ruin the most meaningful night of my life.

He's wanted me all these years.

Sitting here now, sipping my coffee and waiting for my parents to arrive, that's what keeps playing on repeat in my mind. He's wanted me since he was eighteen. How is that possible? I would wonder how I missed the signs, but I know better than anyone how a person can love someone from afar, so well not even those closest to them notice.

"One night or a thousand, you'll always be my goof, Mia. Always." Those words echoed in my mind as I showered and got ready for the day. Preparing for a whole new set of emotions to bombard me when I say goodbye to my parents as they embark on this new phase of their lives.

They should be my priority, and I *am* heartbroken they're leaving. But my emotions are still tangled up in Angus. In the way he looked at me. Needed me. If it weren't for the bruises on my knees and the soreness between my legs, I'd wonder if the whole night had actually been a dream.

"I am going to worship you. And you're going to watch."

Sure, I've heard women talk about their nights in his loft, but I never could have imagined sex with Angus would be so intense. But we weren't in his loft, we were in his bed, in his house.

A knock on the door rouses me from my musings, and I

rush to answer. The need for a comforting hug from my mom suddenly overwhelms me now that I know she's on the other side of the door.

Pulling the door open to find the three most important people in my life beaming at me causes my chest to tighten and my limbs to grow heavy. Sawyer is beaming in his grandpa's arms and Mom is gazing at them fondly, laughing at something Dad said.

When Mom takes in my appearance, she knows exactly what I need. Lunging toward me with open arms, she hugs me like nobody has ever hugged me. She has always given the best hugs, holding on and never letting go until I'm ready. Any other day, she'd stand here as long as I need her to, but today, they need to get to the airport. So, much sooner than I'd like, I pull away.

She takes my hand, gently pulling me away from the open door and closes it behind us.

Dad and Sawyer are waiting a few feet away and I'm surprised to see the somber look on Dad's face again. That same desolation fills his eyes, like it did on Christmas Eve when he apologized for their move. Where Mom seems beside herself with excitement to start their next journey, Dad is anything but.

"Mama! Look!" Sawyer says, holding out a familiar light brown and white stuffed English bulldog. Well, what used to be white has turned to a dingey off-white after three and a half decades.

Tears I didn't see coming overtake me. "Bruce," I say on a shaky breath, studying the faces of my parents. "Are you sure?"

"We're sure, honey," Mom says, shaking the paw Sawyer holds out to her.

Bruce was my brother's most prized possession as a little boy. He went everywhere Chris went. Even through his teenage years, Bruce was always on his bed. Sure, Chris would boot him to the floor at night while he slept, but Bruce was always there.

Chris should be here watching Sawyer grow up. Teaching him how to ride a horse or fish. Instead, my little boy now has Bruce. It's not the same, but it's a piece of Chris I will make sure he treasures.

"Thank you," I say. "For Bruce and for watching him last night."

Dad lowers Sawyer to his feet and he scampers off to his room.

His absence leaves an awkward tension between the three of us.

"Of course. It was fun. You should have seen him jumping up and down on the beds this morning. It was like his very own trampoline park." Dad chuckles. They've been staying in a hotel the last couple of days since all of their belongings are currently en route to their new home in Sarasota.

Mom's fingertips tap my cheek. "Looks like you had a late night. How are you feeling this morning?"

More like an early morning.

I need to play this off. If anybody knows when I'm lying, Mom does.

"Shoot, I forgot I had these on." I peel off the eye masks I put on after my shower. Hopefully, they did their job and it isn't obvious I've been crying since Angus got dressed and walked away. "It was quite the party, wasn't it?"

"It was a perfect day," Mom agrees.

"You guys want some coffee?"

"Mia, honey. We can't stay long. We have to get to the airport."

Dread falls like lead in my belly.

This is it.

Cue the waterworks.

Dang it!

"Now if you keep that up, you're gonna make this old man go all watery, too." Dad pulls me into his arms.

Mom comes up behind me and rubs soothing circles on my back. "Sweetheart, we'll be home to visit, and you and Sawyer will come see us. Besides, we'll FaceTime. Often."

Mom always finds the silver lining, no matter the situation. She's my rock, helping me see the light at the end of every dark tunnel.

"I miss you already."

"Sweetheart, we're so proud of you." Dad kisses the top of my head. "You are a wonderful mother, and the best daughter we could ask for."

"Thanks. But why do I feel like there's a *but* coming?"

"Because you know your old man well." He releases me, holding me at arm's length. "You need to take care of yourself, not just Sawyer. Live a little. Have some fun. Fall in love."

If only it were that easy, Dad.

"What do you mean? I've been out more in the past few weeks than I have in the last few years."

"You have, and there's a light in your eyes we haven't seen in a long time. I'd like to see more of that. Your mom and I worry that with all the wedding festivities ending, you'll go back to work and Sawyer and never leave the house. It's a beautiful house, but there's more to life. Promise us you'll get out?"

"Do Sunday dinners with the McKinnons count?"

"It's something, but how will you ever meet someone if you don't put yourself out there?" Mom asks, genuine concern in her voice.

I'm surprised, today of all days, we're discussing my love life.

"I'm fine. I don't have time to date."

"Sure you do. You just have to make time for it," Mom says, tugging on a piece of my hair.

"What I need to do is get this job, so I can afford to get my own place and stop mooching off old family friends," I retort, hoping to change the topic.

"Nonsense. You are not a mooch. And you are going to get that job. Mark my words, Mia. It's a new year and I have a feeling it's gonna be a good one for you."

"I sure hope you're right."

"I know I am." She walks down the hall to Sawyer's room, leaving me with Dad.

"Mia, tell me you heard me?"

"I heard you," I say sheepishly, embarrassed my impending spinsterhood has them worried. I had no clue.

"You need anything, we're just a phone call away. We're always here for you.

That doesn't change."

"I know. I appreciate it, but it's time for you and Mom to stop worrying about me and focus on sunshine, beaches, golf, and gators."

"It's our job to worry about you."

"I'll be fine. *We'll* be fine. You need to worry about those gators. Tell me you heard *me*," I say, throwing his concern back at him.

"Always the smartass."

Glad to have put a smile on his face, I grin. My first genuine one today. "I learned from the best."

Mom returns with Sawyer in her arms. "You promise to be a good boy for your mommy?" she asks.

He nods his blond head and now it's time for Mom to get emotional. She kisses him on both cheeks and gives him a squeeze before handing him to Dad. As soon as her arms are free, it's my turn. She doesn't speak, and she doesn't hold me for long.

Dad hands Sawyer to me and then hugs us both to him. "I love you, little girl."

"Love you too, Daddy."

They head for the door, Sawyer and I following. We watch them walk down the porch steps, get in their rental car and we wave when they drive away on the snow-covered road that leads to Sharon's and their new life.

Chapter Twenty-One

Mia

"**D**amn, girl. How do you keep it all straight? That rush was insane," Daisy says from her favorite corner booth. She and her laptop are a staple here at the cafe where I wait tables five days a week. She works and we chat when things are slow. She'll never know how much it means to me that she makes this effort to spend time with me. Our friendship is one of the many things that changed when I became a single mom. Luckily for me, we've only gotten closer. "I couldn't focus on my project, because I was too dazed by you zipping around this place like a damn athlete. I'm exhausted just from watching you in action."

"It is what it is." I shrug. "Especially when we're down a person. The bright side is that a busy shift makes the day go by faster. Oh, and there's always my one true love... coffee."

Daisy lifts her Grace's Crooked River Cafe mug in agreement. "Cheers to that."

My hip rests against the other side of the booth. I don't dare sit down and rest my feet. They'll only hurt worse when I get back up. "So, how's it going with the architect?"

She flashes me a devious smile.

"Come on! You know I have to live vicariously through your dating life. Tell me something!"

It's been less than a week since I slept with Angus, and keeping that night from her is the worst sort of torture, yet simultaneously the easiest thing I've ever kept from her. She's clueless to the fact that I've been in love with her brother, well... forever. And she would lose her shit if she knew what went on between us. But to have had the experience I shared with Angus and not tell her is killing me.

Except for my love for her brother and the identity of Sawyer's father, she knows everything there is to know about me. Sure, those are pretty big secrets, but as long as she never finds out, she won't hate me.

She closes her laptop and holds her hands out in front of her, her smile growing as her hands move further apart, one eyebrow lifted.

I gasp. "Wait, are you telling me what I think you're telling me?"

"The architect is huge. Is that what you were thinking?"

I glance over my shoulder to make sure nobody is in earshot. "Good huge, or too huge?"

"Oh, we make it work, don't you worry."

"So, I'm guessing by your smile, you like him."

"For now. He's not *the one* or anything, but it's fun for the time being."

"You sure about that?"

"Besides the fact that he's only here on business and he'll be gone by next month, he isn't much fun outside of the bedroom."

"No?"

"He's nice enough, but he's *so* serious. I'm not sure if that man has had a silly moment in his life."

"Well, that's too bad."

If a man doesn't know how to have fun, it will never work between them. Daisy can be serious when the moment calls for it, but she also loves to be silly.

"Nah, it's all good. Charlie and I are busy getting the new business up and running. I don't really have time for anything more serious than the occasional hook-up."

Daisy certainly doesn't need a man to take care of her, but she gets lonely. Try as she may to hide it, I see through her. She can tell me all day long she doesn't have time for more than a casual fling, but if she met *the one,* she would find the time.

Daisy and Charlie are a lot alike that way. Both already established and successful on their own. Only Charlie found Cal and let him in. My hope is that Daisy doesn't meet *the one* only to let him pass her by because she's too busy working and proving she doesn't need a man.

My phone vibrates in my apron pocket and when I see Dr. Gibbons' name on the screen, my heart skips a beat and I break out into a sweat. I hold my phone up for Daisy to show her who's calling.

Now her eyes grow wide for a completely different reason. "Shit! This is it! Answer it!"

She's right, this is it.

The security I so desperately need for me and my son hangs in the balance of this phone call. My hand shakes as I push the button.

"Hello?"

"Mia, it's Dr. Gibbons at High Desert Health and Wellness, happy new year!"

"Hello. Happy new year to you, too."

"I'll cut right to the chase. We would love to hire you as our lead nurse practitioner if you're still interested?"

Wait. Did she say lead?

"Lead?"

"Yes, it really just means extra paperwork and scheduling. Your references raved about your charting, and we hear you're very organized. We think it's the right fit and it would pay a bit more. What do you say?"

"Yes!" I blurt out a little too fast. "I'm definitely still interested."

"Wonderful! I know you need to give your current employer two weeks' notice, but would you be able to come in this week to discuss your salary and sign your paperwork?"

"Of course, I can come in tomorrow afternoon, if that works."

"Perfect. I'm so happy this all worked out. We look forward to working with you and getting to know your family."

Shit.

"Me too, Dr. Gibbons."

"Great, see you tomorrow."

"See you tomorrow and thank you so much for this opportunity."

All I can do is stare at the phone in my hand once the call

ends. I can't believe this is happening. I just got the job of my dreams and they think I'm married to Angus. My joy and excitement are overshadowed by nausea.

Because I'm a liar.

"You got it, didn't you?"

"I did."

She scoots out of the booth to pull me into a hug. "I knew you'd get it! I'm so proud of you!"

"Thank you."

I collapse in the booth, sore feet be damned, and drop my head into my hands.

"Wait. What's happening? This is your dream job. Insurance and day care, remember? Why are you upset?"

She's right it is, but they also hired me in part because of a lie.

"It is all those things, Daisy." I peek through my fingers to look at her. "But... they... Oh, my God. Daisy, they think I'm married to your brother."

"Louder please. I don't think I heard you right."

"They think I'm married to your brother," I whisper-shout at her.

"Shut up!"

"I know, it's so bad."

"It's crazy is what it is!"

"I agree."

"Uh, Mia. I have three brothers. Which one do they think you're married to?"

"Shh..." I look over my shoulder to make sure there aren't any Nosey Nellies listening. "Angus."

"And why exactly do they think you're married to Gus?"

"I can explain."

"Please do."

The bell over the front door chimes and I'm saved for the moment.

"Hold that thought."

I move to slide out of the booth, but Gracie comes out from the kitchen. "I got it. Take a break."

Shit.

No escaping now.

Daisy's arms are crossed in front of her. "Start talking, lady."

"Listen, I really can explain."

"I'm all ears."

Oh, she is loving every second of this.

"God, it's so embarrassing."

"Spit it out."

"Well, apparently, Dr. Gibbons saw Angus and Sawyer drop me off for my interview. And then while we were talking in her office, wouldn't you know it, they were playing in the park next to the clinic and she had a perfect view of them. She saw Granny's ring and assumed we were married. I started to correct her but in the same breath she raved about the importance of family to the clinic, and how she couldn't wait to meet them. The second time I started to correct her, Sawyer started crying. We thought he might have gotten hurt, and she rushed me out the door."

"Does Gus know?"

"Yep, I told him right away, and he was fine with it."

"I bet he was." She smiles like she's up to something. Like there's more to this than there is.

"Don't be weird."

"It's not like I didn't notice how attentive he was at the

wedding. I've been wondering what's up with you two. I'd say he seemed pretty content playing pretend with you. He was sure honing his husband skills from what I could see."

"You're ridiculous."

"Listen, you could do worse when it comes to fake husbands and baby daddies."

True. Very true.

"I know. He's been so cool about it and said since I'm already staying in his house, the address isn't a lie. You know my paperwork is going to ask me to list my spouse and an emergency contact. How strange will it look to not list my *husband* on the paperwork?"

She sits back, arms crossed. Smile still firmly in place. "You are in a bit of a pickle."

"You're loving this, aren't you?"

"More than you know."

"You're such a brat."

"You have to admit it's funny. Like you would ever marry one of my brothers. Although, after the wedding, I'd say Angus wouldn't mind if you did."

Her playful voice is confusing. Would she be okay with Angus and me, or is this all just a funny predicament to her?

The weight of my guilt from sleeping with Angus the night of the wedding hits me square in the chest. Try as I might to fill my lungs with air, breathing feels impossible. When did I become this person? Daisy is my best friend, yet I'm keeping secrets. Hell, I haven't even trusted her enough to tell her about Sawyer's dad. And now I'm lying to employers to get a job.

Who have I become?

"Daisy, this is bad."

"It'll be okay." She leans forward and takes my hands in hers. "Mia, you got the job. You and Sawyer are gonna be okay and Gus will be cool as long as you need him to be. To be honest, he's a pretty good emergency contact."

"You aren't mad?"

"Why would I be mad? I'm just so proud of you. My brother didn't get you the job. You did that. And we're gonna celebrate. Friday night. The House. Free drinks at your fake hubby's fine establishment."

"That sounds great, but I don't have anyone to watch Sawyer."

"Let me take care of that."

She gathers up her things and puts her coat on, and I begrudgingly stand. And just like I knew they would, my feet hurt worse.

"Listen, we're gonna have to come up with a plan that includes the family."

"Angus said the same thing, but I would really love to avoid that if possible."

"Sweetie, Bend is only twenty minutes from here and, well, not to sound like an asshole, but there isn't anywhere in Central Oregon where folks don't know the McKinnon family. Especially my brothers. We need to cover our bases, and I think the family needs to know so they don't unknowingly blow your cover."

"Daisy, no." Panic overtakes my emotions, embarrassment scorching my cheeks. "I would be mortified if they knew."

Pulling me into a hug, she says, "Okay. We'll worry about it another day. I'm proud of you. Oh, and you're mine Friday night." And just like that, she's out the door.

At once, I'm overcome with an entirely new set of

worries. How do I see Angus on Friday and not want a repeat of what happened on New Year's Eve? Not want to feel that way again.

The knowledge of his feelings has brought back some of the confidence I had before I got pregnant. Knowing Angus McKinnon wanted *me* all these years feels phenomenal.

Empowering.

Something shifted in me that night. I feel different. Like more than Sawyer's mom. Almost like the woman I used to be.

Chapter Twenty-Two

Angus

GOOF

I got the job

GUS

I knew you would. Congrats, Goof. I'm happy for you.

GOOF

Thanks.

They still think we're married.

GUS

Then they likely think I'm a much luckier man than I am.

GOOF

I can tell them the truth.

GUS

Don't do it on my account.

GOOF

I'll have to list you as my emergency
contact.

GUS

Works for me.

GOOF

Gus.

GUS

Mia, just put my name down.

GOOF

You sure? You can back out any time. This
is my problem, not yours.

GUS

That's not the way this works. Your
problems are my problems, wifey.

I've been an anxious idiot since I read my sister's text telling me she and Mia were coming by the bar tonight to celebrate.

When Mia texted three days ago to tell me she got the job, it fucking electrified something deep inside me. I know it's not real but this new connection to her and Sawyer, fake or not, has brought me to life. My therapist is worried this fake connection feels too real. She's worried about how this may end. The thing is, I'm pretty sure heartbreak is the inevitable outcome, on my end, anyway. I'll worry about that later. For now, I'm going to ride this fake relationship as long as I can.

The good doctor also thinks Mia and I should try something real. After examining all the feelings our night together brought to the surface for me, Dr. Laughlin thinks I'm selling myself short. That I deserve Mia. Which means I deserve Sawyer, too.

I would do anything to make a life with them a reality. Our family connection is something we could overcome. I have enough faith in my family to know that much. My secrets and the demons that continue to haunt me, are the real hurdle.

I'd give anything to keep my miserable soul out of their lives. I'm determined to, even though the thought of a life with them consumes nearly every one of my thoughts.

It's been five days since I left her teary-eyed in my bed.

Five days of fighting the urge to show up at the cafe.

Five days of not driving to my house for some bullshit reason just to set eyes on her.

Five days of fucking my hand in the shower every morning to visions of her fisting my sheets, writhing in pleasure while I eat her like she's my last meal. Dark hair spread across my pillow, perfect pink lips swollen from hours of ravaging, her moaning and screaming my name the most sublime sound I've ever heard.

Damn those perfect fucking lips of hers. They were mesmerizing before I knew what they looked like wrapped around my dick. Now? Now, the thought of them on anyone else makes me sick to my stomach.

No matter how tightly I grip my cock, it will never come close to what it felt like to be inside her tight pussy.

Heaven.

Every inch of her is heaven right here on earth and was mine for a night. She was more than I imagined she could have been and more than I deserved, but of course, the selfish bastard I am wants another night. Who am I kidding? I want endless nights with her.

I'll ride this fake husband thing as long as it lasts and love every damn second of it. Along the way, maybe I can earn her trust and encourage her to tell me the secrets she thinks would turn me away.

I want to be her person.

Her protector.

The only one who touches her and makes her feel the way she did five days ago.

I'm mindlessly chatting with Loten, who works at the family hardware store, when the electricity in the room changes.

She's here.

Peeking over my shoulder to confirm my intuition, my heart rate doesn't just pick up its pace, it thunders against my chest like a drum. A strange feeling churns in my stomach, like the one I got as a kid on Christmas Eve when I was too excited to sleep because Santa was coming.

Fuck.

That's what she is.

Christmas.

Every. Damn. Day.

Drawn to her, I don't even excuse myself before striding away from Loten. She and my sister take off their coats and slide onto their two favorite barstools, laughing at the *Reserved* signs I'd taped to the seats. Better to avoid having to kick someone else off them when the girls arrived.

The smile on her face kicks those Christmas feelings into high gear, but when she spots me coming her way and her smile ratchets up a notch, lighting her from within, well, fuck me running, because there's just no feeling like it.

Closing the distance, I open up my arms to her and she walks right into them, accepting my hug and setting me on fire.

"Congratulations, wifey," I whisper in her ear. Her arms tighten around my neck while mine around her waist do the same.

This is the only touching we'll get again, and we take full advantage of it. "Let me know when you tell them you've left my sorry ass, but feel free to take your time."

When she pulls away, our eyes lock on one another too long to be considered friendly.

She's so close.

What I wouldn't give to wipe away the barely there distance between us with a kiss.

One night.

That's all it was.

One. Night.

Letting go of her and stepping away is almost painful.

"Two skinny margaritas coming up."

She nods and sits on her reserved stool, looking as dazed as I feel. The struggle in her eyes tells me she's battling her emotions, too, both of us pushing down the need we have for one another.

Busying myself with making their drinks, I decide it's

safest to keep my pathetic ass behind the bar for the rest of the night. Fortunately, it's busy. I purposely let Laurie work Mia and Daisy's end of the bar, but the struggle is real.

She and Daisy hit the dance floor, and I can't take my eyes off her. I would feel like a creep, but the kicker is… she can't take her eyes off me, either. She watches me, watching her, the magnetic pull between us nearly impossible to fight, yet we do.

When Rhen Mitchell approaches her, gesturing for a dance, I smack a hand on the bar and prepare to jump over it, but she doesn't need me to rush in and save her. No matter how badly I want to. She rolls her eyes, hard, and says something that looks like "I'm good," before walking away, Daisy on her heels with a disgusted look on her face.

Leaning my hip against the counter where Laurie is pouring a rum and Coke, I angle my body in the opposite direction of Mia and Daisy. "Hey, what's the deal with Rhen Mitchell? Why do the women in this place hate him?"

She chuffs. "He's a dick."

"How do you mean?"

"Well, he seems nice enough on the surface, with that pretty face of his, but trust me, he's a dick. He thinks he can do and say what he wants with no consequence. Not to mention he often has to be told no more than once. But his daddy is a senator, so he thinks he's special."

Crimson rage infiltrates my vision. I'm no longer seeing straight.

"Why the fuck haven't you ever said anything? If I had known, I'd never have allowed him in here."

The monster that's been lying dormant deep inside me

for years stretches awake, coming out of his slumber and readying himself for release.

"Hate to break it to you, but if you didn't allow inappropriate men in this place, you'd lose half your customers."

She delivers the rum and Coke to her customer at the other end of the bar. I think about what she's saying. Are there really that many assholes in this bar, in this town? Have I turned a blind eye to things happening right in front of me?

"I refuse to believe it's that bad," I disagree when she returns.

She stops at the register and keys in her code. The drawer pops open. "I'm sure you do, and that's cute and all, but you're wrong." She sorts the cash into the drawer, pushes it closed and turns her eyes on me. "Most men don't even realize they're being gross. This is a bar. They drink too much. They look, they comment, they make us uncomfortable. It is what it is. Most don't step too far over the line. Rhen wasn't like this growing up. He was just like any other cowboy in town. But since his divorce, he's been a dick."

"Has he ever crossed a line with you?"

As shitty as it would be if he had, please tell me he has. Give me permission to jump this bar and rip his arms from his body.

She huffs. "He knows better."

"What about anyone else?"

"Gus, if I knew, I wouldn't tell you. It's not my story to tell. Besides, I make his drinks weaker than most. The more he drinks, the more of an asshole he becomes."

How the hell did I not know this?

The urge to check on Mia and Daisy becomes a necessity I can't resist. Glimpsing over my shoulder to check for perverts lurking in their general vicinity, I'm met with big blue eyes that don't look away when our gazes lock.

MINE!!!

My monster roars, ready to slay any dragon that dares to even look in Mia's direction. The selfish need to bury myself inside her, to claim her as my own, bellows inside me, forcing me to remove myself from the situation. I push through the door to the kitchen and don't stop until I reach my office.

Slamming the door behind me, I move the mouse on my desk, bringing the monitors to life where I can watch her and my sister from the safety of the tiny eight by eight room. Rhen is throwing darts with Loten and the girls are chatting with a couple of their girlfriends who work at Christie's Kitchen over in Redmond.

Thirty minutes later I'm still watching from afar, just like I always have. When the girls begin to put their coats on and appear to be getting ready to leave, it forces me from the safety of my office. Stalking through the kitchen, behind the bar and then out to the main floor, I approach, but I don't touch.

"You two leaving?"

"There you are. Where have you been hiding?" my sister asks.

Mia pulls a baby blue hat with one of those fuzzy balls on the top onto her head, bringing out the blue in her eyes.

"Had some paperwork to take care of."

Daisy eyes me warily, clearly not believing me. Fucking siblings. There's no getting anything past them.

"You two okay to drive?"

"We parked at my place and walked down. We're fine."

The Hell they are. These two must be out of their minds

if they think I'm going to let them walk home at midnight alone. Especially after my chat with Laurie.

"Let me get my coat. I'll walk you."

Daisy huffs. "It's three blocks, Angus. Relax."

"I'll relax when I know you're home safe. Be right back."

I run up to my apartment and grab my coat and hat, but by the time I get back, they're gone.

"They'll be fine, boss," Laurie says. Her expression says she's amused by my antics. She shakes her head at me like I'm ridiculous.

My sister and Mia may be fine. I, however, am nowhere close.

Pulling the bar door open, I can hear the two of them giggling before I spot them two blocks up, arm and arm running like little kids getting away with something. Following behind them but hanging back, my heart speeds up when they round the corner onto Daisy's street and disappear from sight. I pick up my pace and round the corner just as the front door closes behind them. Leaving an unlit front door that I don't hear Daisy lock behind her. Standing on the sidewalk outside the house I pull my phone out, cursing them as my thumbs get to work.

Angus: Lock the damn door and turn on your front porch light.

Daisy: Oh, my God. Did you seriously follow us home?

Angus: Just do it.

Daisy: I think you need to talk to Dr. Laughlin about these new stalking tendencies. It's creepy.

I have a hell of a lot more to discuss with my doctor than making sure Daisy and Mia get home safely, but this will probably make the list. Along with my conversation with

Laurie and how badly I wanted to rip Rhen's limbs from his body. The entire night will make the list, I'm sure.

Regardless, I'm not moving until I know they're safe inside.

The light turns on and I hear the deadbolt slide into place. My blood pressure drops. Not counting my mom, my two favorite women are in that house.

Angus: Thank you.

Daisy: Love you, Gus. Now go away.

Angus: Love you, sis.

I take my time on the short walk back to the bar. The icy air cools my lungs, and I will it to clear my head and quell the burning rage inside me. The one that wants to destroy any man who so much as looked at Daisy and Mia in anything less than an appropriate way.

That's my sister and my wife we're talking about. I would murder anyone who caused them harm.

And yes, I realize I just called Mia my wife.

Fake or not, she's mine and fuck any other man who goes near her.

Chapter Twenty-Three

Mia

"Mia, there you are," Blakely, the clinic's office manager says, popping her head into the breakroom. My heart drops, wondering why she's looking for me.

I've felt sick to my stomach since handing her my paperwork this morning. I did list Angus as my emergency contact but left the box that asks how the person's related to you blank. She must have noticed something off about my forms.

Shit.

"I wanted to give you this." She hands me an envelope with my name written in beautiful handwriting on the front and takes a seat next to me on the ultra-plush couch that matches a second couch and two oversized armchairs. They really spared no expense when designing this place.

"What's this?" I ask, relieved it's not about my employment paperwork.

Adorable, blonde, tall, and thin, Blakely is the epitome of the girl next door. Somehow, she looks even cuter when she bounces in her seat before she fills me in on what's inside the envelope in my hand.

"Well, since we hadn't made our final hires before the holiday, we weren't able to have our company holiday party. We decided a late celebration would be a great way to get to know each other. Since half the staff is from California and the other half from various towns in the area, we thought it would be a good icebreaker of sorts. Besides, it's a good excuse for you and the hubby to have a date night."

No, no, no. This cannot be happening. I need to think of something quickly.

I open the envelope as I rack my brain for any excuse I can.

"Oh, it's this weekend."

"I know, it's super short notice. But if you're worried about a dress, Hailey showed me pictures from the other night at your brother's wedding. You looked stunning. Wear that dress again. How often do you get the chance to wear a bridesmaid dress more than once?"

There are times I really hate small towns.

"Oh, I wish we could, but my parents, who were my primary babysitters, just moved to Florida."

"No worries, we have day care all lined up if you need it."

Of course you do.

"Okay, well, let me talk to Angus and I'll let you know as soon as I can."

She gets up, clapping her hands as she practically skips

out of the room. "Great, can't wait to meet him. This is gonna be so much fun!"

Checking the clock, I have twelve minutes left of my lunch hour. No time like the present to rip the band-aid off. Texting Angus no longer feels like it used to. Easy, breezy, no big deal. Not since our night happened. Since then, everything is different. Even a simple text causes my heart to leap into my chest.

I had almost convinced myself I had made the whole thing up regardless of the marks he left on my breasts or the soreness between my legs the next day. But then I saw him at The House. My body caught fire the moment I laid my eyes on him. When he hugged me in front of everyone, it felt impossible for it not to be obvious, but no one, not even Daisy, caught on. The way he watched me all night, hell, the way I watched *him* all night was all the proof I needed.

Our night really happened.

Other than our hug, we didn't touch or really go near each other, but neither of us hid the fact that we were keenly aware of the other. Neither of us turned away when caught staring, instead our eye contact grew deeper and prolonged. The outright craving in his eyes had me hot and bothered all night long.

But we are not a thing.

MIA

Hey.

Three little bubbles instantly dance at the bottom of my phone's screen and even though I know better, I grin ear to ear because he read my message as soon as he received it. But most of all because he isn't too cool to reply right away.

GUS

Hey, wifey.

Cue the butterflies and the mild throbbing between my legs. Why do I even bother telling myself there's nothing *more* between the two of us? As much as my brain knows nothing further can happen, my body can't seem to get the message.

GUS

Whatever Sawyer told you… it isn't true!

This man knows how to put a smile on my face.

MIA

You're lucky he doesn't speak in full sentences yet.

GUS

You're telling me. So, what's up, Buttercup?

MIA

Well... it's time for you to regret agreeing to this whole fake husband situation

GUS

Never.

MIA

You say that now...

Okay, you asked for it. My new boss is having a late holiday party for employees and their spouses. I tried the babysitting excuse, but they already have that covered, of course.

GUS

Hell, yes! You know I never say no to a good time. Just shoot me the details and what to wear and I'm there.

I got you, Goof.

MIA

I think it's pretty fancy.

GUS

I can do fancy.

MIA

Are you sure? You don't have to do this. I can come up with an excuse.

GUS

Have you ever known me to do something I don't want to do?

> MIA
>
> No.

I'm not sure when I got off the couch, but I'm pacing back and forth in front of it now, just like I used to as a teenager when I was talking to a boy on the phone. It's what I do when I get excited.

> GUS
>
> There's your answer. Send me the details.

Why does he have to be so dang perfect?

> MIA
>
> Thank you. I owe you big time.

> GUS
>
> I'm still waiting for that thank you dinner.

> MIA
>
> You free tomorrow night or do you have to
> be at the bar for the dinner rush?

> GUS
>
> I own the place.
>
> What time?

MIA

6:00? It'll be me and Sawyer.

GUS

Perfect.

MIA

Okay. See you tomorrow. We can brush up on our fun facts to make sure we know each other well enough to keep this fake marriage up.

GUS

It's a date.

The alarm on my phone goes off, letting me know my lunch is over. Tucking my phone in the front pocket of my navy scrubs, I do my best to shove the butterflies in my stomach back in their cage so I can focus on the rest of my afternoon.

If only it were that easy.

Angus McKinnon is a stubborn man and if I let him take up space in my head and let's be real, my heart, there isn't much that can be done.

Chapter Twenty-Four

Mia

"Hey, buddy. How are those yummy goldfish?" I kiss my sweet boy on the head as I bring the first few dishes to the table.

"Yummy, fish!" Sawyer says from his high chair as he pops another one into his mouth. I've been an anxious mess while prepping dinner, and for my sanity, knowing he was safe and sound in one place was a must. A high chair tray full of crackers has done the trick.

"Let's hope Gus Gus is as enthusiastic as you."

The moment I set homemade guacamole and tortilla chips on the kitchen table, there's a knock on the door. As if he's conducting the orchestra of butterflies inside my belly that only perform when Angus is around, they begin their symphony.

It's 5:55. Angus is five minutes early, just like I knew he

would be. Five minutes early has always been on time for him. I wouldn't be surprised if he stood outside and watched the clock not knocking until the second 5:55 hit.

That would be adorable.

However, the word *adorable* hits the road when I open the door and the icy evening breeze gusts into the house. There is nothing adorable about the man standing on the other side of the threshold. His fresh shave has erased the stubble usually gracing his face by this time of day, and if I'm not mistaken, he just got a haircut. I've seen him in his gray Carhart jacket and jeans a million times. He usually pairs his daily uniform of a T-shirt and jeans with his sexy-as-sin work boots; however, tonight, he's wearing cowboy boots.

Holy. Shit.

Was he serious when he said this was a date?

No.

Uh, uh.

No way.

I'm reading too much into his appearance. He probably has an actual date after our dinner. Just because I changed five times before he got here and did my hair in just as many styles, doesn't mean he went out of his way to look good.

"You gonna invite me in, Goof?"

Shit. Busted.

"Oh, of course. Yes, sorry. Come in. It's your house, after all." I'm stumbling all over myself like an idiot.

Opening the door wider, I step back so he can enter, and he breezes by in slow motion, his eye contact unsettling in the best possible way. He's no longer hiding his feelings and in return making it impossible for me to hide mine. The thing is… it's too late. Life has happened and there will never be an *us*.

Once he's inside, I close the door, taking a beat to tamp down my embarrassment from getting busted checking him out before turning to face him. If only the clean, citrusy smell of him didn't linger, clouding my thoughts.

God, he smells so good.

"Little man! Whatcha got there?"

Hearing him talking to Sawyer is my cue that it's safe to turn around. But I couldn't have been more wrong if I had said he was an alien from another planet.

Angus is squatting next to Sawyer's chair while my sweet angel boy feeds him Goldfish crackers. Sawyer opens his mouth like I used to when I would feed him his baby food and it's the cutest thing I've ever seen.

My heart is not okay.

My son deserves a father figure like this. Sure, he has Angus in his life as a family friend. He's as close to an uncle as he'll ever get, but Sawyer deserves a daddy like the man currently eating crackers out of his slobber covered fingers.

Once the kitchen island is between me and the boys, I distractedly finish up the last details of dinner. I'm surprised at how excited I am to cook for him. Especially this meal. I plate everything on serving dishes and start carrying them to the table.

"So, tonight's dinner isn't fancy, but it's your favorite."

"I have a favorite?"

Instantly feeling flushed with nerves, I begin to doubt myself.

This has to be his favorite. It's all he ever wants on his birthday. Right? Shit, did I get this wrong?

"I thought it was your favorite." Keeping my eyes down, I slide around him and set down the tortilla warmer in the middle of the table along with the Mexican rice. "Maybe it's just a birthday thing?"

"Well, hot damn. Did you make me carne asada street tacos, Goof?"

"I did," I say, still not looking at him as I make another trip to the kitchen for the next round of dishes. "I hope that's okay?"

"It's perfect," he says so softly I almost don't hear him.

Glancing up, I find him watching me, a serious yet thoughtful look on his face. Like it means something that I remembered his favorite meal. His expression makes me happy, and I can't help but smile. He releases his own smile, and we grin at each other.

We're both happy.

"Mama, more fishies pease," Sawyer says, breaking the sweet spell we were under.

Angus turns his attention to my son, allowing me a private moment to shake my head free of the inappropriate thoughts jumbling up my mind. Not sexy thoughts, but possibilities for a future kind of thoughts. You know, those even more dangerous kind of thoughts.

"Buddy, you need to eat more than fishies," I say over my shoulder on my way back to the kitchen. "I've almost got everything ready, and then I'll load you up."

"Need any help in there?"

"I'm good, thanks. Almost done. Just take off your coat and sit your butt down. I owe *you*, remember? *I* will do the cooking *and* the cleaning. So, don't even think about asking about helping with dishes later. Got it?"

"Wow, Sawyer. Is your mommy always this bossy?"

"Mama, bossy." Sawyer giggles as I set the last of the dishes down.

"Hey, now. No ganging up on Mommy."

"We would never, would we, buddy?" He winks and I melt.

Making my last trip to the kitchen, I pull out two bottles of Gus's favorite Mexican lager, steadying myself with yet another deep breath.

You can do this, Mia. It's just Angus. Your lifelong friend.

Approaching the table with a little bow, I hand him his beer.

"Wow, you really thought of everything."

"If there is one thing I know about you, it's that you only drink *this* beer with *this* meal."

I clink my bottle to his and sit.

"And you're worried we need a study session tonight to make sure we convince your co-workers we're husband and wife."

"I don't think knowing what kind of beer you like will be enough. Study time is a must."

"Like I said, bossy."

"Oh, I'll show ya bossy." I stand, taking the plate sitting in front of him.

On one side of the plate, I lay out two tortillas and build Angus's tacos. Carne asada, onions, cilantro, and a lime wedge on the side. On the other side of the plate, I add rice and my favorite little side dish of black beans, sweet corn, and more cilantro.

Placing his dinner in front of him, I point to each item in the center of the table. "Homemade quac, homemade salsa, jalapenos if you want 'em, and Juantia's chips, because duh. And if you're good, you might get dessert." I end the sentence by sticking my tongue out at him.

He settles himself in his seat. "I like this side of you, Goof."

I like it too. Not the bossy part. The feeding him part.

"Mama, me too?"

"Yes, baby."

I pick up his Paw Patrol plate and fill one section with rice. In another section, I already have his applesauce and cut up cheese quesadilla. His matching Paw Patrol spoon is clutched in his chubby little hand, and don't forget the matching sippy cup of milk. He'll likely wear more of his meal than he will eat, but that's okay tonight.

With his plate in front of him, he says, "Deet do."

"You're welcome, sweetie."

"Seriously, I think the way he says thank you is the cutest thing I've ever heard," Angus comments, watching Sawyer in wonder as he devours his applesauce.

"I know, right? However, the mess he's about to make won't be so cute, but we'll let him have some fun tonight. I promise no harm will come to your floors."

"I noticed the tarp under his chair. You think of everything, don't you?"

"It's part of being a mom."

"Well, he's got a pretty good one, if you ask me."

The heat on my face tells me he likely knows his compliment did something to me and that's the last thing I need. So, I pretend he didn't say anything.

"Don't let your food get cold. Eat up."

"Eat up!" Sawyer exclaims, lifting a spoonful of his rice

into his mouth. Most of it falls down the front of him. He tries to catch it, scooping it up and shoveling it in his mouth.

Angus chuckles and takes a bite while I load up my plate. By the time I'm seated, he's swallowing the last bites of his first taco, looking at me like I've done something wrong.

"What's wrong?"

"Not a thing. It's just so damn good it pisses me off."

I chuckle. "Glad you like it."

"Woman. Like doesn't come close to covering it."

All I can do is shrug, because I don't really know what else to say.

"So, how's the job?" he asks as he dips a chip into the guacamole.

"It's great. Everyone's nice."

"I know you were worried you were rusty. Did it all come back to you like you hoped?"

"Did I say that?"

"You did, after your interview."

I did?

"You were worried they'd hire you and then you'd let them down because you were rusty."

That's right. I did.

"You're an elephant, you know that?"

He takes a bite of his rice mixed with my black bean concoction and tilts his head to the side, confused.

"You never forget. Anything!"

He shrugs.

I shake my head. "Yes, it all came back. The clinic is very state-of-the-art, though. Lots of new techie things to learn."

We eat and chat, and it's fun. My mind is already racing with what I can make him next.

There may not be a next time, but a girl can dream.

When we finish our tacos, I move to the kitchen to prepare dessert. It doesn't take much since it's his favorite flan from his favorite restaurant. Walking from the kitchen with the plate, it feels like I'm about to deliver his birthday cake to him, but by the time his birthday gets here in August, our little charade will probably be over.

"Ooh, what do we have here?" he says with Sawyer in his arms. I'm impressed to see that he cleaned him up while I was in the kitchen.

"This is from your friends at *Matador*. I can't take the credit."

"Sawyer, have you ever had flan?"

"No, he has not," I answer flatly.

"Your life is about to change, my friend."

"You are not giving my child that nasty stuff."

"How dare you?"

"Sorry, it's gross!"

"We'll let Sawyer be the judge of that."

He scoops up a piece with the spoon and lets my boy try it. It comes out of Sawyer's mouth almost as quickly as it went in. Angus catches it in his hand.

"Ucky."

The drool doesn't faze Angus as he puts the wet bite in his napkin.

"That's my boy." I reach my hands out to take Sawyer, but Angus shakes his head. "I'll take him while you eat," I say.

"He's fine. No dessert for you?"

"Nope, but it is time to work on our story."

He pulls his spoon from between his lips, his tongue

swiping over them as he waves his spoon in the air. I hate knowing what he can do with that tongue, because it's making this much harder than it needs to be.

"Proceed."

"Okay, for starters... How did we meet?"

"That's easy. The truth is all we need. I've known you since the day you were born. I was two, our moms are best friends, and we grew up together. What do they call it? *Friends to lovers?* Don't think I haven't heard you and Daisy discussing your books at Sunday dinner. Pervs." He winks.

Why is he so nonchalant about all of this? Angus McKinnon is not a nonchalant person. He rarely pokes his head out of his hard shell, but since Sawyer's birthday party, I've gotten to know a whole new side to him. His lighthearted take on our situation is throwing me for a loop, and I swear he's enjoying every moment of this.

"But, if we call each other husband and wife, that is far from the truth. So, we will have to lie at some point."

"What if we purposely never say those two words? If you never call me your husband and I never call you my wife, technically, we aren't lying."

"You are all about technicalities, aren't you?"

"If it helps you feel better about the situation, I will find every technicality I can."

I've always known him to be a kind person, but lately he's acting like my well-being is his responsibility. Giving me his home and pretending to be my fake husband and father to my child goes above and beyond the whole family friend responsibilities. I'm so confused.

"And if they ask, when did we realize we were more than friends?" I push back.

"Well, I don't know your answer, but I know mine."

"Have you actually been working on your story?"

"No need to work on anything. Again, all I have to do is tell the truth."

What?

"What?" I ask, on a confused whisper.

"You don't remember me telling you about your prom."

"You meant that?"

"Sweetheart, you will never hear a lie from this mouth." He bounces Sawyer in his arms. "Like I told you that night, it felt like a punch to the gut to watch you going to prom with someone else, but I knew you could never be mine. I enlisted the next day. Safer that way. You were off-limits and there was no way I was sticking around to watch you with other guys. I had to get out of town."

"Angus, no. Tell me that's not true."

That can't be the case. He's been through so much. Horrible things. It can't be because of me.

"Well, I was ninety percent sure I was joining, anyway. That day solidified my decision and sped things up a bit."

He takes another bite of his flan, then offers a bite to Sawyer, who shakes his head vigorously.

"More for me." He kisses my little man on the top of his head.

Sawyer snuggles into him, causing my heart to break a little.

I clear my throat nervously. "I have a hard time believing you have felt this way for so long. I mean, I can't be that oblivious, can I?"

"I'll lie *for* you, Mia. But I'll never *to* you."

I'm not sure my heart can take more of this conversation, but I wouldn't stop it if I could.

"But you never showed any interest in me. I would have noticed. Trust me."

"I've learned how to put my walls up over the years. We can never be, so why instigate something? It wouldn't be fair to either of us."

"So, why now?"

"Honestly?"

"You said you'd never lie."

"Doesn't mean you want to hear the truth."

"I do."

"I can't really explain it. Since the day you said you were pregnant, but wouldn't tell us who the father was, I've had this overwhelming need to protect you, and this little guy." He rubs my yawning boy.

Am I dreaming? I must be dreaming.

"I've been able to keep myself in check, but when you needed help and I knew I could provide the solution to your problem, I couldn't *not* step in. The relief I felt the day I drove away from this house, knowing the two of you were inside... Mia, I can't explain it. It took a weight off my chest I hadn't realized was even there."

"Gus, you don't have to protect us. You know that, right?"

My mind races with all the moments I must have missed over the last two and a half years. When I look back now, Angus was always there. I was so wrapped up in my pregnancy and then Sawyer; I saw it for what I'm sure everyone else has: a good friend who was there for all the important moments. Including the night I went into labor. He was there all night long and didn't leave until after family and friends could come in and see the two of us. I remember him kissing me on the forehead, but I was so out of it, I didn't see it as anything other than platonic.

"But I do need to protect you."

"Why?" I'm absolutely baffled. None of this makes sense.

"I don't know why. It's just the way it is." He shrugs the shoulder not weighed down by a two-year-old whose eyelids are growing increasingly heavy. "The day I drove you to your interview and hung out with this guy," he places another small kiss on Sawyers' head, "I hadn't felt that relaxed in a long time."

I don't know what to say. All I can do is watch the two of them from across the table. He looks natural with Sawyer in his arms. He notices him nodding off and lowers his voice when he continues.

"You two staying here feels good. It's *right*. I may not be here with you, but that's okay because you're right where you're supposed to be."

"Angus, I don't know what to say."

It's true. I'm baffled. It makes all the mixed signals I was getting from him much clearer, but it's still too much to wrap my head around.

He can't feel this way about me. About us. He can't.

"There's nothing to say. I still shouldn't have crossed the line like I have. I should have left it at friends. Taking care of you two should have been enough. And it was. Until I selfishly kissed you. All it took was one kiss and you obliterated my well-built walls."

Right back at cha, cowboy.

"I don't regret that night, Mia. Never. But I also know that night was as far as we can take it."

"Agreed."

"Good. Now, if someone asks to get me a drink at the party, you should probably know what my favorite drink is."

And just like that, one of the most meaningful conversations of my life ends. We're back to our fake relationship. A relationship I wish was anything but fake. Regardless, I roll with the conversation change.

Besides, the answer to his question is easy.

"EBC if we're talking beer, and an old-fashioned for a proper drink."

"Seems I'm not the only one paying attention. I mean, you knew my favorite meal."

There are so many flirtatious replies on the tip of my tongue, but I go for the safety of our new direction of conversation. Besides, he's got me. I did know exactly what to make him tonight, but I'm going to pretend he didn't mention it.

"Whatever. You think you know my favorite drink?"

"Sweetheart, it's not even a question. Wine is always red, beer is always EBC. Before the baby, your mixed drink of choice was a vodka cranberry, but post baby, you prefer a margarita on the rocks, if you drink at all."

Holy shit.

I am so turned on I squirm in my seat to keep my body distracted from the pulsing between my legs.

"Okay, well, we can check that one off the list."

"Mia, I know you're worried about being caught in a lie, but we know nearly everything about one another. I can tell them where you went to school, everywhere you've worked, and your favorite color."

A small laugh escapes me. "You can't possibly know my favorite color."

"Sure do. You like that retro baby blue color. Like the shade they used on old school convertibles. I have no idea what you call it, but I know it when I see it. It always reminds me of you."

"How do you know that?"

"Like I said, I think you're making a bigger deal out of this than you need to."

Sawyer's limp little arm falls from Gus's neck.

"He's out cold. Here, let me take him. I'll go lay him down."

"I got it," he whispers as he stands, supporting Sawyer's back.

"You don't have to do that."

"No, I don't. But I want to."

How do I argue with that? Especially after everything he's shared tonight.

Nodding, I walk ahead of them into Sawyer's room. I turn on the truck nightlight on the dresser Angus built and pull back the bedding he bought.

"Do you need to change him?" he asks.

"No, we'll just let him be for now. You cleaned him up after he ate. We'll let things slide tonight," I say as my hand reaches out to rub soft circles on Sawyer's back.

In the glow of the low light, Angus's eyes lock onto mine. Something real is brewing between us. As much as I know I should, I can't look away from him. Not when he's looking at me like this. He doesn't need to confess his years of repressed feelings, because now I see it all in his eyes. He wishes there could be an us.

Needing to break the spell, I close my eyes for the count of three, then step aside, letting him gently lay my angel down. He pulls the blankets over him and tucks his new favorite stuffed bulldog close to his side.

Tears threaten to fall at the heartfelt moment, so I turn my back on them, striding through the door to gather myself. Besides my parents, I've never watched anyone else put my child to bed, let alone the man who just told me his life is better when he's taking care of the two of us. My emotions hover just under the surface and I'm afraid I'm about to fail at holding them back.

Would it be rude to ask him to leave his own house? I'm not sure how much of this I can take.

He meets me outside the bedroom door and I pull it until it's almost closed, leaving it cracked.

"Thank you," he says, his voice still hushed.

I point my head toward the great room and he follows me, but before I can say anything, he speaks.

"Dinner was perfect..." He puts his hands in his front pockets and the distance between us grows as we walk. "I... I really enjoyed myself, but I think I should head out."

"Of course. Sure. Yes, it's getting late."

It's not getting late. I'm just fumbling over my words because I wasn't expecting him to bail already, even if it's what I need him to do to protect myself. Still, disappointment takes a firm grip on my heart.

"Hey, I keep forgetting to ask. How's your car holding up? Everything okay since you got it back? Need me to look at it?"

He steps closer, and my heart rate accelerates, but he only grabs his coat from the chair next to me. Nothing more.

"Oh, uh, my car. Yep, it's fine. Thanks for asking."

"And you've got snow tires, right?"

"Yes, I live in Central Oregon and I'm thirty-three years old. So, I'm all good. You don't have to worry about me, Angus."

If he wasn't reaching for the door, I would say he was stalling, but no. He's just Gus, being Gus.

"Okay. Well, I'll see you Saturday night then." He seems uncomfortable. As if he doesn't know what to do with himself. "Text me and let me know what time to pick you up."

"Um, okay. Sure."

"Have a good night, Goof."

"You too," I say to the door because he's already gone.

Chapter Twenty-Five

Angus

Yes, it's colder than a witch's tit outside, but I'm pretty sure my body is shaking for a whole different reason. I'm about to spend the evening pretending to be Mia's husband and I'm amped to know at the very least I'll get to touch her all night long.

After dinner the other night, I was a man on fire, every nerve ending blazing to touch her. I had to get out of the house, or I would have crossed the invisible line keeping the two of us from repeating the best night of my damn life.

I know it was just dinner, but it had felt more like a fairytale.

I'm still adjusting to being alone with her.

It's new.

It's everything.

Throw Sawyer into the mix and it's downright perfect.

When she served my birthday dinner, including my favorite Mexican lager, it felt like Christmas all over again. She knows me as well as I know her, which only makes staying away harder and harder. Dinner had me shoving the reasons I couldn't be with her into a nice little box.

When I built the ranch house, I didn't really give any thought to who would sleep in the four bedrooms. But seeing Mia and Sawyer move around the house so comfortably has me giving it a lot of thought. I like them moving within the walls I built with my bare hands, filling the house with laughter, and for the first time, joy. They're fulfilling a dream I hadn't realized I had.

One I didn't want to wake up from.

What I *did* want was crystal clear as I laid in bed later that night. The years of nameless, faceless women who had been in and out of my loft, never to the ranch, ran through my head. And I felt nothing. Because none of them were worthy of the house I unknowingly built for Mia and Sawyer.

Unfortunately, this isn't a fairytale, and I'm no Prince Charming, deserving of a happily ever after. Regardless, come hell or high water, I'll be damned if any harm comes to them on my watch. I will always be there for them.

Exiting the highway, onto the road that takes me to the property I grew up on, my stomach flips and my excitement grows. I know it's stupid to be this excited. All I'm doing is orchestrating some perverse self-inflicted torture. But she needs me. At least, that's what I tell myself.

The truth of the matter is I want more time alone with her.

Scratch that, I *need* to be alone with her.

She has quickly become an addiction.

All I think about.

The self-control I've shown to Daisy's best friend, and Chris's baby sister, is gone.

All logic is out the window.

I'm sure she feels the same. I feel it in my bones. Something special happened when I laid Sawyer down the other night. There was a connection, much stronger than lust, between us. Like some sort of invisible string binding us together.

My relentless craving to kiss her had been so intense it took every ounce of my willpower not to press my lips to hers the other night. Even though it felt like I may never breathe again if I didn't.

Knowing we get to play make-believe tonight has been the only thing keeping me breathing.

To call her mine, even if just for a night.

The truck sways side to side as I navigate the bumpy snow-plowed road leading to my house. It's cold out, but I'm not wearing a coat. My worn work jacket wouldn't go with the very expensive Tom Ford suit I'm currently wearing thanks to Knox and the occasional dress up functions he's dragged me to. Tonight is a big night for Mia, and I want to look my best, so, I'll freeze my balls off for her.

I'd do anything for her.

Hopping out of my truck, I'm happy to see the walkway to the front door is clear. I've been paying one of the ranch hands to plow the road to the house and shovel the path to the front and back doors every morning. The last thing Mia needs is to be late to work or God forbid slip and fall. I had been showing up early every morning myself to make sure the porch steps were clear, but that became too much of a risk after New Year's night.

Fixing my suit like a prom-bound teen, I knock on my own front door and hold my breath as the lock clicks before the door pulls open. I sigh in disappointment when my sister comes into view instead of Mia.

She gives me a quick once-over before nodding her approval. "Well, don't you clean up nice?"

"Nice to see you too, sis."

Unmoving, her expression turns venomous as she studies me.

"Dais, it's fucking freezing out here. You gonna let me in or what?"

"I don't know, Angus. How about you tell me what intentions you have with my best friend?"

Suddenly, it's hot as hell despite the snow on the ground.

What are my intentions?

Not knowing what Mia has told Daisy, I have no idea how to answer her question.

Does she know what happened the night of the wedding?

After Mia told Daisy I'm playing the part of her husband and father to her son she took it upon herself to inform the immediate family about our situation. So, she knows the deal, but not much gets past her. She likely sees right through me. Likely knows there's more between us than a fake relationship.

"I'm doing a friend a favor. Relax."

"And that's all?"

"Yes. Now let me in before I freeze to death."

Finally, she swings open the door. I sneak past her, grateful for the warmth of the fireplace burning in the great room. It's not as hot as the feel of my sister's watchful eye on my back, though.

"Your *wife* will be out in a sec. She's just finishing up."

Well, that answers that question.

A nod is my only reply.

"Where's Sawyer?"

"In his room playing."

Itching to get away from my sister, I weave around furniture and down the hall until I reach Sawyer's room. His back is to me, so I lean against the doorframe, watching him drive his fire truck over the roads on his bedroom rug. My heart swells to see him happy and flourishing. Especially knowing I played a small part in his happiness.

The sound of Mia clearing her throat snags my attention.

You could knock my ass over with a feather.

She's absolutely breathtaking in a black velvet floor-length dress with a slit that reaches her upper thigh. The bodice hugs her body as though the designer intended for only her to wear it. Her long silky waves hang over her shoulders and down her back.

She looks like a goddess.

Stepping away from Sawyer's door, closer to where she stands at the end of the hall, I whisper for only the two of us to hear. "You look beautiful."

She blushes, but her eyes don't leave mine.

There's only a couple of feet between us now. "So do you," she whispers back.

One corner of my mouth lifts, because I'm a lot of things, but beautiful isn't one of them.

Without thinking, I reach to take one of her hands in mine. Her eyes widen as she looks over my shoulder.

Daisy.

"You ready?" I ask, a little louder than necessary.

"Yep." She runs her hands over her hips, taking a step forward.

Stepping aside, letting her walk in front of me, I'm not surprised to find my sister at the end of the hall watching us like a disapproving parent who knows we're up to no good.

Mia stops by Sawyer's room to say goodnight and to tell him to behave for Daisy. He shows me his truck, then gives me a high five as I do my best to move us out the front door without catching my sister's eye again.

The tension in my shoulders eases as I step across the threshold, relieved we're in the clear and have made it past the five-foot nothing inquisition inside. Mia is a couple steps in front of me and I've turned to close the door when the she-devil appears in the open space.

"Hurt her and I will make your life miserable."

Shit.

She already knows.

What she doesn't know is that if I hurt Mia, my life will be miserable without her intervention. It's one of the few things I'm sure of. My peace of mind relies solely on Mia and Sawyer's well-being.

Closing the door in her face without acknowledging her threat, I find Mia standing at the bottom of the porch steps. Her long leg peeks out of the slit of her dress and she trembles from the cold, momentarily wiping my sister's warning from my thoughts.

"Didn't you bring a coat, Goof?"

"I don't really have a coat that goes with this."

Not caring that my sister is likely watching from the front

window, I grab her hand and rush her to the truck. I left it running so it would be warm when she got inside.

Pulling my coat from the back seat, I slip it over her shoulders. "What am I going to do with you?" I wonder aloud while I bundle her up.

She doesn't speak, but her eyes say it all. They tell me she can think of several things she'd like me to do with her.

Or is that wishful thinking on my part?

Once we're in the truck driving down the dirt road, I ask her what's been on my mind since Daisy opened the door.

"I know Daisy and the family know about our fake relationship, but does my sister know more than that?"

"She knows you're my fake husband. But that's it."

"You may not have told her any more than that. But she knows there's something more going on."

"What makes you say that?"

"Uh, you've met her, right? She knows everything. She can probably smell our pheromones. At the very least, she can read our minds."

"And what would she read in your mind?"

"Before or after I saw you in that dress?"

She giggles and swats at my arm. "You're so stupid."

She's trying to keep things light between us, and I can't blame her. We've drawn a line. One I've been determined not to cross. But something happens when it's just the two of us. Our walls tend to crumble, and things feel easy between us. Right. Like we're already a foregone conclusion. When it's just us, I don't care that she deserves better, or that she has a secret so big she thinks I would run for the hills. Instead, I hop right over the line, keeping us apart.

"And you're too scared to ask what's been going through my head since I first saw you in this dress."

She rolls her eyes and shakes her head before going quiet, her attention focused out the window, proving my statement to be true. She's too scared to ask what's going through my head, because she knows that imaginary line will be obliterated before we make it to the party if I tell her the truth.

Chapter Twenty-Six

Mia

"I remember when my little Archie was two. He wouldn't eat anything but Cheerio's."

"Not Sawyer," Angus says, continuing his conversation with my co-worker, Blakely. "Don't get me wrong, he could eat Goldfish all day, but he loves his mama's cheese quesadillas or any kind of fruit you throw at him. Luckily, he's a good eater."

He's not lying.

Nothing we've said has been a lie. Angus could talk about Sawyer all night and not tell a lie, because he loves my kid. Clearly, he's paid more attention than I ever noticed. Angus didn't study for tonight, because he didn't need to. He knows us as well as my parents. He cares about us. Listening to him talk to my co-workers makes that crystal clear.

When I saw him watching Sawyer in the hallway tonight,

he took my breath away. He looks like a model in one of those fancy cologne commercials. Wearing a sleek black suit, white shirt, and black tie. He even wore shiny tuxedo shoes that can't be comfortable compared to his usual work boots. I kinda wish he had worn his boots, because they're hot as hell, but I'll take him as he is.

Because as he is, is magnificent.

It's not that I've never seen him dressed up, but knowing he's decked out for *me* only adds to his hot factor. The man oozes sex appeal. Yet the hottest thing about his look tonight is that, as elegant as he appears, I know the details of the intricate tattoos covering the chiseled body hiding under his expensive clothes.

His manners are an aphrodisiac all on their own. After covering me in his jacket to keep me warm, he opened the truck door for me and didn't shut the passenger door until I settled myself and he had secured my seat belt.

After teasing me about not wanting to know what was going through his head after seeing me in my dress, things went quiet. My heart was pounding and my stomach was somersaulting from his care, attention, and unexpected playfulness.

I was feeling way too much. Like I always do when the two of us are alone together. It's not as easy for me to share what I'm feeling, yet he seems to have no issue voicing his thoughts.

We were silent on the drive, while we parked and as we walked hand in hand into the hotel lobby. But once we strolled through the ballroom doors where everyone believed we were married, some sort of switch flipped.

He's been polite and engaging with everyone and hasn't

left my side for even a heartbeat. His hand rests on the small of my back as we walk through the room. When we stop to chat with others, he pulls me to his side, lowering his hand to my hip.

And the kisses to the cheek... Oh... dear... Lord.

He knows what he's doing, and he's doing it well.

Putty in his hands, that's what I am.

So I follow his lead, enjoying his gentle caresses while I've got them.

Dinner is over and we're chatting as the dancing part of the evening begins. I'm tucked into his side while he brags about Sawyer like he's the proudest dad on the planet. I can't help but feel like I'm right where I'm supposed to be.

As he holds court, I examine his features and honestly, can't imagine there is anyone more handsome than Angus McKinnon. His nose is straight with a barely detectable bump from being broken on more than one occasion. Long lashes frame his caramel eyes. His perfectly shaped lips have been innocently kissing me all night long, though they feel more like a branding iron. With every brush of his mouth, I lose a little more of myself to him.

He catches me watching him, and I don't look away. Instead, I relish in the freedom the night is giving me. Tonight, I'll let him see everything I'm not willing to admit to either of us out loud. Heat flashes in his eyes, and I know he sees exactly what I intended him to.

He is the most beautiful man I have ever known. Inside and out. I appreciate his presence in my life. I care about him, and God, I want him.

Clearly, I've misread things, because as quickly as desire flashes in his eyes, it's gone. Closing the distance, he places a kiss on my temple, before addressing the group. "Please excuse me."

No explanation.

No eye contact to give me a clue as to what might be wrong. He simply rushes out of the ballroom as if he can't get away from me fast enough.

My heart sinks to my stomach while embarrassment heats my face. How could I have been so wrong?

Dr. Goff fills the quiet left by Angus's quick departure with a story about the first time his dog played in snow after his move to Central Oregon. I grab a glass of red wine when it's offered, taking a big gulp to calm my worried nerves.

He's only been gone ten minutes, but it feels like hours. Blakely and her husband and the doctors and their spouses are all dancing to a slow Adele song and I'm standing where Angus left me.

Alone.

"You look way too pretty to be standing over here all by your lonesome," Devon, one of our lab techs, says as he joins me at the high-top table where my wine glass sits empty and my ring spins around my finger. "Where did Angus go?"

Smiling, I ignore his observation and his question. "Where did your date go?"

I'm not sure what else to say, because Angus's location is a mystery to me. Hell, I don't even know if he's coming back.

He wouldn't leave me here, would he?

"Who, Cindy?" He looks at me incredulously. "She's not really a date. Just a good friend."

"You sure about that? She wasn't looking at you like a friend."

"Okay, you got me. She wants more than the friend situation we've got going, but she's a single mom and I'm not ready to be anybody's daddy."

Wow. Devon is kind of a dick.

"So, why did you bring her?"

"Well, she's still a lot of fun when the kid is with his dad."

Devon, you're an asshole. That's what I want to say, but unfortunately, I don't think that would make for a productive working relationship. But seriously, what an asshole.

"So, while we wait for the ones we brought, should we dance with the one we're with?"

I don't have to shoot him down, because a hand reaches around my waist to rest on my hip and electricity races through my veins.

Angus.

He came back.

"Sorry, but my wife only dances with her husband." There's not an ounce of humor in his voice. "It was in our vows, so them's the rules." He tries for lighthearted but sounds anything but.

Wife.

He called me his wife and, by doing so, told his first lie of the night.

It's the most beautiful lie I've ever heard.

Without another word to Devon, the hand resting on my hip releases me, seductively sliding over my low back before his hand finds mine as if they were magnets drawn to one another without effort.

Angus walks us to the dance floor, taking me in his arms just as the Adele song ends. I assume the next song will be a fast one, but strangely, the same song begins to play again. A song about wanting to be someone's one and only.

I look over my shoulder to see if anyone else has noticed, but everyone continues to sway in the arms of their dates.

"That's strange. I wonder if they realize they've restarted the song?"

"I asked them to play it again."

"You what?"

"Let's let Adele do the talking for now."

"Angus?"

"Unless you don't want to dance with your husband."

"You don't have to--"

"Shh."

He pulls me to his chest and rests his cheek against the top of my head, bringing our joined hands between us, resting mine against his heart as we sway.

Listening to the lyrics I know by heart, I couldn't be more confused. Why would he request this song when Angus and I have made it clear we can never be together?

What is he trying to say?

After a few moments, his other hand caresses my cheek, and when our eyes meet, his are full of something powerful. Meaningful. He doesn't blink. Doesn't speak. He simply looks at me as if I am the answer to every question.

Or possibly his one and only.

Even though my pulse is racing, I'm not scared. Because nothing has ever felt so right.

When he leans down to place a soft kiss on my lips, all awareness of our surroundings drifts away. Angus and I are the only people in the room. He places gentle kiss after kiss to my mouth and I melt into him.

His tongue doesn't seek permission. He isn't causing a scene. It's almost as if he's trying to show me what he's trying to tell me through the lyrics of the song. It might be the most honest moment of my life.

As the chorus begins again, there is nothing but Angus and the music. I let them both consume me.

He's daring me to take a chance on him.

To give him my heart.

But how can I give it to him when it's already his?

He has to know I want to be his. If only I were worthy of his love.

He pulls back to wipe a stray tear from my cheek with his thumb. His eyes flicker with a hint of sadness, as if he knows no matter how true the lyrics may be, it doesn't mean it will ever be our reality.

Smiling ever so slightly, he grazes one last kiss on my forehead and pulls me back into his arms, our hands once again joined over his heart. We're pressed together so tight it would be impossible to get closer.

The song ends and an upbeat song begins. I couldn't tell you who sings it or the name of the song because all I hear is the one we just danced to, playing on a loop in my head.

Eventually, the rest of the team and their plus ones shake me out of my lovesick puppy haze. We sing, dance, and drink with everyone for another hour.

As the night winds down, people are saying their goodbyes when Dr. Gibbons approaches. "Mia, I'm so glad you and Angus could join us tonight. I hope you had a good time."

"We had a great time. Thank you so much."

"No, thank you. You're a wonderful addition to the team and I'm glad we did this after the holidays so you two could join us. Now, we have a car service all set up for those who need a ride home."

"Thank you, ma'am, but we won't be needing it," Angus replies for us. "We've got a room here at the hotel."

I gasp, unable to hide my shock. My boss's eyes sparkle as a cheeky grin lights her face.

"Surprise, baby," he says, squeezing my hand.

"That's where you snuck off to, isn't it? You went to surprise your wife. How romantic."

"Guilty as charged. We don't get nights like this often. I thought we should take advantage of it while we can."

"I remember those days. Little ones are exhausting. It's easy to forget about the two of you as a couple."

Is this happening right now?

Are we really having this conversation with my boss?

"Thank you for the offer of a ride, though." Angus oozes with charm I've never seen before this evening. "We've had a wonderful night and I'm glad to have met everyone."

"Our pleasure. Now, you two get. Don't waste anymore of your evening here with me. I'll see you on Monday, Mia."

The sound my name pulls me out of my stupor. "Oh, yes. Monday. I'll see you on Monday. Thanks again."

In a daze, we walk hand in hand through the dimly lit ballroom, out into the brighter lights of the lobby. It's a public place where anyone can see the two of us glued to one another.

What happened to one night?

As if he doesn't have a care in the world, Angus saunters to the elevators and presses the up button. He is the definition of calm while I exist in a state of confused anticipation.

Just as the elevator pings, I remember I forgot to stop by coat check.

"Angus, I forgot my coat," I say, taking a step away from the elevator doors.

He doesn't let me go, though. "You didn't wear a coat. Remember?" The elevator doors open and for the sake of my heart, I know I shouldn't follow him in, but I do.

Of course I do.

"What about Sawyer?"

"I already called Daisy. She'll stay the night with him."

His voice is almost stern, his face solemn, yet there is still a fire in his eyes.

His mood swing sends a chill down my spine, a reminder of our other night together. Not the part of the night in the tack room where he gave me the reins, but back at his house, when he was very much in charge. It was the best night of my life.

"Daisy is gonna know something is going on."

"I really don't want to talk about my sister right now."

We stand side by side, hand in hand, looking at each other in the reflection of the closed doors in front of us.

The way he looks at me, never breaking his gaze, is something I'll never get used to.

It's intense.

When we reach our floor, my hand is still in his as we walk to the last door at the end of the hall. Using the key he snuck away to get, he holds the door open for me as if nothing out of the ordinary is happening. Like Angus and I spend the night in hotel rooms together all the time.

My body hums when I brush past him. Everything but the bed is a blur. The white duvet is pulled back and there are two robes laid out across the foot of the bed. A side table holds two champagne flutes and a silver ice bucket chilling a bottle of champagne.

He was gone so long because not only did he get the room, but he came up here to prepare. I'm not sure what to do. Or what to say. We shouldn't do this, but leaving this room isn't an option.

I want this.

I want him.

Not yet daring to look at him, I can hear the shake in my voice when I finally speak. "We said one night."

He strides past me to the table, where he lifts the bottle of bubbly from the bucket. My body is on high alert, jumping when he pops the cork. The sound reverberating against my anxious heart. He fills both glasses, then turns to face me, leaving them on the table.

"We did. But I need more."

He slips his shoes off.

"We can't," I say, turning Granny's ring around and around my ring finger. Willing myself to stay strong when I know there's no way I'm turning back now that I'm here. Now that the second chance for a night of bliss has presented itself. At least I can tell myself I tried to do the right thing.

"Why not?"

He tosses his suit jacket on the desk below a big mirror.

"Because if we keep doing this, one day you'll hate me. Trust me on this."

"Well, we're in the same boat, then. If you knew the things I've done, you'd never

let me touch you again."

He pulls his shirt out of his pants as he takes a step toward me.

"I don't believe you."

One more step and he's close enough to reach out and trace my neck and collarbone with his finger, so he does. It's all I can do not to lean into his touch.

"And I don't believe I could ever hate you. So, it looks like we're on the same page."

"Angus, I can't do this again without my heart getting involved."

He's close.

So close.

"Honey, mine's been involved for years."

He brushes my hair off one of my shoulders, so it falls down my back.

"What?"

He repeats the motion, leaving me feeling exposed.

"You heard me."

Did I?

It's one thing for him to be attracted to me. To want me. It's another for him to admit his feelings run deeper than lust. To confess his heart is involved.

His confession is a straight shot of adrenaline to my heart, bringing it to life as though it's never fully beaten before. But my brain... my brain can't quite comprehend the implication.

He gently presses my back against the wall. The look in his eyes says he's never wanted anything or anyone as much as he wants me right this very second. And as much as I find it hard to believe, it's the hottest thing I've ever seen. And that's saying something, because I've seen all of him.

At least, I thought I had.

Between the passion in his eyes, the warmth of his body against mine, and the flame he's stoked inside me all reason to fight my desire ceases to exist. Because this... Angus... feels like home.

"Angus..."

"No more talking." He brushes a gentle kiss across my lips. "You keep your secrets and I'll keep mine."

He leans in to kiss my neck and I gasp at the feel of his lips and tongue trailing their way across my jaw.

"We shouldn't," I say in jest, as my hands travel under his shirt, tracing the defined muscles of his torso.

"I know," he breathes against my ear, and that's all it takes.

No more talking. No more delaying what we both want and know is going to happen.

Chapter Twenty-Seven

Mia

My finger traces the eagle, globe, and anchor of the Marine Corps tattoo on his shoulder as he sleeps. His head is on my stomach, like the last time we spent an entire night together. This seems to be his thing. Is it his thing with all the women he sleeps with? Or is it a *me* thing? The thought of him sleeping this soundly wrapped up in another woman makes my insides twist in knots, so I push it to the back of my mind.

Last night I memorized all of his tattoos. He explained the meaning behind each piece of art. However, there were a couple that didn't need any explanation. Like the McKinnon family crest over his heart, or the folded flag with my brother's dog tags draped over it on his other pec. I kissed them both and carried on with my exploration of his body and the art covering it.

It was another perfect night, but it was a mistake.

We can't keep doing this.

I'm not sure I'll survive the aftermath that comes with more of him. Yes, he sets my body on fire, but with Angus, it's much more than that. It's not just the attraction between us, there's respect. Friendship.

His confessions of the heart keep messing with my head. The lyrics to Adele's "One and Only" continue to play on repeat, and I want so badly to ask why he requested the song, but of course I don't. The way he worshipped my body last night… it's all more than I deserve.

We can't keep slipping into situations that lead to us waking up in bed together. It's not fair to either of us.

A low groan vibrates against my belly just before the heat of his words scatter across my skin. "Morning, Goof."

"Morning."

"Can we stay here forever?"

I chuckle in reply, wishing we could remain in our fantasy land.

His lips press against my stomach as he begins his ascent up my body. Kissing his way to my breast before taking a nipple in his mouth. He adjusts himself so his morning wood presses against my leg, then switches his attention to my other nipple.

"Angus," I whisper.

He nuzzles the crook of my neck and in one swift move buries himself in my weeping core, lazily working his cock in and then almost completely out of me, before easing back in. His body is warm and heavy on top of me, and there is nothing between us.

He fills my body and soul as he rocks in and out of me.

God, why is this even better than last night? Every inch of him feels amazing. Sex with Angus is next level, but nothing has ever felt this phenomenal.

Then it hits me and I gasp.

"Angus, you forgot the condom. We have to stop."

Without a word, he pulls out, lifting to his knees, my legs still around his waist. With no shame, he kneels before me, his beautiful length glistening as he works himself.

"Touch yourself."

Not giving it a second thought, my fingers find my clit and I do as he asked.

"Fuck, Mia. Do you see what you do to me?"

Too distracted by the sight of his hand wrapped around his cock and the sensation of my fingertips, I don't reply.

"Mia, answer me. Tell me you see what you do to me."

Ripping my gaze from his hand to examine his face, I'm surprised to find his features almost feral. Hovering above me, he looks like a mythical creature. His beauty is unreal. Body taut, abdominals rippling, his big hand and strong arm move at a leisurely pace. The muscles in his jaw tic as he watches me.

I'd do anything he asks me to at this moment.

"Yes."

"Look at you. You are perfect, you know that?"

"You're beautiful, Gus."

Our free hands come together, and our fingers interlace, closing in on our climax.

"Come for me, Mia. Let me watch you fall apart from your own touch."

Spurred on by his request and hoping to give him something to remember this morning by, I let my fingers slide from my clit through my wetness before slipping two inside my pussy.

"God, damn," he says, as he picks up the pace of his own self pleasure.

I pump my fingers in and out of my center, the feeling nowhere near as good as having Angus inside me, so I slide them back to my sensitive bundle of nerves, applying pressure and friction and it's only a few seconds before the sensation of my orgasm builds.

"Angus. I'm going to... I'm going... I'm... I'm coming."

He growls above me, his brows furrowed as he watches my body come apart. "That's it, Mia. Fuck, yes."

Once the last pulse of pleasure subsides, I lift my wet fingers to his lips, and he sucks them clean right before he comes all over my stomach, my name tearing from his mouth so fiercely he sounds angry.

Still holding my hand, he leans forward, bringing my arm up above my head. He kisses my mouth for the first time since he woke. It's slow and gentle, not lust fueled and all tongue. Small, sweet kisses full of affection. Maybe even appreciation.

"Don't move," he commands.

He leaves me on the bed and a minute later, he's back with a warm washcloth that he uses to clean me up.

"Get dressed. I'm taking you to breakfast."

"I need to get home, Angus."

He checks his watch. "It's only 7:30. We have plenty of time."

He's right. I doubt Daisy is expecting us home this early. So, we get dressed in last night's fancy clothes and head to Jackson's Corner for pancakes.

* * *

"It feels like the morning after the prom I never got to take you to." He winks, as he takes a bite of his waffle.

"I still find it hard to believe you've had feelings for me all these years. That the attraction hasn't been one-sided."

I also can't believe that in the light of day, in a public place, dressed in our clothes from last night, we're comfortable enough to talk about our feelings with each other.

He opens his mouth to say something, but we're interrupted.

"Well, looky here. Angus McKinnon and Mia Powell. Who would have thought?"

Rhen Mitchell.

Leave it to this asshole to ruin whatever moment I had just been enjoying.

"Rhen," Angus says with a nod of his head, not engaging any further.

"You are full of surprises, aren't you?" he asks, his eyes on mine.

Ignoring him, I take a bite of my pancakes.

"If you don't mind, we'd like to get back to our breakfast."

What he's trying to say is, go back to wherever it is you came from, asshole.

"The apple doesn't fall far from the tree, now does it? You get knocked up by some stranger and now you're having breakfast in clothes from the night before. You really are your mother's daughter."

Silverware clanks to the ground as Angus flies out of his seat, nose to nose, with Rhen in the blink of an eye. Keeping his voice low, he snarls. "Who the fuck do you think you're talking to?"

Eyes still on me, Rhen doesn't back down. The idiot ignores Angus and continues. "Just a man who calls 'em like I see 'em. Sluts seem to run in the Powell family."

Rhen seals his fate and before I can register the magnitude of his accusations, Angus's fist cracks against his nose and he falls to the ground. Standing over him, Angus seethes. His chest heaving, his hands still in fists, ready for more.

Patrons at nearby tables scatter and hushed voices whisper around us. Grabbing my things, I throw cash on the table. Clutching Angus's wrist, I lead him out of the restaurant and away from Rhen who's smiling on the ground.

I don't stop until we reach Angus's truck parked a block and a half down the street. My heart is beating out of my chest. Not only has no one ever treated me like that, but what in the world was he talking about? I've always known Rhen was a dick, but to call my mother a slut! That's next level.

"What the hell was that about, Angus?"

"He got what he deserved. Who the fuck does he think he is speaking to my wife like that?"

Whoa!

"Angus—"

Clearly realizing his mistake, he interrupts me. "You know what I mean. Nobody speaks to you like that, Mia. Nobody."

Closing the space between us, he pulls me into his arms, cradling my head with a hand. "Are you okay?"

"I'm not really sure," I say, honestly, stepping back to examine his hand. "You okay?"

Releasing a deep breath, he steps away, pacing back and

forth on the sidewalk. "No, I'm not okay, Mia. I cannot believe he had the audacity to say those things to you. I had heard he was an asshole, but I had never seen it for myself. If he thinks he will ever step foot in my bar again, he is out of his damn mind."

As much as I appreciate him coming to my defense, my mind is reeling.

"Angus?"

He stops his incessant pacing, bringing his attention back to me.

"What was he talking about? What was all that stuff about my mom?"

He stills. Looking anywhere but at me.

"Angus..."

He opens the passenger door, holding it open for me. Following his lead, I climb into my seat but don't buckle myself in. He closes the door and rounds the truck, getting behind the steering wheel.

I turn in my seat to face him. Gaze locked on the road ahead, his hands scrape over the scruff on his face. He doesn't buckle up, and he doesn't speak.

"Angus, do you know what he was referring to?"

"Goof, he's just spreading unfounded rumors. Don't listen to him. He's a piece of shit."

"But you know the rumors he was alluding to?"

"I... I'm sure it's all nonsense. You know how people in small towns love to gossip."

My heartbeat thunders in my ears. The cab of the truck closing in on me, oxygen somehow not reaching my lungs. If Angus has heard the rumors, who else has? And why haven't I?

"What have you heard?" I whisper.

"Mia... "

"I want to know."

"Why?"

"Why? What do you mean, why? If there are rumors about my mother cheating on my father, I think I have a right to know. What if it was your family?"

"I don't take part in town gossip. You know me better than that."

"I would rather hear it from you."

From someone I trust.

"Are you sure?" He reaches across the console, lacing our fingers together. "The last thing I want to do is hurt you."

"Please." I squeeze his hand, letting him know it's okay.

"Fuck, I don't want to be the one to tell you this." He drops his gaze, as if he can't stand to see my reaction. "Mayor Collins."

"What?" I shriek.

He winces but doesn't answer.

"My mother is sleeping with the mayor?"

"It's a rumor, Mia."

"The mayor and my mother?"

"I'm so sorry."

Dad's despondent face flashes in my mind. "Is this why they're leaving?"

"I don't know."

"Oh, my God. I think I might be sick. How could she do this to him?" Releasing Angus's hand, I throw open the door, needing fresh air. Angus is there before my feet hit the pavement.

Taking my face in his hands, he brings us eye to eye. "Mia, I work in a bar. People are drunk. They talk shit. All it takes is one look between a man and a woman, and this town will have everyone sleeping with each other before it's over. Rumors are not the gospel. They're just petty people talking shit."

The below freezing air and his words loosen the grip my panic has on me, but it doesn't wipe it away. He's right. A rumor doesn't make it true. But what if it is?

"Do you think it's true?"

He doesn't hesitate. "I know your parents love each other very much."

He also doesn't answer my question.

"That's not what I asked."

"Maybe not, but it's all I know for certain. I can't imagine there is any truth to the rumors, but I can't sit here and tell you I haven't heard them. I respect you too much to lie to you."

He places a kiss on my forehead, holding my hands until I give him a nod, letting him know I'm okay.

I'm not okay, but there's nothing he can do to help to stop my anxiety from spinning out of control.

Like puzzle pieces fitting together, things that had seemed so out of character for my parents now make sense. The sudden move to the other side of the country. Mom's tears about leaving and Dad's somber demeanor.

Yes, my mother works with the mayor regularly in her role as a Goose Hollow council member. But sleeping with him? Seriously?

Angus jumps back into the truck and starts the engine, turning on the heat. We sit there in silence for who knows how long before he asks. "What are you going to do with the information?"

That is the question I am racking my brain with.

If I ask Mom and it's not true, she may never forgive me for doubting her. If I ask her and it is true, then what? Will my relationship with her ever be the same again? Will it embarrass Dad if I know? If I don't ask, will it always be in the back of my mind?

"I don't know. What would you do?"

"I couldn't tell ya. As you may have noticed, I can be a bit of a hothead."

I chuckle, considering he just knocked Rhen on his ass.

"I likely wouldn't be thinking straight and would demand answers. But I have a feeling I would end up wishing I had thought it through first."

He's telling me to sit on it for a minute.

To think before I react in a way I won't be able to take back.

"Do you think your mom has heard what people are saying?"

"I don't know. We've never discussed it."

"Thank you for telling me."

"I'm sorry you had to find out this way."

"Me too."

"C'mon, let's get you home to Sawyer."

Chapter Twenty-Eight

Angus

It's been the longest three weeks of my life.

Twenty-one days ago, I had one of the best nights of my life and I know the precise moment the night held that significance.

The moment everything clicked for me.

I was chatting with Mia's coworkers about Sawyer, and I could feel her watching me. When I turned to meet her gaze, she didn't turn away. Instead, her eyes softened with the same wonder and appreciation I feel for her.

It was at that exact moment; I knew there was no way I could simply take her home when the party was over. Leaving her to go book our room made more sense than anything ever has. I needed to touch her again. Taste her again.

It was selfish on my part, of course I knew that. But we both wanted another night. Needed another night.

We made love all night long, falling asleep around dawn. Once again, I was wrapped up in heaven on earth.

Silence accompanied us as we dressed and walked hand in hand to my truck. But at breakfast, we both relaxed. Our conversation picked back up. Maybe it was because stopping to eat delayed the end of our time together and we were embracing what time we had.

Then Rhen cast a shadow over our table and dimmed the light in Mia's eyes.

Should I have hit him?

Probably not.

Would I do it again?

Abso-fucking-lutely.

The last thing I wanted to do was tell her about the bullshit rumors that have been going around about her mom and the mayor for the last year or so. I've known Erin my entire life and refuse to believe what people say. But I could see Mia's wheels turning as soon as the insult rolled off his damn tongue.

On the way to breakfast, my mind was working double time, trying to figure out what I wanted to say. How to tell her I wanted more than one more night. That I wanted all of her. But first, she needed to know. Everything.

Then the morning went to shit and the last thing she needed was me complicating our already complicated relationship.

When I pulled up to the house, she spoke for the first time. "You don't need to walk me to the front door."

"Of course I will," I insisted.

"No. Just let me go. You know Daisy is going to have questions about our sleepover."

"Exactly why I should be there to answer them with you."

"No need. I'll tell her there's nothing going on between us. It's the truth, after all."

The defeat in her voice ripped my heart out of my chest.

I reached for her, but she pulled away. It felt like she had dropped my heart on the driveway and drove the truck over it.

"Mia, talk to me."

"I can't do this again. It already hurts too much."

"Okay."

Okay? Really asshole? That's all you got?

I wanted to punch myself in the face, but what else could I say after the morning she's had? Especially when she was telling me to let her go.

The awkward part of me wanted to apologize for last night, but I wasn't sorry. Like I told her, I'm a selfish bastard. I wouldn't change a thing.

The front door opened and my sister filled the doorway, arms crossed, letting all the heat out of the house.

She didn't look happy, but I didn't give a shit.

Mia let herself out of the truck and walked away without a goodbye or so much as a look over her shoulder, which threw me into a desperate panic. The woman has a death grip on my heart and was unknowingly walking away with it.

I've been to Sunday dinner every week since. After three no-shows, Mia and Sawyer are finally here.

Shit, they're a sight for sore eyes.

I've barely slept since dropping her off three weeks ago. I

texted her later that morning to check on her and she thanked me, but said she needed some distance.

Respecting her request was one of the hardest things I've ever done.

There have been a million times I almost texted her, called her or drove to the house when I was at the ranch to visit Mom. But I didn't. I'm not strong enough to hear the pain in her voice. If I saw the heartbreak on her face again, I may just say fuck it and claim her as mine. Consequences be damned.

Tonight, things are back to normal. She greeted me with a platonic hug, as if she hadn't let me bind her up with the tie from the hotel robe as I feasted on her. As if she hadn't come all over my face and we hadn't fucked ourselves senseless.

With these memories occupying space in my head, it's still the defeat and sadness on her face when I dropped her off the next morning that won't leave me alone. It refuses to let me pretend everything is okay.

Although what I think is playing pretend on her part may not be. Maybe the space between us over the last few weeks was what she needed to get over things. Over me.

I haven't been so lucky.

My feelings have only intensified.

I miss her.

I miss Sawyer.

At the moment, Mom, Cal, Charlotte, Daisy, and I are video-chatting with Knox. During the call Mia snuck away to change Sawyer's diaper. I'm a man obsessed, waiting for her to come back into the room. So much so, I've barely heard a word Knox has said. Before I know it, we're saying our goodbyes.

Getting up from the table, I'm about to make up an excuse to go find Mia when Daisy swoops in. Taking me by the arm, she forcefully drags me out the back door to the privacy of the deck overlooking the pastures. I've made sure not to be caught alone in a room with her for three weeks now, and have avoided eye-contact with her all night. Hell, I've been avoiding my sister as much as Mia's been avoiding me. Daisy is a damn tornado when she wants to be. I'm afraid I'm not prepared for the storm she's about to bring.

The Sunday after our sleepover, my sister cornered me. Once again, warning me not to hurt Mia. That she was going through enough after the Rhen debacle and didn't need any other drama in her life. I told her she was freaking out over nothing. Of course, she didn't believe me, but when I refused to answer any more of her questions, she let it go.

However, Daisy is like a dog with a bone. She may bury the bone for safekeeping, but when she's ready, she'll dig it up and chew until she's gotten to the core and eventually until it's all but gone.

Once we reach the far end of the deck, out of view from the dining room windows, she turns on me and hisses, "What the hell are you doing?"

It could be the cool early March evening air, but it's more than likely the venom in my sister's voice that sends a chill racing down my spine.

"Not sure what you're talking about, sis," I lie through my teeth, keeping my gaze on the fence posts between me and the darkening horizon.

"Mia! You idiot! What is going on between the two of you?" Her finger as pointy as ever when she stabs it into my shoulder. "This is more than a fake relationship for her bosses, and don't tell me it's not."

"I'm sure you've had your girl talk. Why don't you tell *me* what's going on?"

I mean it. I want to know what Mia has told her. How she's feeling. What she wants.

"Gus, this is Mia we're talking about. Not one of your never-ending one-night stands."

She doesn't have to tell me the difference between Mia and every other woman I've had in my bed. There is simply no comparison. That's why there has been no one else since New Year's Eve and fuck me, but I don't want there to be.

"You don't have to worry, sis. I know I'm not good enough for her and Sawyer."

"Shut up," she hisses. "Don't be ridiculous. I didn't say that, but this is Mia, Gus. She's part of the family. If you hurt her, you hurt me."

Same, sis. Same.

"She's not going anywhere," she continues. "And she'll have to look at you at every Sunday dinner and family event from here until, well, eternity."

I fucking wish.

"Dais, I get it."

"Do you?"

"I don't need a lecture, baby sister."

"Gus Gus!"

Sawyer is running toward us at full speed with his head leaning forward like he may topple over any second, but he crashes into my leg just in time.

"Hey, buddy. Whatcha doin'?"

Knowing I shouldn't, but I've always been a glutton for

punishment, I look at my sister. Her arms crossed over her chest, the irritation on her face says it all. *Don't fuck up their lives.*

Message received loud and clear, I say back with a nod of my head.

I scoop Sawyer up and he wraps his arms around my neck. His body relaxes against me like dead weight. Instantly comfortable.

"Sorry, it's past his bedtime."

Mia's voice instantly brings me peace. After three weeks of silence, knowing she's near is enough to loosen the knot of anxiety that's tied me up since I dropped her off that morning. Not knowing what she's doing or how she's spending her day has had me balancing on the edge of insanity.

She steps up beside me to rub her son's back and I'll be damned if I didn't want to put my arm around her and pull her against my side so they're both in my arms.

"No, worries. You know I don't mind," I say, swaying from side to side to soothe Sawyer.

She looks at Daisy out of the corner of her eye before offering me a small smile. She seems uncomfortable under my sister's watchful eye.

"So, how have you been?" I ask, trying to pretend we don't have an audience. And stopping myself from telling her exactly how many days, screw that, how many hours it's been since I've seen her.

"It's okay. I told Daisy everything when you dropped me off. We can talk about it in front of her."

My hackles go up, ready to battle Daisy, because of course she's going to have something to say about me screwing her best friend all night while she babysat.

Eerily, she remains mute. It's out of character for her. I don't trust it. If she's known for three weeks, why hasn't she hunted me down and busted my balls?

"So... what exactly did you two talk about?" I don't dare say too much before I know the details.

"My mom," she whispers.

A surge of disappointment waves through me. Of course, she wasn't talking about our night together. She was talking about her mom. She meant what she said when she told me she couldn't do it again. That she didn't want her heart to get involved. But I'm the asshole whose heart has always been involved and thought our night together meant more to her than the bullshit Rhen brought up.

I'm an idiot.

Of course, Rhen's comments rocked her.

"Right. So, you doing okay?"

"I don't know. I mean, I don't want to believe it's true, but it explains the sudden move to the other side of the country, when they had never talked about retiring anywhere but here."

"Are you going to say anything to her?"

"No. I figure it's their relationship and really none of my business. And hopefully, it's not true. Can you imagine if I confronted her about it and it wasn't true?"

"Makes sense."

Her eyes meet mine and I can see her heartbreak. "I hate that part of me believes it. And if it's true, I hate to think of how much it hurt Dad. I'm not sure I'll ever look at them the same again."

With my arm not holding her son, I pull her into my side. "I'm sorry, Goof." On instinct, I kiss her on the top of her head. She turns her body into me, so her cheek is on my chest and her hand goes back to rubbing Sawyer on the back.

The three of us fit.

But one look from my sister and I know I'll have a lot to talk about in my therapy appointment with Dr. Laughlin tomorrow.

Chapter Twenty-Nine

Angus

Her long hair tickles my chest. Her kisses brand my skin as they make their way over my abs, on their way to my cock, where I know the heat of her mouth will bring me to my knees in seconds flat. Her tongue traces the vein on the underside of my length before it licks circles around the tip, lapping up the pre-cum waiting for her.

The vibration from her humming around me elicits a growl from deep in my chest, causing her to giggle before taking me to the back of her throat. Bright blue eyes order me to watch her take me. My hand fists her dark hair —

BANG!

A loud noise accompanied by a strange hissing sound wakes me from my dream. Unable to see anything in the dark, I jump out of bed, naked as the day I was born, and flip on the lights. At first, as my eyes adjust to the light, I can't figure out where the sound of rushing water is coming from. Walking toward the kitchen, I don't need my eyes to figure it out. The icy cold water lapping at my bare feet tells me all I need to know.

The pipes under the kitchen sink have burst, and there's water everywhere.

Fuck!

Rushing back to the bed, I pull on the shorts I had left on the floor and dial Cal, putting the phone on speaker.

"What the fuck, Gus? It's one in the morning. You okay?"

"Dude, so sorry to wake you, but I have a situation. The kitchen pipe burst. There's water fucking everywhere."

"Shit, okay. I'm on my way. You need to turn the main waterline off and disconnect your appliances."

"Roger. Thanks, man."

I end the call and run outside to the main waterline. By the time I've figured out what I'm doing, Cal's truck lights illuminate the line and I shove my phone in my pocket, no longer relying on the flashlight feature.

After the water line is off, Cal follows me inside with an arm full of towels and the toolbox he brought with him. It doesn't pass me by how fortunate I am to have the family I do. Always just a phone call away. Always there when I need them.

By the time we reach the top of the stairs, there's water covering the floor from the kitchen to the full length of the space.

"I fucking told you to upgrade the loft when you fixed up the bar. This is what you get for cutting corners."

"Can we save the lecture for another time?"

Cal drops a towel at the top of the stairs, likely trying to prevent any water from going down the stairs. Wishful thinking on his part.

He works some sort of magic under the sink while I use every towel I own before remembering the wet vac we have down in the bar. Cal unhooks the appliances while I do my best to clean up and wipe things down, but it's still a mess. It's gonna take a lot more than a wet vac and some towels to clean up this shit show.

"Pack a bag. You can crash at my place tonight," Cal offers.

"I'll crash at the cabin," I counter, shoving enough clothes for a few days into a bag.

"No can do. A producer friend of Knox's is using it to hide from the paparazzi. Some cheating scandal with a pop star, or some shit like that."

"Shit."

"We'll figure it out. In the meantime, I'll reach out to my buddy in the morning and see how soon we can get them here. Where you land, you're gonna need to be there for a while. I'm thinking you'll need to store your shit somewhere for the duration as well. No skimping this time. You need to upgrade the whole place."

"Great. But I'm not gonna stay with you for more than tonight. You're a newlywed and I'd rather carve out my eardrums than listen to you have sex."

"You can always stay with Mom."

"I could, but I work late and I don't want to keep her up. I'll figure it out."

God, this is gonna cost a pretty penny. I hadn't planned for a situation like this, but luckily the bar renovations paid for themselves and the business is doing well. This isn't what I wanted to spend my money on, but life's a bitch.

As much as the cost and the general pain in the ass of the whole situation sucks, there is a masochistic silver lining, because I know exactly where I can stay.

Chapter Thirty

Mia

I've been nauseous since receiving Angus's messages this morning. So shaky inside and out that it took me three times to take my first patient's blood pressure. Unable to hear the pumping of their heart through my stethoscope over the thundering of my own. Half of what my patients said to me went in one ear and out the other because my brain had no room for anything other than Gus's text.

It took until the end of my lunch break to contain my shaking fingers enough to text him back.

ANGUS:

Morning, Goof. I have a huge favor to ask of
you. The pipes in the loft burst and I need a
place to crash. If I promise to stay out of
your way, are you cool with me moving into
the house temporarily? You keep my room.
I'll use the spare.

MIA

Of course, it's your house. But I don't mind
changing rooms when I get home. I'll start
looking for a new place so we can get out
of your hair.

He answers right away, as if he was waiting for me to reply all
morning.

ANGUS

Don't you dare. My place is still your place.
That hasn't changed.

MIA

I don't mind though.

ANGUS

Stop. I'll see you when you get home.

Our text conversation ended over four hours ago, yet it's lived
rent-free in my head ever since. So, when Sawyer and I pull

up to the house and find Angus's pickup parked out front, my insides twist and I break out into a cold sweat.

I can't do this.

I cannot live with Angus McKinnon.

Not after our night at the hotel. Having my heart involved with this man isn't new, but it feels more fragile than ever. Like it may shatter into a million pieces if I'm not careful.

Stepping out of the car, into the chilly evening air, I take a deep fortifying breath before I open the back door to get my baby boy out of his car seat.

"Come on, my tired little man," I say, pressing a kiss on his fuzzy winter hat on our way up the porch steps. "I love you, my sweet boy."

"Wuv you, Mama," he says with a sleepy voice.

My steps stutter and the part of my heart reserved only for the boy in my arms swells. There's no stopping the tears that fall as I open the front door and am hit with the smell of something delicious coming from the kitchen.

I drop my purse and Sawyer's backpack on the floor to wipe my tears away.

Angus's deep voice startles me. "What's wrong? Are you okay? Did something happen to Sawyer at day care?"

"Gus?" Sawyer lifts his head, instantly reaching for the concerned man who's now standing far too close.

Angus takes Sawyer from me, only adding to my emotional state. It's too much. Seeing the two of them together is already breaking my heart.

"Mia, please." He sounds desperate. "Who did this to you?"

I can barely see him through the pools in my eyes, but

there's no hiding the concern in his voice. It's apparent he thinks someone has hurt me and wants to come to my rescue.

Pointing to Sawyer, I can't help but chuckle through my sobbing. "He did."

"What do you mean, Goof?"

"Mama, no cry," Sawyer says from Gus's arms.

"Babe, please tell me what's wrong?" He takes a step closer, bending to look me in the eye.

Babe?

Nope.

Not gonna address that at the moment.

Nope. Nope. Nope.

"He told me he loved me for the first time," I blubber.

Angus's face lights as he smiles from ear to ear. Closing the gap between us, he presses his forehead against mine. Sawyer wraps an arm around each of our necks. "Good job, buddy."

Angus doesn't kiss me, but the moment is more intimate than it could ever be with his lips on mine, because it's the three of us. The two men in my life. He may not be mine, but Angus is incredibly important to me. He always has been.

Sharing this sweet moment with him means the world to me. Moments like this are what I dream about, but what I'm most afraid of is that too many moments like this will turn into a living nightmare in the end.

This is dangerous.

Space. We need space.

"Something smells good." I try to change the subject and step away, but Sawyer still has a hold on each of us, keeping us connected.

Angus's breath tickles my face when he replies. "I'm

making you dinner. My way of saying thanks for letting me invade your space."

My heads spins with the need to kiss his beautiful lips hovering only inches away. Instead, I take a step backward.

He clears his throat. "Come on, little man. Let's let Mommy take a load off." They move to the great room, where he sets Sawyer down on the couch. When he pulls his hat off his head his fine toddler hair, full of static, sticks straight up. "Bud, look at your hair. You're stylin', dude." Angus carries on, helping him with his coat and shoes. Sawyer is wide awake and ready to play now.

"Gus, play vroom truck!" He jumps from the couch, running to his room, leaving us alone.

"Sorry about the silly waterworks," I say, shrugging off my coat, hanging it on the hook by the front door.

"Not silly at all," he says, crossing the room to hang up Sawyer's coat and drop his shoes next to the ones I just took off.

And just like that, we obliterate the distance between us.

"You didn't need to make dinner."

"I know, but I wanted to." He reaches for me and just as his thumb caresses my cheek, the patter of socked feet running down the hall has him dropping his hand, but his gaze remains fixed to mine for several heartbeats before he turns toward my boy.

"Vroom, vroom." Sawyer soars a plastic dump truck in the air with one hand, his other carries a tow truck he holds out for Angus.

"You get them warmed up for me and I promise to play after dinner."

"No! Gus play now!" he whines, stomping his feet.

"Sawyer Brian Powell," I say, using my mom voice.

My tired boy drops himself to the ground, landing on his diaper-clad bottom. His lower lip quivers and I know the waterworks are on deck. He's exhausted and melting down. I'm about to step in, but Angus beats me to it.

"Bud, I made you a special spaghetti dinner and it's time to eat. I promise we'll play after dinner."

Sawyer's lower lip still quivers as one giant crocodile tear hangs onto his lower lashes for dear life.

"I will never break a promise to you, buddy. Never."

Angus means what he says with everything that he is. He is one of the most loyal, dependable people I have ever known. The only lie he's ever told me was that we would only have one night together, because he gave me a second.

Sawyer nods his head in understanding.

Easing Sawyer's toys out of his hands and then picking him up, the tattooed man who just promised my son he would never go back on his word, walks to the already set table and secures Sawyer in his high chair.

"Come on, Momma, time for dinner. Go get out of your scrubs."

In a daze, I follow his instructions, and change out of my work clothes and into equally comfortable yoga pants and an oversized off the shoulder sweater. When I meet them at the table, Sawyer is chewing on a piece of garlic bread while Angus pours two glasses of red wine.

Why is he doing this? Why the effort? Has he changed his mind about the possibility of there being an us?

"There she is."

"Momma!" Sawyer holds out a fist full of slobbery bread.

"Hey, sweetie. Looks yummy."

"Yummy, Momma."

My eyes drift over to Angus. He's watching me and when I catch him, he doesn't look away. Instead, he says barely above a whisper, "Hey."

One word. That's all it takes and I am a mess. If I hadn't just landed in my seat, I would be a puddle on the floor.

"Hey," I reply.

"It's nothing fancy. Just a Caesar, spaghetti, and garlic bread. I wasn't sure how you wanted to handle the sauce with this little guy, so I gave him bread to start."

"Thanks."

I'm not sure what else to say.

"Dig in, Goof."

* * *

"It's amazing how much work taking care of a kid is. It's a good thing he's the cutest thing I've ever seen." Angus plops down on the couch on a heavy sigh.

"I'm convinced it's nature's way of keeping them alive while they're young. I mean, that face of his, it's hard to stay firm with him sometimes," I say from the kitchen, where I'm finishing up. Dinner was fantastic, but wow, did he blow up the kitchen.

He hung out with us during bath time and while I brushed Sawyer's teeth and got him into his pajamas. Angus read him a bedtime story or three and I've been cleaning up in here after the bomb that went off while dinner was being made. It's nice to know the man isn't perfect after all.

His phone rings, but before he answers, he rises from the couch and heads toward the front door. "I'll be right back."

Waving a hand in acknowledgement, I don't miss the flex of his jaw or the seriousness of his tone.

Done with the kitchen, I grab my e-reader from my bedroom. Well, *his* bedroom and settle myself into my favorite corner of the oversized couch, cover myself in a soft fleece blanket that hangs over the back, and attempt to read the sexy billionaire romance I'm halfway through. If only I could get past the first sentence on the page. My mind is a roller coaster of questions and crazy thoughts.

Why did he have to go outside to take his call?

Who is he talking to?

Is he seeing someone?

Should I be moving my things to the spare room instead of sitting here reading?

I should start looking for a new place to live, so the man can have his house back.

But I don't want to move out. In fact, I want the plumbers to take their time, lose parts and maybe never finish the loft. Not only would I get to keep Angus as a roommate, but he wouldn't have his den of sex to take women back to.

The front door opens and keeping my eyes on my tablet, I wait until he's sitting in the same spot he was when he got up, before I say anything.

"Everything okay?"

"Just one of my old army buddies. There's this podcast host who's been asking me to be on their show for the last couple of years. He's resorted to reaching out to one of the guys from my platoon, but I'm not interested."

"Why don't you want to do it?"

"There aren't too many CMHs around and I get a lot of offers, but I'm not a fan of all the special treatment. I'm no different from any of the other soldiers I served with. I was just one of the lucky ones who survived."

He never discusses his Congressional Medal of Honor. This is not where I thought our conversation was going, but I'm glad he trusts me enough to talk to about it.

"Yes, but you also saved others. You weren't lucky, you were brave," I say, from the other end of the couch. "You *are* special, Angus. I wish you could see that."

His eyes search mine. I'm not sure what he's looking for, but all I want to do is crawl into his lap and hold him. Make him feel as special as he is.

"I've talked to my therapist about it, and she thinks it might be good for me. I'm just not sure."

He has a therapist?

Why this surprises me, I'm not sure, but I'm glad to hear it. My heart warms at the thought. He portrays himself as this stoic man who doesn't offer smiles freely, but if you're fortunate enough to be on the receiving end of one, it's everything. After the trauma he's been through, I'm glad he's talking to someone. I'm glad to see him smiling more these days.

"You know we're all really proud of you. CMH medal or not."

His gaze falls to his hands resting in his lap. He almost looks ashamed, which was far from my intention.

"I'm really glad you're alive." It's true. Losing Chris was the worst thing I've ever gone through. I cannot imagine if we had lost Angus, too.

This brings his gaze back up to me. He doesn't speak, but there's an unspoken question in his eyes that I don't know how to answer.

The man is breaking my heart.

"You deserve good things, Angus. You deserve gratitude from those who are grateful for what you've done and for just being in their lives. I bet people could learn a lot from you."

"I'm no teacher."

His tone is somber. Maybe the compliment route isn't the way to go.

"What kind of offers have you gotten?"

"Speaking engagements. Book deals. Podcasts." He shrugs.

"Wow, my roomie's a hot commodity."

I reach out with my foot to nudge his leg and he grabs it. Before I know it, he's giving me a glorious food rub. My instinct is to pull away, because he's the one who deserves the pampering, but it seems to relax him, keeping him busy while he shares a part of him we've never talked about.

"I wouldn't go that far, but there have been some quite lucrative offers over the years. It just doesn't seem right to profit off the worst day of my life, you know?"

"I get it."

"I'd do anything for those I care about and those I served with were my family. It's what you do."

He doesn't mention Chris. He doesn't have to. It's too hard for him. They may not have been brothers by blood, but they were brothers, nonetheless.

"Kind of like what you're doing for me and Sawyer. Giving us a place to live and pretending to be my husband."

"When are you gonna realize I'd do anything for you?"

"Because we're family?"

Where the hell am I going with this?

"If that's what you need to tell yourself."

His mood seems to shift as we watch each other. One of

his hands slides up my calf. My body heats from his touch along with the implications of his reply. Before his hands can slide any further, I pull my leg away, tucking it under me.

Say something, Mia.

Say something!

As if throwing me a lifeline, Sawyer cries. I bolt to my feet at the same time Angus does. Both of us grasping the flotation device.

"Goodnight," he says, sounding frustrated as he walks out of the room.

I follow, stopping at Sawyer's door. Angus saunters to the spare bedroom he insists on sleeping in. He doesn't look back at me before he closes the door.

How did I get myself into this mess?

Chapter Thirty-One

Angus

"So, how are things going at the house with Mia and Sawyer?" Dr. Laughlin asks during my weekly online therapy appointment.

When I first sought help, I didn't mesh with any of the local therapists. I tried I really did. I met with one psychiatrist and two psychologists in Bend, but none of them were a good fit.

I had all but given up when I mentioned my struggle to my buddy, Jimmy, on a visit to the East Coast. There was no way I was missing his college graduation.

After our time in the military came to an end, I received a veteran small-business grant and opened The House, whereas Jimmy, always the smart one in our platoon, took full advantage of the GI Bill, earning his bachelor's degree in only three years. He then went on to get his masters. He said meeting with the Doc during those first three years of school was the only thing that got him through it.

After what we experienced... what we lost... Most of the surviving men and women who served in my platoon weren't the same people we had been when we joined the military. Many of us were too guilt-ridden or scared to seek help. It would mean recounting our trauma out loud. At least for me, that's what it was. Sure, the images played like a movie in my head, but saying it out loud... Hearing myself talk about what happened... I worried that if I dove too deep into the past, I wouldn't be able to find my way back to the present.

There was no way I could share what I was going through with friends and family. They would never look at me the same.

Then, I met Dr. Laughlin.

Well, I've never met her in person, because she lives in Virginia, but we talk via video call every Tuesday at 11am. It's been years now and even though I have a long way to go, I feel like a different person. I'm not sure I'll ever get eight hours of sleep in a night again, but I only wake up in a cold sweat from a nightmare once or twice a week these days. If getting regular sleep is all I get from therapy, it will have been well worth it.

Since I still can't use the loft and my office at the bar isn't private enough, I'm on my couch at the house holding a throw pillow that smells like Mia. Everything in the house smells like Mia now.

"To be honest, it's confusing as hell, Doc."

"How so?"

"Because being around the two of them is the happiest

I've ever been, but she pulls away or I pull away, because we both know we can never be."

"Why is that?"

"You know why."

"I know what your reasons were in the past, but things between the two of you have changed. Your feelings have grown stronger and I'm curious if your reasons might be different now."

"You're right. As much as it should be at the top of the list, I don't really care if being with Mia pisses my sister off anymore. She'd get over it, eventually. Besides, it's obvious she already knows."

"So if Daisy isn't the reason, what has you holding yourself back?"

We've talked about it before, but it's been a while since I've said his name out loud. My chest tightens. My breath shallows. My best friend's face flashes in my head. His face the moment before he died. Right before my eyes. The knowing look he gave me as he patted his chest, where, unbeknownst to me, he'd kept a letter that he had written in case something happened to him.

"Chris," I finally get out after several silent moments.

"Your best friend and Mia's brother. You don't think Chris would approve?"

Leaning forward, my elbow on my knees, I hang my head and close my eyes for a beat before finding the strength to look into the camera. "His letter said to take care of his sister. I'm not sure this is what he had in mind."

"Is that all?"

She knows it's more than that. Chris is the main reason I

sought help. I haven't gotten over losing him. Or how I lost him. I'm not sure I ever will.

"She doesn't know it's my fault. That I could have saved her brother, and chose not to."

"Angus, is that really what happened or is that what you continue to tell yourself? Do you think Chris would have done things any differently had it been him in your position?"

"Doc, don't." My chest tightens and my insides twist.

"Given your training would Chris have done anything differently?"

"No," I exhale. The truth in my answer lessens the tension in my body.

"Do you love her?"

"With everything that I am."

"What else did Chris's letter say?"

There's a lump in my throat. I swallow past it and answer, "To get back to the real world and live a full life. To be happy."

"And Mia and Sawyer make you happy, yes?"

"Doc, you know they do."

"You deserve to be happy, Angus. Chris would want that for you."

"I'm not sure I deserve to be happy, but God, the two of them make me happier than I knew was possible."

"You deserve to be happy," she repeats.

"Doc..."

"Angus, you deserve to be loved, the same as Mia and Sawyer deserve to be loved. They deserve you and you deserve them."

"But if she knew I could have saved her brother.... That I could have but I didn't...."

"If you tell her what really happened, your orders, the circumstances, not the version you continue to tell yourself, but the facts, I think she could love you the same as she does today."

I huff out a laugh. "Let's not get ahead of ourselves. Nobody said anything about Mia Powell loving me. A childhood crush and sexual chemistry do not equal love."

"But you love her," Dr. Laughlin counters.

"I do, but I never said she loved me."

"Maybe if you told her how you feel, she would do the same."

"And what if she doesn't?"

"If she doesn't, she may have her own reasons. Daisy, being one of those reasons. But from everything you've told me, it's clear she has feelings for you. It may be too soon for it to be love for her, though. She may not be ready. She's a single mother, and that comes with a lot of responsibility. You need to understand where she's coming from. It's not just Mia, you would be in a relationship with. It's Sawyer too."

"And if it's not for any other reason than she simply doesn't feel the same way?"

"Then at least you'll know you put yourself out there. You'll never have to wonder. You've earned the right to know how she feels. Who knows, you could be depriving the both of you of something special."

* * *

Getting the doc's words out of my head has been impossible. I've been useless since our call ended.

I went to work and stayed until closing time to sort out

the side effects from today's appointment. I barely spoke two words as I slogged through the motions while guilt, love, fear, and desperation to make Mia mine wreaked havoc on my head and my heart.

Today left me with more questions than answers. Is there a remote chance this is more than a crush and intense sexual chemistry on her side, too? Could she really love me? Even without her knowing about Chris, does she think I'm good enough to be a father-figure in her child's life?

It's 2am when I walk through the front door of the quiet house. As usual, she left the light above the kitchen sink on. The ambient glow highlights Mia and Sawyer's belongings littered about the great room and dining room. Sawyer's favorite dump truck waits on the bench next to the front door, where both of their jackets hang. Mia's favorite fluffy gray blanket is folded and draped along the back of the couch. Sawyer's high chair is tucked under the table. Their things make this house feel like a home for the first time.

I stand in the entryway taking it all in, telling myself not to lean in and bury my nose in her favorite red scarf that I know will smell like her.

That would be creepy.

Forcing myself to walk past the coatrack and through the house amongst their things, I head to the kitchen, hoping to distract myself with something to eat. Except what I find in the fridge is anything but a distraction. There's a container of food with a note on it.

Sawyer missed you tonight. Hope you like stir-fry?

She didn't confess her undying love. She said Sawyer missed me, not her. So why is it suddenly so hard to breathe? Why is my heart thundering in my ears? She said she hoped I liked stir-fry, not that she wanted to stay here with me forever.

You deserve to be happy.

Mia and Sawyer deserve to be happy.

You'll never know if you don't put yourself out there.

The same words that have been torturing me all day spin round and round through my head, but now that I'm here in the house where they lay sleeping, standing in the kitchen with leftovers in my hand, those words hit me like a freight train.

I fucking love Mia and her little boy.

There is nothing I need more than to make them happy. For a lifetime. Can I really spend the rest of my life pretending she isn't it for me? Am I going to watch her eventually meet someone else, fall in love, and live a life with him?

The thought makes me sick.

My world has been out of focus for far too long. Now it sharpens, turning crystal clear, as if I'm seeing it in HD.

It's time to tell her everything. The truth about Chris. The extent of my feelings for her.

Tomorrow I'm not hiding at the bar.

Tomorrow night, I'll be home for dinner. Bath time and

bedtime. I'll read Sawyer a story or two or three, then I'll pour his mom a glass of wine and bare my soul.

What could go wrong?

Feeling good about my decision made by the refrigerator light, I pop my dinner in the microwave. I've just hit start when I hear a cry coming from down the hall.

Sawyer.

My dinner all but forgotten, I race to his room where he's sitting up in his fire truck bed holding his stuffed dog. Tears stream down his face.

"Hey, buddy. What's wrong?" I ask, wiping tears from his cheeks.

When he sees it's me, he holds his arms up, his lower lip quivering. "Gus Gus."

Seeing him upset like this is a punch to the gut, and I can't pick him up fast enough. "I got you, bud. I got you."

He wraps himself around me. Arms around my neck, legs around my middle, he holds on for dear life. He rests his head on my shoulder. His crying has ceased, but his body shakes with every breath as he settles himself in my arms.

"That must have been a nasty dream. I'm so sorry. I know how scary they can be. But I got you. I'm not going anywhere." I rub soothing circles on his back. His little body, growing lax.

An unexpected pride sneaks its way into my psyche. He reached for me to comfort him, and that's just what I did. I comforted him. And it worked.

He is one of the most important things in my world and to be there for him in this tangible way validates everything I've been feeling.

Turning away from his bed to walk around the room until I'm sure he's completely back to sleep, I find the rest of my world standing in the doorway, watching us.

255

Chapter Thirty-Two

Mia

Angus and I were naked in a pasture. Our horses tied to nearby fir trees as we made love on a red and gold Pendleton blanket. I'm in the middle of a recurring dream I've already had several times this week, only tonight, when I got to the part where my best friend's brother moans my name, as he rocks in and out of me, he says "Sawyer."

"What?"

Rolling off me, he says his name again. "Sawyer."

It's then that I wake up because of the crying coming from the room next door.

In a rush, I step into my slippers and race to his room only to find him in the arms of the man I had just been dreaming about.

"That must have been quite a nasty dream. I'm so sorry. I

know how scary they can be. But I got you. I'm not going anywhere," Angus says against the top of his head.

My hand covers my mouth as sobs threaten to overtake me. The emotions of seeing this man from my dreams so sweetly calming my little boy mixed with the heartache of hearing him acknowledge his own nightmares takes me by surprise.

What I wouldn't give to soothe his pain, to rescue him, like he's rescued Sawyer and me these last few months.

When he finds me watching them, he drifts in my direction, a slight bounce in his step to help Sawyer fall back to sleep if he isn't already. He doesn't stop in front of me, though. Instead, he gives me a soft smile as he passes by, walking circles around the room.

After four more passes, he stops in front of me. "I got him. You can go back to sleep."

Shaking my head in reply, I stay rooted to my spot in the doorway.

We do what we do far too often. We stare at each other. Neither of us hiding from the other. Not saying the things we're both too scared to admit. There's no need to share feelings that will leave me in even more pain than I'm in already. Playing house. Nights of passion. It's confusing and unrealistic to think there could be anything more.

Gus's lack of movement has Sawyer squirming and whining in his arms, interrupting our silent conversation.

"Here, let me take him," I offer.

"I don't mind," he whispers.

"He may need to be changed."

He relents at this, gently passing him to me. Once he's in my arms, Angus places a kiss on the top of his head, and I want to cry. He really loves my kid, and doesn't that just make all of this that much worse?

I expect him to leave, but he stays. Watching us in the gentle glow of the nightlight on the other side of the room.

That is what the two of us have been doing most of our lives. Watching. Only I'm used to admiring him from afar. Now that we're living under the same roof, the distance usually between us has evaporated.

I know what he tastes like.

What his skin feels like under my fingertips while I trace his tattoos.

I've heard him moan my name in the throes of passion.

Everything between us is different now.

He's no longer a fantasy. Well, he is. I fantasize about him every night as I fall asleep in his bed. He may not be lying beside me, but he always finds me in my dreams. Always.

As if I'm not emotional enough, the man who has forever held my heart in his hands breaks the silence.

"You are so beautiful."

His words ignite the panic I've been trying to keep at bay since I came home from work yesterday to find him cooking in the kitchen. When I went to bed last night, I couldn't help but wonder if he remembered our conversation in his loft. When I told him, a man cooking for me was better than flowers. He called it my love language. I was sure I was reading more into it, because each time my heart flutters with hope and desire, panic reaches through my ribs and clenches my heart in its fist, reminding me I'm not allowed to want more with Angus McKinnon.

Besides, he wouldn't be looking at me the way he is right now if he knew my secret.

Chapter Thirty-Three

Angus

Moonlight sneaks through a space in the curtains dimly illuminating the room, projecting an ethereal glow over Mia's perfect fucking face.

She and Sawyer deserve love, and I want to be the one to give it to them.

Leaning against the doorjamb, in the middle of the night, while she changes her sleepy little boy's diaper, isn't exactly the most romantic time or place to tell her everything I've had running through my mind. But, God, do I want to.

I want to tell her that the more time I spend with them, the more I *need* them.

That everything I want in my life is right here in this room. Their laughter gives me life and, if given the chance, I'll do everything in my power to make them happy every single day. Hell, the two of them make me want to be a better man. After talking to her about the podcast offer, I've thought more about what to do with my CMH. I want to tell her about my ideas, but that can wait. We have other important matters to discuss first.

I want to share my moment of clarity, but there's no denying the look of despair on her face. It's another punch to the gut, but I get it. I've felt the same anguish for years, but never more so than the last few months. I'll give her the time she needs to meet me where I am, but I need to let her know I no longer think of us as an impossibility.

With Sawyer changed and dressed, Mia stands in the middle of the room, swaying back and forth while his eyes close with two slow blinks. She looks tired, almost pleading with me to stop making this connection between us so real.

Impossible.

She lays him down, tucking his stuffed animal under his arm, and pulling his blanket over him. Hesitantly, she turns around, facing me, but doesn't make a move closer. Almost as though Sawyer had been some sort of shield she was hiding behind.

Unsure how to start the conversation I decide to get right to it. Whispering, I finally risk it all. "You know, I talked to my therapist about you today."

Her eyes go wide. "You did?"

"I did. It wasn't the first time either."

I take two steps. I'm only a couple of feet from her now.

"Is our being here causing you stress? Anxiety? If so, I can figure something else out," she whispers. "I'm so sorry."

Her eyes are wild. As close as I am, I can see them growing glossy with tears. This is not how I wanted this to go.

"On the contrary." I can't help but reach out and take her hand in mine. "I told her how happy I've been since the day I became your husband."

"Angus..." she breathes on a gasp.

"You and this little guy make me want to be a better man."

A tear escapes down her cheek, and I wipe it away with my thumb.

"Angus... I can't. You don't know what you're saying."

"That's where you're wrong. I'm done making excuses, Mia." She tries to pull her hand out of my grasp. I don't let her. "I know you think the secrets you keep will make me feel differently about you, but I'm not sure that could ever be true. But as much as I want you, there is something I need to share with you first. I need you to know everything. And after, if you want to share your secrets with me, fine. If not, that's also fine."

"I don't deserve your secrets."

"Why? What could be so bad, Mia? Why won't you trust me enough to give me a chance to make that decision for myself?"

"I do trust you, but you need to trust me, too. Trust me to know that you would never see me the same again. You would hate me."

Closing the gap between us, I use my free hand to wipe away the tears streaming down her face. "Come on. Let's go talk."

"I can't. I just can't."

Pulling away from my touch, she strides past me into the hallway, leaving me in the middle of Sawyer's room with an ache in my gut. It hurts but doesn't deter me. I'll give her time, but I won't give up.

Her, bedroom door clicks shut, leaving me to watch Sawyer sleep. God, it feels good to have this kid under my roof. In his room, right here where he belongs.

Chapter Thirty-Four

Mia

"Mia, thanks for staying late. I know it's not ideal. But Dr. Rivers urgently needs to be seen tonight and I need you to run an IV while I run tests. He has patients until we close, so after hours it will have to be."

"Of course, I completely understand. I know it's hard for doctors to take care of themselves when they take care of everyone else all day. I just need to make arrangements for Sawyer."

"Well, go take a break and call that hubby of yours." She walks away from the nurses' station. "Thanks again."

Shit.

It's been three nights since Angus declared he was through making excuses. Since then, he's been like he's always been. Perfect. He hasn't mentioned our 2am conversation, but he has cooked dinner every night. We eat together and then he goes to the bar for two or three hours and is back before I'm in bed.

When he gets home, we talk and watch old episodes of *Friends*. We've started from episode one and I hate knowing we won't get to spend this time together long enough to make it to episode 234.

He's giving me space, yet things are different. Casual touches when we're moving around the house, goodnight kisses on the cheek and don't get me started on how wet I get every time he calls me babe. He's not pushing, but he's not holding back either.

Realistically, I know he won't mind picking Sawyer up. If I know Angus, it will make his day. I've never seen him as happy as when he's doing all the domestic daily activities that come with sharing a home with the two of us. Still, it's not his problem. He's running a business, he has a life, but he's my only option.

I would rather text him, because every time he says my name with that deep gravely voice, be it my actual name or my childhood nickname, I let my guard down, forgetting the reality of our situation. However, this favor deserves more than a text.

Taking a deep breath, I select his name on my phone.

"Goof. To what do I owe this honor?"

I've never heard anything more beautiful than the smile in his voice. Not just any smile, but a smile that says he's happy to hear from me. If only we were on a video call and I could see those caramel eyes of his.

"Well... I have a favor to ask?"

"I am at your service, m'lady. What is it I can do for you?"

"I am so very sorry about this, and I wouldn't bother you if I had another option."

"Woman, there isn't anything I wouldn't do for you. Spit it out!"

Why does he have to be so sweet?

"Okay, I really cannot believe I have to ask this of you, but would you be able to pick Sawyer up from day care tonight?"

"Is everything okay?"

"Yes, everything is fine. We just have a late patient that will keep me here after the on-site day care closes. Are you able to get away from the bar?"

"If you haven't noticed, I've been able to get away every night this week and if it means time with my little buddy, well, you don't have to ask me twice."

Of course, I've noticed. You're killing me with your nightly dinners and goodnight kisses.

"You're sure?"

"Don't you dare ask me again, Goof." There's a hint of humor in his voice, but not much.

"Okay, okay. Thank you so much."

"What about a car seat?" he asks.

"I'll take it out of my car and leave it with the gals in the day care. You remember how to put it in the truck, right?"

"Yes, ma'am."

"You're a lifesaver."

"Is it okay if I pick him up a little early?"

"Really?"

"If you don't mind?"

"He'd love that."

"Nice! I'll take good care of him and we'll have some fun,

too. Will you be home for dinner, or should we eat without you?"

"I don't know what time we'll finish up here. Eat without me. I would tell you what to feed him, but you've mastered all his favorites. You're good to go on that front."

"Sounds like a plan. You take your time and don't worry about a thing."

"Thank you." Someone walks by and I lower my voice to whisper, fearful of blowing my cover. "I know this is more than you signed up for when you offered your home to us. I hope this doesn't wreck your plans for the night?"

"When are you gonna realize it's not a bother when you and Sawyer are involved?" His voice softens. "You can wreck my plans anytime you want, Goof."

Dumbfounded by his words, I don't have any in return.

"Mia. Don't freak out. All I'm saying is I've got you."

He knows me so well.

"Thank you."

"Stop thanking me. We'll see you when you get home."

"Okay, see you when I get home."

"Bye, Goof."

"Bye."

My heart is galloping all over itself and there's nothing I can do about it.

* * *

If I thought moving into his home was a mistake, agreeing to stay in his house with him also in it, was a monumental error in judgment on my part.

My little boy and the man I have always loved are out

cold on the couch, *Paw Patrol* silently playing on the TV. They didn't hear me come through the front door and are oblivious to the fact that I'm standing in the family room, tears dripping from my chin as I cover my mouth with my hand to hold in my sobs.

I've dreamt of this exact scenario so many times. It's everything I could ever want, not just for me, but for Sawyer. He deserves a life like this more than I do. And as much as Angus tells me he's tired of making excuses to keep us apart, it's only because he's naïve to the reality of our situation. I've got to put an end to this before the three of us get in any deeper. I need to find a new place to live. Maybe I'll find an apartment in Bend close to the clinic. I'll start making calls on my break tomorrow.

Slipping off my shoes, I tip-toe through the house to the kitchen where I keep my to-do list, crossing off one item and adding two more. One is a reminder to pick up laundry deter-gent at the store tomorrow, and the other will change our lives forever.

Gently, I attempt to pick Sawyer up, but Gus's arms squeeze him tighter to his chest as his eyes open. When he sees it's me, he gives me a soft smile that melts my heart.

"Let me go put him down," I whisper.

"Okay," he relents, relaxing his grip.

Sawyer, already in his pajamas, is heavy in my arms. He's getting so big. So fast. Life is flying by without a care in the world for my need to slow it down. Sooner than I'd like, he'll be too old for his mom to hug and kiss him in front of his friends and then he'll be in college, then married.

Good grief, woman! Get a hold of yourself! He's two!

I chastise myself, because my tears are back and one falls

on his little head as I lay him down. Kneeling next to his bed, I watch my baby sleep as I run my fingers through his blond hair. Taking in the moment of peace with him, because his life is about to change irrevocably.

"I'm so sorry, baby boy," I whisper.

I'm still on the floor with him when I feel Gus's presence. My moment of peace is over. Who knows if I'll ever have one again.

Standing, I take a fortifying breath and turn to face the man in the doorway. He's no longer the childhood crush that kept me up at night. He's more than any of those things, because I am *in love* with him. It's not the kind of love you feel for a family friend, it's an all-consuming kind of love that you only get once in a lifetime. Only, I don't get to keep my once in a lifetime, because I'm about to lose it. But before I do, I want one more night.

One more night of the most devastating love I've ever known. Before I bring it all crashing down.

"You okay?" he asks, as I approach him.

My reply is to link my pinky finger with his as I pass by, leading him out of the room, and closing Sawyer's door behind us. Angus follows me to his bedroom.

"Mia, as happy as I am to see where your mind is going, I'd like to talk about something before we go any farther."

Closing the door behind us, I make my way to my bedside table where I turn on the baby monitor, lowering the volume to barely audible. The obsessive mom in me has to have it on, but the woman in me doesn't need to hear him sleep while I take what I want from the man standing behind me.

"Mia." His arms wrap around my middle as he whispers in my ear. "We need to talk."

The caress of his words on the shell of my ear fuels the fire inside me. The last thing I want to do is talk.

"I need to talk to you, too. But it can wait until tomorrow."

He turns me around so he can look at me. "I don't want to go further until you know everything. Because that's what I want from you. Mia. *Everything*. And I can't give that to you until we talk."

Another tear falls. "Same. But tomorrow, okay?"

"Please." He wipes away my tear. "I want to do the right thing here, and something's upset you. Talk to me."

I'm not upset, I'm devastated. Because you won't want me come the light of day.

Shaking my head slowly, I stand my ground. "I promise to listen to whatever you have to say tomorrow."

Not allowing him to protest any further, I lift to my toes and kiss him. His hands land on my hips, all protests gone. What starts as slow and gentle, is deepened by him. Our tongues dance together and his hands on my hips pull me against him. His erection begs for attention I'm dying to give him.

Pulling away, I only put enough distance between us for me to pull his shirt over his head and slide his gray sweatpants down as I follow them to the floor. As much as I love Angus in a pair of tight jeans and boots, you won't hear me complaining that he's barefoot before me, thankfully going commando under his sweats, providing me easy access.

"What are you doing?" he asks, gloriously naked and all mine for the taking.

In reply I slide my hands up his muscular thighs to his hips. With the bed right behind him, I give him a little push and he understands what I want. He takes a seat on the edge of the bed, while I unabashedly take him in.

Tonight, I will make a point of memorizing every inch of his body I may have missed the last time we were together. Every intricate tattoo covering his olive complexion and taut muscles.

"Baby, you don't need to do this."

I don't want to talk. I just want to feel. Taste. To tattoo this night onto my heart.

So, I don't reply with words. Instead, I show him how I feel with actions. Dropping my gaze, I watch as my hand strokes down his thick length until the first bead of pre-cum glistens from his tip. I stop to lick it off. Only now do I dare to look at him. He's gaping at me in awe, so I make a show of licking around his head while my hand continues to stroke him.

Hissing through gritted teeth, he tries to stop me again. "Mia, this is fucking hot, but you don't need to—"

With my eyes still locked on his, I silence him by taking him into my mouth, all the way to the back of my throat.

"Fuck," is all he says as I take him over and over, my eyes watering from his size.

One of his hands glides through my hair and holds on for dear life. He's not directing the rhythm, he's just holding on. My eyes had drifted shut, but the light sting of his hand in my hair has me opening them. I'm met with a look on his face so feral it nearly brings me to orgasm. Watching him watch me turns me on. My need to come is overwhelming as my center throbs. Without thinking, my hand slips down my pants as I desperately seek release.

"Fuck, baby. You know I love to watch you touch yourself, but tonight all your orgasms are going to come from me. You won't be using your hand when you can ride mine. Got it?"

I moan around his cock, and the vibration makes him grit his teeth.

"Give me your hand," he growls.

Pulling my hand from my pants, I present it to him, glistening with proof of how turned on I am. He stuffs my fingers into his mouth and sucks my wetness from my fingers, causing me to moan again.

"Fuck, Mia. I'm gonna come if you keep doing that. You sure you want that so soon?"

"Hmm, hmmm," I groan around him.

I'm not worried about him coming already. Experience tells me he'll make me come several times and then be ready again. This man has the stamina of a fictional book boyfriend.

"One last time, Mia. You sure?"

Taking my hand away from him I tug on his balls, giving him his answer. The tension in my hair increases and his abs flex as his body grows stiff. He moans my name, releasing my hand so he can fist the sheets as he throws his head back and comes down my throat.

Rising to my feet, I blatantly take inventory of him. He's spread out before me, post orgasm, his broad chest rising and falling from exertion. The V of his muscles acts as a flashing neon light, directing my attention to the heavy cock resting between his thick thighs.

He is a masterpiece.

"You like what you see?"

I nod. Still afraid to speak.

"I'm glad because I'm all yours, Mia. You know that, right?"

A fresh tear escapes, and I don't bother stopping it from streaming down my face. Tonight, I'm giving him all of me.

When I don't answer, he stands, lifting my sweatshirt over my head, then pulling my yoga pants down. I brace my hands on his shoulders as he strips me until I'm standing before him in only my bra and panties.

He takes my face in his hands, bending his knees until we're eye to eye. "I'm yours, baby, and you're mine."

Chapter Thirty-Five

Angus

Her tears shred my soul.

Moonlight streams through the window, lighting her face as the pools in her ocean eyes overflow. I've confessed that I'm hers, but when I told her she was mine, her body shook with barely suppressed sobs that haven't eased.

Naked with her only in her underwear, I hold her as she breaks down in my arms, next to the bed where she just rocked my world. Her tears brand my skin as her emotions quake through her body. She hasn't said a word. All I can surmise is that she believes the talk we need to have will ruin this thing between us. Until recently, I thought the same. Now I'm so confident I'm meant to be hers, I believe we can make it through anything. But I'll hold her until her sobs subside, reassuring her I'm not going anywhere.

Minutes later, she steps back, her pale face red and splotchy from crying. But still so damn beautiful. She reaches behind her and unclasps her bra, her gaze never leaving mine. Presenting herself to me. Her eyes begging me for something. The optimistic part of me believes she wants me to take her pain away and tell her that after we share our secrets, I'll still be here. But the realist in me can see she's saying goodbye. She wants this one last night together, because that's all she thinks we've ever been. Secret nights. Nothing more, and after we talk, we won't even have that.

Living in the moment and pushing future worries into the deepest recesses of my mind, I take control when she begins to remove her panties.

"Don't you dare," I demand.

Her hands freeze where they are. I slide a teasing finger beneath the last piece of clothing preventing her from baring her full self to me, touching the part of her she used to hide away. It's fucking beautiful to see her comfortable in her own skin. My cock, that is always in a state of arousal when she's near, is growing hard again.

Sliding my hand inside, I find the material soaked, just as I had expected. "You're so wet for me, baby."

Finally speaking, she whimpers my name. I think it may be my favorite sound. Scratch that, it is my favorite sound.

I slip a finger inside her warm pussy and she gasps. "You like that?"

She nods.

"You want more?"

Another nod.

"You want my tongue, baby?"

"Yes, please," she whispers in desperation as my finger slowly pumps in and out of her.

"There she is. I need you to talk to me, Mia. Tell me what you want, what you need. Don't shy away from me. I need you to give me all of you." I slip a second finger in. "Can you do that?"

"Yes," she promises, her gaze still on mine.

"You want me on my knees for you, baby?"

"God, yes," she shudders, fire in her eyes.

"My girl gets what she wants."

Sliding my hand out of her lace, I drag her wetness over her skin. She watches my every move. Her eyes blazing as I drag her panties down her legs and drop to my knees, ready to worship her. Her hands scrape over my barely there hair as I place kisses across her pelvic bone.

I stand and point to the bed. "Sit."

She takes the spot on the bed where she had previously placed me. Her gaze still locked on me; she leans back on her hands. The room is dark, only able to see her thanks to the moon shining in her through the windows, but she's as bright as the damn sun. Her pale skin glows against the dark comforter and those baby blue eyes of hers are like a beacon calling to me.

"Open for me."

She spreads her legs, giving me the view I've been craving.

Kneeling between her legs I drag my finger over her clit and through her wetness, I tell her the most honest thing I have ever said. "You are fucking perfect."

Her legs open wider, begging for my mouth. I can still feel her watching me, but there's no way I can take my eyes off my finger. This is all still unbelievable to me. Sure, I dream of moments like this with her, but for it to be real is fucking overwhelming. If I have my way, I'll be the last man who ever touches her like this.

Sliding another finger into her, I leisurely thrust in and out of her tight heat for a few beats before looking up to find her biting her lower lip. Her nipples are hard and she's rocking her hips, looking for more.

Unable to resist, I lean forward and suck her clit into my mouth as my hand continues its leisurely pace. She tightens around my finger, always so responsive. I close my eyes and circle her sensitive bundle of nerves, teasing her with my tongue by licking her everywhere, but where she wants it the most. Edging her closer and closer, but never giving her what she needs.

When I open my eyes, she's still leaning on one hand while the other teases and pinches one of her nipples. The sight of her finding such pleasure in the moment is so damn sexy I grip my cock and work myself as I devour her.

I. Am. Insatiable.

Need courses through my veins. Releasing myself so I can push her legs even wider, I remove my fingers and feast on her, pumping my tongue inside her center while my thumb works her clit. When her body tightens, I thrust two fingers inside her, working her G-spot, and my tongue finds her sweet spot once again. She writhes against my face, soaking my hand as she comes and comes and comes. I'm relentless, spurred on by the intensity of her climax, continuing to work her body until the waves of her orgasm cease and she collapses.

Lying back on the bed, she releases her grip on the

comforter, sounding intoxicated when she asks, "How does it get better every time?"

"Because we fit, baby." Rising from my knees, I crawl over her as she scoots back on the bed, teasing a nipple on my way up her body. I nip at the soft skin of her neck and her fruity scent infiltrates my senses. All I want to do is ravage her. But I also want this to last until morning.

I force myself to roll off her, hating the air between us, much preferring her skin against mine. Resting my head in my palm, keeping one leg wrapped around hers, my forefinger circles her breast. "Hi."

"Hi," she giggles, and I realize she didn't say a proper hello when she got home.

"How was your day?"

She rolls to her side, mirroring me, her eyes locked on mine. "I don't want to talk about my day, Angus."

"What *do* you want to talk about?"

"What do you say we skip the talking altogether?"

"What if I want to tell you how beautiful you are?"

She pushes my shoulder. "Shut up."

"What if I want to tell you I think you might be my best friend?"

Ripping her gaze from mine when she rolls to her back and covers her eyes with her forearm, she whispers, "Don't."

"Why?" I ask, because it's clear she doesn't want to venture into a serious conversation.

"Because I don't want to talk. Not tonight."

"What *do* you want, then?"

Lifting to her knees, she pushes me to my back, straddling me. "You."

"Babe I'm yours for the taking. Do your worst."

Leaning forward, she presses her breasts against me, kissing my lips, then pulling back, licking the taste of herself from hers.

"You taste good, don't cha, baby?"

Nodding, she lays her body on mine, stretching so our legs tangle. Her lips find my mouth again and I let her take what she wants. How she wants it. She lingers there for a time before her kisses intensify, her body creating the best kind of friction against mine. Her clit rubs against my cock, and she gasps.

"Angus, I need you inside me."

Chapter Thirty-Six

Angus

Stretching myself awake, flashes of last night play like a movie on my still closed eyelids. After rushing to my room to get protection, we made love all night. Well, not all night long.

Shortly after midnight, Sawyer woke after a leaky diaper left him wet and uncomfortable. Mia, in my T-shirt, and I, in my sweatpants, worked in tandem as she changed and cleaned him, and I changed the sheets. His fire truck bed is cute and all, but damn if it being so low to the ground doesn't kill the back and knees when making it.

Sawyer went back to bed easily and was fast asleep two seconds after his mama laid him down. That wasn't the case for the two of us.

We had worked up quite an appetite and needed a snack. Over the last week, we discovered our mutual love for peanut butter, so we grabbed the jar and two spoons and dug in for some much-needed protein to get us through the night.

Once we were back in bed, I put her right where she belonged, in my arms.

Spooning her, holding on tight so she didn't slip away, I whispered into her hair, "We make a pretty good team."

Her body tensed as she fidgeted. Disappointed by her reaction, but not surprised, I lightly squeezed her back to my front even tighter, not letting her out of my grasp. I didn't let her distract me from what I had to do before things went any further.

"Shh.... You know it's true." This time, I kissed her head.

"Angus—"

"I don't want to hear the reasons we can't be together. I don't care about your secrets. And I don't care what Daisy or the rest of the family think. Shit, Daisy already knows this is much more than a fake relationship. You and I belong together, Mia. You know it. I know it. So, let's get over our shit and do what makes us happy. What do you say?"

"You can't be serious."

"As a heart attack."

She shifted in the bed to turn toward me, so I released my hold on her. Her eyes were glossy, yet she somehow looked elated that I wanted to be with her, scared shitless at the same time. She didn't speak, instead taking me in as if waiting for me to drop the other shoe. And damnit if that wasn't what I did next.

I told her about that day in Afghanistan. About the mission the five of us were given to secure a high value target who had been supplying weapons that were being used against not only us, but also the civilians in the region.

As hard as it was, I recounted the worst day of my life. I explained how we gained entry into the compound, and how Chris took a bullet to the leg as soon as we did. Instinct told me to rush to my best friend, but my training kicked in, reminding me that the medic was right behind me and better equipped for the job. I continued as planned around the walls of the enclosure we had been studying for the last week. I let the rage consuming me after watching my brother in arms fall wounded fuel my determination to not only hit our target, but to make sure the asshole on the other end of the gun never saw another sunrise.

Seeing red, I ordered the other three into positions where they were protected by what little shelter we could find while I ran into a barrage of gunfire. I didn't stop firing until the shooter was dead, along with the supplier we were sent there for.

There was no need to go into much more detail. When I was awarded the CMH, the story of what happened on the mission became public knowledge. She knows I was shot in three places that day. Her fingertips have traced my scars, her lips have kissed them. According to the Army, I sacrificed myself to protect my fellow Marines and take down one of the biggest weapons suppliers in the war.

Nowhere does it say I chose the mission over my best friend. Over Mia's brother. But I tell *her* all of that.

That by the time I got back to him, it was too late. Little did I know, but Doc had taken a bullet to his arm. Both he and Chris were bleeding out. Chris was fighting to stay conscious, but he made me promise to take care of his sister. It was the easiest promise I ever made, but the last one I ever wanted to make. Richards and Cano carried Doc. I had

Chris, and Nibbs carried our shit as we made the mile long trek to our evac team. They worked on Chris in our rescue vehicle all the way back to base, but he had already lost too much blood. The citation doesn't say that I held him as he took his last breath. That they had to pull him from my arms because I refused to let him go.

Swiping a tear from her cheek, I continue. "Goof, when I promised your brother I would take care of you, I don't think this," I motioned between our naked bodies, "was what he meant. But I need you to know I would have taken care of you with or without my promise to him. Deep down, Chris knew how I felt about you. We didn't discuss it, but he knew. There wasn't anything about me he didn't know. He saw the way I looked at you."

She scooted closer to me, caressing my face with her hands.

"I need you to know my role in Chris's death before we go any further. You deserve the truth, not the bullshit the president read the day he put that medal I never wanted around my neck. You deserve the choice to be with a man who could have saved your brother but chose not to."

I waited for her to pull away.

Ask me to leave.

Anything but to lean forward and kiss me. To tell me it wasn't my fault, as she wrapped her naked body around mine.

At first, I wasn't sure she understood what I'd said. "Mia, did you hear me? I left him there."

"I heard you." She pressed her lips above my heart. "You were doing your job. It wasn't your fault."

"You don't understand."

"Angus, you can't change what happened that day. I'm heartbroken that I lost my brother. My life will never be the same. But *you* came home." Another kiss against my chest, where my heart is begging for her to listen to me. To understand that my action, or lack thereof, caused her heartbreak. But to no avail. "I'm glad you came home."

Her words confused me.

Relieved me.

Broke me apart and put me back together again.

She wrapped me up in her love while I wept in her arms. She held me, telling me over and over that it wasn't my fault.

It wasn't my fault.

Once my tears subsided, she kissed every inch of my face before she climbed on top of me, telling me with her body that it wasn't my fault and that she wasn't going to run away. At least not because of this.

It was more than I deserved.

This morning as she got ready for work, I laid in bed and watched her go through her morning routine. She told me I was stupid, as she so often does, and stuck her tongue out at me. I didn't care. I could gladly turn watching her do the most mundane tasks into a full-time job.

She also told me to stay in bed when I offered to help with Sawyer. Her reply was quick. Adamant. Almost as though she didn't want Sawyer to realize I was here. Likely, so he didn't get used to me being a part of their daily routine. After everything we shared last night, it stung, but I stayed in bed as requested.

They've been gone at least an hour, but I'm still between the sheets, my mind all over the place. Talking about the day I lost Chris made sleeping dangerous. Choosing to stay awake all night rather than drifting off and risking a nightmare. I tend to thrash in my sleep when I get trapped in one of those nightmares and I would never forgive myself if I hurt her. Granted I've never had anyone sleeping beside me during a nightmare, but I wasn't taking that chance.

I'd also never talked about that day with anyone other than my therapist. Nor had I cried since the day they pulled me away from Chris. And I didn't cry last night. I sobbed until I had nothing left in me.

She accepted me as I was, didn't blame me, and didn't walk away. But there's no denying the look in her eyes when she kissed me goodbye this morning. Fear and sadness lingered behind her cerulean eyes. It was the same sorrow she wore when she took my hand and led me to the bedroom last night.

The ringing of my phone interrupts the barrage of thoughts and emotions threatening my sanity. Grateful for the distraction and to see it's my brother on the other end, I answer.

"What's up?" I answer, because Cal isn't the type to call for a chat.

"You busy this morning?"

"Nope, not going into the bar till noon."

"Meet me at the barn. I need to go for a ride."

"See you in twenty."

"Thanks."

When Cal says he needs to '*go for a ride*', it means he's stressed out and needs to talk. I'm more than happy to talk about *his* problems. Anything to stop replaying the fear in Mia's eyes when she left.

I heft my exhausted body out of my bed that still smells

of her. I saunter to the spare bedroom where I'm staying, get dressed, brush my teeth and head to the kitchen, relieved to see she filled a thermos of coffee for me with a sticky note on it.

Thank you.

Thank you for what?

A nice roll in the hay? Telling her the truth about Chris? Or thank you for the place to stay?

Callen has the right idea. A ride is what I need to get my head straight.

Patting my pockets for my truck keys and coming up short, I look around the kitchen counter, finding them next to Mia's ever growing to-do list. I'm not purposefully snooping when I read it. It's her writing that calls to me. It's rare you see a person's handwriting, what with texting and technology, so seeing her writing draws me in. Anything and everything about this woman captivates me.

The list is your regular laundry list of things to do around the house, but at the very bottom she's crossed out a line that says, *Tell Angus about bar invite email.* Below it, she's added two words in all caps...

TELL HIM!

My heart plummets to my stomach. Nausea swirls in my gut. My mind races once again.

A small part of me is relieved she wants to move forward with our relationship. She wants me to know her truth. But the way those two words sit on the page makes me queasy. Not in her sweet swirling writing, but in harsh block letters written so hard she nearly ripped the paper.

Not to mention the force she used to cross out the line above it.

My fear is short-lived, though. Whatever she has to tell me won't matter in the least. She's it for me. Let her tell me her worst so I can prove my loyalty and stick by her side.

Standing a little taller, I say out loud to the empty house, "Hit me with your best shot, Goof. I'm not going anywhere."

Checking my email for an invitation, I see one sent from Mia's work email two days ago that I somehow missed. An invite for a casual after work night of dancing at The Cross-Eyed Cricket next weekend. "Scratch it out all you want, woman. You aren't going dancing with anyone, if it ain't me. You better believe I'll be there."

We're finally crossing the imaginary bridge we've always had between us. I never thought we'd get this far, but now that we have, I'm not giving her up for anyone or anything.

Tell me your secrets, Mia.

You don't scare me.

Chapter Thirty-Seven

ANGUS

Taking in a deep inhale of sun-warmed earth and the hint of manure, my soul breathes a little easier.

There's nothing better than a spring day on the ranch. At the moment, the horses are tied to a tree, grazing on a fresh mix of grass and clover while Cal and I fix a hole in the fence line.

We haven't talked much, but I know my brother. His job is at the store, the ranch and riding are what he does when something is on his mind. However, he prefers to figure things out on his own. He asked me out here for a reason, but I'm not gonna push. If there's anyone who knows how hard it is to say what's on their mind, it's me.

Finished with the fence, we climb back on the horses, taking our time as though neither of us have businesses to run. Like there is nowhere else in the world we need to be.

Instead, we mosey along at a leisurely trot, traversing the endless pastures side by side without a care in the world. Cal even stops Mabel here and there in search of blackberries. It's early in the season but wouldn't you know it? He turns up with a handful.

That's how his life has gone since Charlie showed up in our little town. The man won the damn lottery when she found her way back to him. And with their announcement this past Sunday his life just keeps getting better. Charlotte is pregnant. Apparently, she found out on their wedding day, but they've kept it to themselves until they were through the first trimester.

"So, how's the mom-to-be feeling?"

"Not too bad. Her morning sickness is more like all-day sickness, but considering, she's doing good."

"Glad to hear it."

He scratches at the couple days' growth on his face, tilting his head in contemplation, like he's trying to make a tough decision.

Hmm... What's bothering you, big brother?

"And how are you?" I ask. Keeping my inquiries short and sweet. Too much digging and the man will take off at a full gallop.

He exhales, his body sagging as he confesses, "I'm scared shitless. That's how I am."

And there it is. That's what's on his mind. Callen McKinnon, who can defeat any foe, is afraid of becoming a dad.

Is there anything scarier?

Or fucking cooler?

"What is it that has your panties all twisted up?"

"Make fun all you want, little brother. You'll get it one day."

"Well, help me get it now. Because there is no doubt in my mind that you're gonna be a great dad."

Moments tick by, but only the song of a sparrow and the horses' hooves on the dirt answer. Cal, as usual, is working out what he wants to say next. He gets there eventually.

"Not worrying about Charlotte's safety, not having her at arm's length at all times, is a day-to-day struggle. I know she's safe. I do. But since I found out she was carrying my child; my anxiety is off the charts. What the hell am I gonna do once the baby is actually here?"

"Well, you know Charlie's safe. You made sure of that," I say, referring to the stalker that showed up in Goose Hollow last summer. "And when the baby gets here, you'll take care of her or him like you do everyone else in this family. If any of us are meant to be a parent, it's you, dude. C'mon, you know that."

"You think?" His eyes are dark with worry.

He's not fishing for compliments. The man really doesn't think he's ready for the next and biggest part of his life. He wants to know I'm not blowing smoke up his ass.

"Cal, what's got you so wound up?" I duck under a pine tree branch along the path back to the barn. "I thought you were excited."

"I was. I mean, I am. It's just a lot, you know? Running the store, building the house, and now Charlotte is pregnant. What if I'm not around enough? What if she feels like I'm not pulling my weight? What if the dog doesn't like the baby?"

I hold my chuckle in, enjoying this vulnerable side of my big brother.

Careful not to let my smile show, I do my best to ease his mind. "Listen, I get that you're scared, I do. But you'll figure out how to prioritize all the balls you're juggling. It's not like you'll be building the house for the next twenty years. It's your dream house, on your dream piece of land. It will all be worth it. As for Ruby, she's gonna be that kid's best friend. She'll protect the baby just as much as you will."

"You're right. I know you're right." He says the words, but I'm not sure he believes them.

"You got this, big brother. I think you're just so damn happy you're waiting for something shitty to happen. Sorry to tell you, but I think you're finally living the life you've always deserved. Quit worrying about what could happen. Live in the moment and count yourself lucky as hell."

He gives me a nod. The turmoil behind his eyes has lightened and hopefully, the load weighing on his shoulders has lessened. He may not realize it, but it means a lot that I was the person he reached out to. Cal has been there for me countless times. It's nice to be on the other side of the equation.

The moment is fleeting, because what Cal says next nearly knocks me out of my saddle.

"So, you've been into Mia our whole lives and we all missed it, didn't we?"

Now I'm the brother with the zipped lips. Shocked at the change in conversation, I measure the words in my head before allowing myself to reply. Seems to be hereditary.

"Charlotte noticed it the first time she saw you two

together, and I told her she was crazy. But then I saw you carrying her to the barn the night of the wedding."

"What?"

"Yep, you cock-blocked me on my wedding night, asshole." He chuckles. "Charlotte and I were about to make our way to the tack room to consummate our vows, but you beat us to it."

"Sorry for the cock-block, but I'm not gonna apologize for Mia. Never." I know how defensive I sound. I've known one day soon we'd have to face our families. However, I am not prepared for today to be that day.

"So?"

"What do you want me to say, Callen?"

"This is a lot more than a fake relationship, isn't it?"

"I'd do anything for Mia and Sawyer."

"Because you love her." It's not a question.

I won't deny it, but I'm also not ready to confess my love for Mia to my big brother before I actually say the words to her. She deserves to hear them first. So, I leave his statement blowing in the wind.

"Well, if you're worried about the family, don't be. You know how we feel about her. You've got our support. Daisy will require a conversation, but you know she'll come around. Besides, I think she already knows. She's been shifty anytime the two of you and your fake marriage come up."

"Shit. Does it come up a lot?"

"As much as you would expect. Not a lot happens around here. We have to get our entertainment where we can. But the look on your face tells me it's not as funny as we thought."

"What does Mom say?"

"Like I said, it's all good. All any of us want is for you to be happy. Both of you. But she's a package deal, Gus. You ready to be a daddy?"

"I love that kid."

"We all do. But this is different. If it doesn't work out, it's not just her heart. It's Sawyer's, too. And they aren't going anywhere. So, there's that."

"I'm well aware."

"Good."

"Is that all?" I ask, because it feels like he should have a lot more questions.

Shaking his head, he shivers in his saddle. "Normally, I would ask for details, but this is Mia, and I don't wanna know a damn thing." He signals to Mabel, and they take off.

And just like that, our conversation is over. I give River a squeeze to his rib cage, and we take off at a breakneck pace after them. Between the rush of the wind against my skin as we race back to the barn and the relief that I seem to have the support of my family to move forward with Mia, I feel lighter than I did when we met at the barn this morning.

My feelings for Mia aren't a secret anymore, and I like it that way.

Now we just need to take care of her to-do list and see about getting our real life started.

Chapter Thirty-Eight

The hint of Italian herbs attempts to override my senses when I walk through the front door, but try as they might, they don't stand a chance at distracting me. Not when I feel as queasy as I do. My nerves have been going haywire all day, because my life changes tonight. I wish I could say it will be for the better, but I'm not that delusional.

As soon as I have his coat and shoes off him, Swayer takes off at the speed of light to find his Gus Gus. Pieces of my heart crumble to the ground and the words haven't even left my mouth yet.

"Hey, buddy. How does spaghetti sound?"

"Hmm... yummy," Sawyer replies as Angus picks him up.

"What about you, Mom?" he asks, turning his attention to

me. "Spaghetti work? I know I'm repeating my recipes already, but my skills in the kitchen only run so deep."

Does spaghetti work?

Who cares about dinner when my world is about to come crashing down around me?

The domestic scene in front of me has my head spinning and my insides churning, but I play along. "Sounds perfect." As soon as the words are out of my mouth, bile crawls up my throat. "Can you watch him for a minute? I'll be right back."

Not waiting for his answer, I sprint down the hall barley reaching my bathroom in time. With the reality of my situation staring me in the face, the sour stomach I've been keeping at bay all day wins the battle. If only retching what little was in my belly into the toilet made me feel any better.

Once I have control of my body again, I brush my teeth, change out of my scrubs and do my best to clean myself up. Pasting on a brave face, I leave the safety of the bedroom.

It's a herculean feat to control my emotions when I find them at the table, waiting for me. Sawyer is in his high chair, one fist holding a toddler fork, the other holding his spoon, with a bib tied around his neck. Angus, his twin, has a napkin shoved into the collar of his T-shirt and silverware in his fists.

I will not cry tonight. I have done nothing but cry for months now. I'm all cried out. I've cried sad tears, angry tears, happy tears. Tonight, I need to be strong. For Sawyer.

I force a giggle, shaking my head at their adorableness. "You didn't have to wait for me."

"We're gentlemen. We wouldn't start without the lady of the house."

Faking a smile, I pray I'm hiding the anguish slowly suffocating me. "Well, I'm here now. Eat up."

"To be honest, manners aside, he got so messy last time I wasn't sure how to approach Sawyer and red sauce. I'll have to defer to you, Mom."

Grateful for the distraction, I cut up noodles and throw together a bowl of spaghetti, busily helping Sawyer and avoiding eye contact with Angus, praying he hasn't noticed I'm not eating. My stomach may be empty, but it won't tolerate more than the two bites I've taken.

Dinner is peaceful, but messy. Once Sawyer is full, I sneak away for bath time, leaving Angus to do the dishes. It's early, but once he's in his jammies, I tuck Sawyer in bed and read him three different books until he finally closes his eyes.

Lingering in the moment, I stare at my little boy and hope he understands how much I love him. That I've only ever tried to do what was best for him. I have no idea what our futures hold after I leave his bedroom, but I know I'll fight for my little boy, no matter the cost.

Running my fingers through his hair, I whisper, "I love you, baby boy. I hope one day when you're old enough to understand, you'll know I did what I thought was right for you. I'm so sorry for whatever we lose after tonight, but you'll always have me."

I sure hope that's enough.

Planting a kiss on his forehead, I watch him for a couple more heartbeats before walking out of his room, closing the door to the quiet, beautiful life we've been living.

Angus is leaning against the kitchen counter, a dish towel over his shoulder, scrolling on his phone. He's distracted and doesn't notice me, but I notice everything about him. His tan, McKinnon skin, the intricate details of the guitar on his forearm that symbolizes his father's love of music as well as the other art that cover his arms. There's no ignoring the muscles straining the cotton covering his tattooed and scarred torso. But it's his face I can't tear my eyes away from. Long lashes line caramel-colored eyes that always seem to see more than I want to show him. His pillowy bottom lip is begging for me bite it again. He's like a priceless painting. More beautiful the longer I admire him.

Sensing me in the room, he looks up and a smile lights his eyes. The final brush of brilliance to his magnificent face.

The man is a priceless work of art.

And he was almost mine.

Pushing off the counter, he slides his phone into his back pocket before picking up my to-do list. Pinching it between his thumb and forefinger, he waves it in the air. "Tell me something, Mia."

"What's that?" I manage around the panic strangling me.

"Why'd you cross off talking to me about the invite to your work thing? Because I got the email and I'll be there with bells on."

This is not how I wanted this to go down.

"Why do you have my list?"

"You left it on the counter."

"So, you read it?"

"Not the point, Goof."

"What is your point?"

"Why did you scribble out talking to me about the invite?"

Shit.

"Does it have anything to do with the last item on your list?" he asks, leaving my list on the counter where he found it and crossing the kitchen.

Shit. Shit. Shit.

"Babe, you know you can tell me anything." He's standing a foot away from me.

Babe.

I don't deserve his term of endearment.

"I don't know how," I admit. Because no matter how many times I've rehearsed what I need to say in my head, I don't know how to tell him.

"Sure you do. You trust me, then open that pretty little mouth of yours and lay it on me."

He's trying to keep things lighthearted.

It's a futile effort.

"Even if it means it will change everything for everyone?"

"Your secret is safe with me."

"You don't get it. Once I tell you, it will change every-thing. And not just for you and me."

"Mia, I know you're scared, but I got you."

"You'll hate me."

"Why don't you let me decide who I hate?"

Rip the band-aid off. It's the only way.

I memorize the way he's looking at me right now, etching it into my mind.

Inhaling through my nose, I release my breath and change the trajectory or our lives forever. "Knox is Sawyers' father."

Angus doesn't react. Doesn't move or ask any questions. He says nothing. Does nothing for what feels like forever.

After the silence between us goes on for far too long, I dare to break it. "Can I explain?"

"Does he know?" The tone of his question gives nothing away.

"No."

Ripping his gaze from mine, he takes his first step away from me—away from us—he walks past me on his way out of the kitchen toward the spare bedroom. I flinch when I hear the gentle click of the door shutting. The calmness with which he closed the door is more unsettling than if he had slammed it.

Frozen to the spot, I'm still standing in the middle of the kitchen when he appears again. His military duffle hangs over his shoulder. He doesn't spare me a glance. Doesn't say goodbye.

He simply walks out the door like I knew he would. Although I expected some sort of conversation, I always knew this was how it would end.

And just like that, it's over. Not the fake life I've created here in Angus's home, but the real life I've created for my son and me. There's no way he keeps this to himself and when the family knows I've kept this from them, from Knox, they'll never forgive me.

Tired and on the verge of tipsy, but not quite, I do my best to touch up my face before joining the rest of my favorite people out in the throng of people at tonight's party. It feels like I'm living in some kind of dream scenario.

I am currently in Nicolette Gwen's bathroom. No big deal, she's just the biggest pop star in the world.

Knox paid for the whole family to fly out to Los Angeles on a private plane. He put us up at the famous Sunset Marquis and earlier this evening we all attended the

Grammys and were there when the Hollow Knocks won record and album of the year. We followed that up with a fancy after-party before ending up here at Nicolette's house with the likes of Josh West and other members of the Holly-wood elite.

I've been sipping my champagne slowly all night, trying to keep my wits about me, so I don't miss a thing. It's doubtful I'll ever be here again, and I would kick myself if I forgot even a second of it. Knox is beyond drunk, and I hate to think he'll forget anything about this special night in his life, but he's a big boy and not my problem.

I reapply my lipstick, give my cheeks a pinch and do a half turn to see the back of my sequined black gown and my bare back. It's simple, and though it looks like it's painted on me, the material is light and flowing and easy to move in. My hair is in a messy on purpose up-do, leaving my neck exposed. I've never seen myself all glammed up like this. These days, I spend my life studying in sweats and interning in scrubs.

I look good.

I feel good.

"Maybe I'll meet the man of my dreams when I walk out of this bathroom." I chuckle to myself. I laugh because it's been a while since I've had any kind of man in my life. I'm too busy and when I get to escape school and go home, it's all the same people I grew up with. Tonight, I'm not back home, or at school, or working. I'm living in fantasy land, and you just never know what might happen.

A girl can dream.

And a girl could use a little sexy fun in her life.

Ready to meet my prince charming in a sea of famous faces who want nothing to do with the small-town girl here as a plus one to a famous person's sister, I open the door just as Knox is reaching for the handle. He falls across the threshold, but I put my arms out to stop him from falling on his face.

"Whoa, big guy. Looks like you've had a bit too much to drink."

My hands press against his black tux shirt. He's gained a bit of his composure, shuffling his feet closer to mine, shutting the door behind him. But I'm still holding him up.

"Knox, I don't think you need my help to take care of your business. I'm gonna let you do your thing."

Knox McKinnon, my best friend's big brother, one of the most famous, most beautiful men alive, is staring at me in an unfamiliar way. His long dark brown hair is pushed behind his ears, putting his high cheekbones, golden eyes, and tan skin on display. I've never felt attracted to Knox, but he's also never been this close.

"You havin' fun tonight?" he asks, his voice low. Seductive.

"I am. Thanks again for including me."

"I'm glad you came." He moves closer, a light in his intoxicated gaze and a slight lift to one side of his mouth.

This is so strange.

"God, Goof, when did you get so beautiful?"

"What?"

Dropping my hand from his pecs, I step back, but he gently grabs one of my wrists as his other hand cups my cheek.

"You're fucking gorgeous, Mia."

"Knox, I think you've had too much to drink."

"I think I was stupid for never noticing how hot my little sister's friend is. I mean, look at you." He spins me around to get a good look at me and in a move I've no doubt he's used

before, my back is pressed against the door. I hear the click of the lock.

Why is this happening? Why am I locked inside Nicolette Gwen's bathroom with Knox, when all I've ever wanted was his brother? After all these years, a McKinnon brother finally sees me, and it's the wrong brother.

"Knox, what are you do—"

His lips tenderly touch mine. One of his hands slides down my side to my hip.

"What are you doing?" I ask, against his mouth.

He pulls away. The smell of the alcohol skates across my cheek on the way to my ear. He licks my earlobe and the heat of his words sends a shiver through my body. "Nobody has to know, but I need to know how tight your pussy is, Mia. You look too good not to take a bite." He sinks his teeth ever so gently into my shoulder.

Holy shit. Nobody has ever spoken to me like this.

"You're drunk."

He is drunk, but he's not being rough or forceful. I could step away if I wanted to. So why haven't I? Am I really that horny and desperate? I'm tipsy, but not that tipsy.

"Not that drunk." Moving one of my arms that has been hanging lifelessly at my sides, he presses my hand against his suit pants.

Impressive. He fits the rock star mold to a T.

"Knox, this is stupid."

Not as stupid as the squeeze I just gave his cock with my hand.

Wrapping one of his huge hands over mine, he moves it up and down his erection. "Might be stupid, but feels like it might be fun, doesn't it?"

"*Knox, we can't.*"

"*Why not? We're two consenting adults. I won't tell anybody if you won't.*" His glazed eyes don't leave mine as he clutches at my dress, dragging it up my legs while I consider his proposition.

I know he's drunk, but he's hot. He could have anyone he wants, and he wants me. Much to my dismay, my defenses are slowly falling. My head knows this is wrong on multiple levels, but my neglected body wants this. Not him. This. I've never had a secret hook-up in a bathroom before. It may be just what the doctor ordered.

With my dress gathered around my waist, his hands slide to my ass. "*C'mon, Mia. What do you say? One time. It'll be our little secret.*" He trails a finger over my hip until he reaches my embarrassingly damp thong, the only thing between us.

I don't answer him with words, instead I step my high-heeled feet apart, opening to him.

As if this was all the answer he needed, both hands grab my bare ass. He picks me up, placing me on the cold marble countertop. He tugs my dress out of the way as I fumble with his belt and then pants button. My hands are too shaky to make any progress. He swats my fingers away and has his pants down in seconds, releasing his massive cock. Knox is a big guy, but this is more than being proportional to his body size. I have no idea how that thing is gonna fit.

Wasting no time, he pushes the material covering my weeping center to the side. "*Last chance to run,*" he says, slipping a finger inside me. "*But I don't think you will.*"

I gasp at the intrusion. Sliding his finger free, he brings it to his mouth and licks it clean of me.

I give a small shake of my head, telling him I don't want to run. Without another word, he pulls me to the edge of the counter, tapping the outside of my thighs, signaling for me to wrap my legs around his waist. Once he has me where he wants me, he pushes into me. No foreplay. Just in and out, inch by inch, until all of him is inside me.

Resting his forehead against mine, he grunts. "Tight, just like I knew you would be."

That's all he says for the next minute, maybe two. He doesn't kiss me. His hands don't explore my body. There are no tender words. He pumps in and out of me until he comes.

His forehead still against mine, he says, "Damn, Goof. You feel as good as you look." Pulling out of me, he tucks himself back into his pants, putting himself back together.

I'm still on the edge of the counter wondering what in the hell just happened when he unlocks the door. Turning to me, he lifts his finger to his lips as if to say we'll both be quiet about whatever this was and then he's gone.

You have got to be kidding me. That's what sex with a rock god is like? I'll stick with cowboys, thank you very much.

This secret won't be hard to keep, because there is absolutely nothing to share. I may have been a willing participant, but that was about all I contributed to the exercise.

It's kinda funny. I have sex with the most famous man on the planet and it's the worst sex of my life.

Hopping down from the counter, I gasp when I feel it. His cum. Dripping down my leg.

No! No! No!

We didn't use protection.

No, no, no, no, no!

Any bit of champagne that may have had my defenses

down disappears. The clarity I needed minutes ago finally making an appearance. Knox does this all the time. He has random sex as if it were getting a coffee. Who knows how many diseases he has?

Gross.

That is how I feel.

Gross. Gross. Gross.

Things aren't so funny anymore. They're just well, gross!

I shamefully hide the pristine white washcloth I used to clean myself up in the wastebasket next to the toilet. I don't think Nicolette will miss it, nor would she want it if she knew what I had used it for.

Feeling stupid and extremely sober, I make my way toward the party and join the McKinnon clan, who are right where I left them. Sean and Matt from the band are there with their wives. Sean's hand rests protectively on Samantha's pregnant belly.

I sit next to Daisy feeling awkward and thanking the stars above sex with her brother was awful and something I never want to think about ever again, preferring to pretend it never happened.

Thirty minutes later, Knox enters the room, a bottle of tequila dangling between his fingers as he stumbles his way toward us. He's officially blato. "Helloooo family."

Cal is the only one who replies. "Hey, brother. Why don't you come sit with us?" He gets up, offering his chair.

Knox takes the seat and a swig off the bottle. Cal plants himself on the other side of Daisy. We make small talk and then Sean and Matt say their goodbyes.

Once his bandmates are out of earshot, Knox begins a long

diatribe about how they're ruining the band by having families. Repeating over and over how selfish they are.

Angus interrupts him. "Dude, calm down. Just because you haven't met the love of your life yet doesn't mean they're assholes because they have. There's more to life than the band, you know. Shit, the way you get around, I'd be shocked if there aren't any little McKinnons running around that you don't know about."

Everyone chuckles. It's a joke, but he's not lying. I now know firsthand.

"Dude, I will never have kids. Don't want them. Never have. Never will."

"Well, you may not want them, but if you keep living this lifestyle, you may find yourself with one anyway. You better be gloving up," Cal says.

He's not, Cal. Trust me on this. I think to myself.

"Dude, any woman that shows up on my doorstep saying she's pregnant with my kid is only after one thing." He lifts the bottle in the air, pointing his forefinger. "Fame and fortune."

"C'mon, you don't mean that," Daisy says, shocked by his attitude. The looks on all our faces say we all are. I've never seen this side of him. Never.

"Sorry, little sister, but it's the truth. Fame and fortune, that's all any of them want. They don't want me. They want the idea of me, and of course, my money. They don't want the real me and I don't want a kid. I'll write them a check and they can be on their way."

"You're an asshole," Daisy says, standing.

"Sorry if the truth hurts."

Angus stands. "You're drunk, Knox. Why don't we head out?"

Knox takes the hand his brother offers and we all follow them through the massive L.A. mansion. It's time to leave fantasy land behind.

In the limo, Knox bitches about women only wanting him for his money. All the way to his place. Angus stays to take care of the drunk award winner, while the rest of us go back to the hotel. Watching Angus help his brother inside his palatial estate at 4am after the biggest night of his life, I can't help but wish it had been him who locked himself in the bathroom with me.

Chapter Thirty-Nine

Angus

Knox is Sawyer's father.

Of all the things that could have come out of Mia's mouth, that confession never crossed my mind.

Knox is Sawyer's father.

Knox is Sawyer's father.

Knox is Sawyer's father.

This is why she said I would hate her. Because he had her first. My big brother has been inside the woman I've loved my entire damn life. He fathered her child.

When I pull up to the barn, I have no idea how I got there. My bag is on the passenger seat, although I don't really remember packing it. The moment the words came out of her mouth, I blacked out, functioning on autopilot, arriving here.

The crisp April air hits me as soon as I shove the truck

door open, and I think I might be sick. Not allowing myself to pause long enough to lose my spaghetti, I stumble into the barn as though I were ten shots of tequila deep.

The first thing I spot is the tack room door. The door that leads to one of the best nights of my life. My life that is now fucked. In so many ways.

My stomach wants to empty itself as my heart aches and my eyes begin to leak, but that's not my style. Instead, I let my fists take over. The instant the skin on my knuckles splits open against the oak wood of the door, my shocked stupor turns into a white-hot rage, all of my feelings rising to the surface.

Left. Right. Left. Right. Left.

"What the fuck is wrong with you?" an angry voice bellows in the distance, not breaking through the roar in my head. I keep pounding on the door.

"Angus! Stop!"

I don't think so.

A freight train tackles me from my left side, sending me flying to the ground on my right. "Christ, Angus! Enough!"

Callen.

He shifts me to my back but stays on top of me, pinning me to the ground. This happened a lot when I was a kid, but eventually, I bested him. Today, I don't even try.

"What the hell are you doing?"

"Fuck off, Cal."

"Sorry, bro. Not gonna happen."

"Dude, get off me!" I struggle under him, but my heart isn't in it, because it's been torn out of my chest and trampled on.

"Tell me what's going on and I'll think about it."

I want to scream that Knox is Sawyer's father. But then the look on Mia's face the night she told us she was pregnant flashes in my mind. It's not my story to tell. And just like she said, this news changes everything for everyone.

"Get off me."

"Tell me what the damn door did to you first."

"I can't."

"Sure you can."

God, I want to. I really do.

Rage is building inside me. The need to get everything off my chest is so intense all I can do is open my mouth and bellow until the rafters shutter and the horses whinny. After I've screamed for what could have been a few seconds or minutes, my chest is heaving and my throat is sore.

Cal sits us up, pulling me into his arms. "What is it? You're scaring the shit out of me."

I can't tell him Mia's truth, so I tell him mine. "I love her, Cal. I fucking love her and that kid so damn much it hurts." My words are so low, I doubt he would hear them if he wasn't hugging me as tight as he is.

Hearing myself admit my feelings out loud opens a floodgate of pain that rushes through my soul. Deep down, I knew that's what this was. Of course I did. It's always been love when it comes to Mia. Dr. Laughlin has asked and I've answered, but I've never said it out loud to myself or anyone else, including her. And now, what does it even matter? She was out of reach before, but now...

Why couldn't I have stayed on the sidelines? I should have continued to watch from afar. Sure, I was a miserable bastard, but this pain.... I've felt nothing like it before. It's not the same hurt you feel with the loss of a parent. It's not even the same as the devastation of losing Chris and the others that day. Now I know what it's like to eat dinner with her and Sawyer every night. To help with bath time and story time. I know what she tastes like. Feels like. Sounds like when she comes. I could only imagine all of this before. Now, I know what I'll be missing and the future I had been naïve enough to think might be ahead of me has been erased.

Cal pulls back, leaving his hands on my shoulders. There's a small smile on his face. "Of course you do. But that doesn't explain the door."

"What do you mean, of course I do?"

Why is he not surprised by my confession? Yes, he questioned me the other day, but I never confirmed his suspicion.

He scoots away, pressing his back against the door I was trying to murder mere moments ago. We're still sitting on the barn floor, but my chest is no longer heaving, and my violent range has tamped down.

"The way you two look at each other is hard to miss, little brother. I'd venture to say the feeling is mutual. So, what sent you into such a fit?"

"You think she loves me?"

"Don't be stupid. What's not to love?"

"Seriously?"

"Gus, if the way she looks at you is any indication, I do."

I let his words zip around my head and, unfortunately, my heart. A childhood crush doesn't mean love. She may want me. But loves me? Could my idiot brother be right? And what if he is? What does it matter now?

"You still with me?" Callen says with a snap of his fingers.

"What? Uh, yeah. I'm still here."

"So, what's got your panties in a bunch?"

"Listen, it doesn't matter. None of it does. We can never be, so fuck it. You know?" I stand and brush the dust and hay from my clothes. Avoiding my brother's eyes as he stands too.

"Why? Because of Daisy?" he challenges.

"I have a feeling Daisy would have a lot to say about the matter, but it's more than that."

"Please tell me it's not about Chris."

"I would say the fact that she's my sister's best friend, mom's goddaughter, and her brother died in my arms are pretty sizable roadblocks. Besides, I don't deserve her."

It's taking every bit of willpower I have not to tell him about Knox. Devastated or not, I don't share. Hell, Knox doesn't even know.

How could she not tell him?

This whole situation is just so fucked up.

For now, if Cal thinks Daisy and Chris are what's holding me back, so be it.

He shoves my shoulder. "That's bullshit and you know it. She'd be lucky to have your love. You know that, right?"

Unsure what the hell I'm supposed to say to that, I shrug.

"Angus, you are—" Callen stops short when the distant sound of a car horn blaring interrupts us. "You hear that?"

"It's coming from my place. What the fuck?"

Without another word, we're both on our feet and in a split second, jumping into Cal's truck. He points it in the direction of my house worry extinguishing my rage as we bounce along the dirt round leading to Mia and Sawyer.

Shaking from the inside out, my body doesn't know if it's coming or going with the swing of emotions it's been through in the last what? Thirty minutes? If it's even been that long. I have no idea what to feel, but I know I need to get to her. Put eyes on them both and make sure they're okay.

The moment the house comes into view, Cal bursts out into a fit of laughter. "God, I love that damn cow."

"For fuck's sake," I mutter at the sight of Bernadette's back end in the front doorway. Mia has her car door open and is honking her horn and yelling to get her attention. She's out of luck, though. Bernie doesn't work that way. Bernie does what Bernie wants.

Relieved the two of them are likely fine, I wish I was anywhere but here. As much as I may love her, I can't look at her. Not now. Not yet. But here we are.

Cal parks the truck next to Mia's car, getting her attention. The mist of rain that started a few minutes ago plasters her hair to her face, her eyes filled with frustration until she sees me. My favorite bright blue eyes have lost their sparkle. They darken with shame as she lowers her head.

In the seconds I've studied her face, Cal has gotten out of the truck. I follow suit just in time for him to say, "Well, you've got yourself in a pretty little pickle, don't ya?"

Focusing on my brother, she speaks only to him. "I don't know where she came from."

Cal, chuckles. "You missed a thousand-pound cow? She's pretty hard to miss, Mia."

Twirling her granny's ring around her finger, she tells the truth. "I wasn't in the right headspace to notice much of anything."

Cal lifts an eyebrow, his eyes flicking to me for the briefest of moments. "What had you so rattled?"

She moves her ring from one hand to the other and back again before she answers. "I needed to talk to Angus, but by the time I made it outside, he'd already left. I needed a moment to collect myself, so I stayed outside to take in the fresh air. When I snapped out of it and went back to the house, there she was. Half in. Half out."

"And honking a car horn was what you thought would move her?" The smile on Cal's face says he's loving every second of this.

"Well, I went through the back door to get into the house and try to push her out, but she wouldn't budge."

"You left the back door unlocked?"

My question earns me a glance over her shoulder, but it's fleeting. Her attention returns to the grinning asshole in front of her.

"Well, it looks like Bernie did you a solid. You needed to talk to Angus, and here he is."

There is no way we are having a conversation with Callen here. No way in hell. "I'll go get her."

Stomping along the side of the house, it's only a second before I hear another set of boots marching over the soggy ground behind me. I speed up, but Cal catches up to me at the back door.

"You know she only told me she came after you so you would hear her, right? She wanted you to know that whatever led to you bloodying your knuckles on the tack room door, she wasn't done."

"Stay out of it, Cal. You don't know what you're talking about," I spit at him as I push through the back door.

"Whatever you need to tell yourself."

Siblings are so fucking annoying.

Even though I saw her in the doorway out front, seeing an adorable, albeit huge, highland cow in my house brings a smile to my face and a shake of my head. Bernadette is a beauty and a pain in the ass simultaneously. Always has been. She's the perfect McKinnon family mascot.

Callen laughs. "Dude, there's a cow in your house."

"Why wouldn't there be? My life can't get much more fucked up."

We each take her by a horn, gently guiding her all the way inside. I push the couch out of the way and Cal walks her in a circle around my great room and out the front door.

"I've got it. I'll load her into the back of the truck and take her back to Mom's."

"I can help."

"No need. I've got the built-in ramp on the back of the truck. I've got it." He gives me one of his famous, I'm older and know better looks. "From the sound of it, you and Mia need to talk."

Bernadette and Cal slowly, at her pace, tromp out the front door. I take the moment inside alone to check on Sawyer. He's tucked into his bed, Bruce hugged tightly to him as he sleeps on his side facing the door, giving me a perfect view of his chubby cheeks and blond head of hair. Squatting on the side of the bed, I examine Sawyer Brian Powell, the little boy I had been daydreaming about being a father figure to. My chest hurts when I think about the fact that I'm actually his uncle and will never be his daddy.

I don't know when that yearning started for me, but now that the possibility is gone, I realize how bad I wanted it. A life together. The three of us. It was just a couple days ago when I finally came to the conclusion I no longer cared what the family thought about us being together.

Mia and I were endgame.

At least I had hoped we were.

Looking at Sawyer now, I see the resemblance. His wavey hair, his perfect nose, the dimple on his chin, matching the one on Knox's. And his middle name. She kept his true identity a secret but gave him a part of us by giving him the same middle name all the men in my family have.

How did I miss it?

As I did earlier this evening, I feel sick to my stomach thinking about Knox with Mia. Knox has the honor of being Sawyer's daddy, and he doesn't even know. The myriad of emotions swirling through my body brings angry tears to my eyes. I need to remove myself from this situation before my emotions get the best of me. Placing a kiss on Sawyer's head, I stand and watch him sleep a few seconds more. He's gonna be so sad he slept through a cow being in the house. The thought brings a small smile to my lips.

Exiting his room, I close the door quietly behind me and take a fortifying breath before heading down the hall to face his mommy. A lifetime of images flash through my head as I slog to what feels like my death. All memories of Mia. Decades of friendship, longing and, for the last few months, the intimacy we've shared. It feels like I'm losing it all.

My best friend.

The love of my life.

Finally summoning the courage to face her, I make my way through the house to find Mia leaning against the front door. Her arms are crossed in front of her as she shivers from being outside in the rain. When she sees me, her arms drop and her hands fists at her sides.

She's blocking my way out. When I'm only five feet in front of her, she locks eyes with me, not letting me slip away so easily this time. "This is why I was scared to start something with you. I knew you would hate me one day."

"I could never hate you, but I need to wrap my head around this."

"Of course."

"Knox needs to know."

"Angus, you were there at the Grammy after-party. You heard the things he said about any woman who claimed to be pregnant with his child. I never meant for this to happen, and I refuse to be accused of being the kind of woman he described that night. But most of all, I refuse to let my child feel unwanted or like he was a mistake. I knew falling in love with you would end like this, but that little boy is my entire world. He will never be a mistake."

The conversation she's referring to rings a bell, but that's not the part of her statement that has my heart trying to break through my chest. "What did you just say?"

"My son is not a mistake."

"Before that."

She takes two steps away from the door. She's so close my skin tingles from her nearness.

"You mean the part where I fell in love with you?"

My pulse quickens hearing her say it again. I'm unable to control the heaving of my chest as her words sink in.

"And not the love I felt for you growing up. That was a teenage crush. It was nothing compared to what I feel for you as a woman. I have fallen madly in love with you. And even though I knew telling you the truth would end us, I couldn't be with you and keep the truth from you. Daisy, my parents, nobody has mattered enough for me to risk coming clean, but you... you needed to know. Is that the part you're talking about?"

"Do you think loving me was a mistake?"

"Never. But I'll never forgive myself for hurting you. I'm sorry about that. You'll never know how many times I've wished it had been you."

"But it wasn't, was it?"

Images of her with my brother flash through my mind for the hundredth time since her confession. My rage threatens to rush back to the surface. Space. I need to put space between us so I can think clearly.

Pushing past her, I storm through the front door and into the heavy Oregon drizzle so familiar this time of year, but before my feet hit the last porch step, her voice reaches me. She's so quiet at first, I'm not sure she meant for me to hear her. But her words pierce through my chest as they splinter my heart.

"Maybe it was because all I ever wanted was for you to see me. But you never did, and I knew you never would. That night, a McKinnon brother finally saw me. It was just the wrong one. He wasn't you, but he was the next best thing."

Frozen to my spot on the stairs, I don't dare move. I don't turn to look at her. It hurts too much. To hear her truth. To know she's wanted me all these years, and I missed it. She continues, slicing my heart through and through with each word.

"A two-minute indiscretion changed my life forever. It gave me my son. Angus, as sorry as I am for hurting you, I will never apologize for Sawyer."

My first tear falls, mixing with the rain soaking me to the bone. How could she ever think I would expect her to be sorry for Sawyer? She shouldn't be. He's amazing. But I don't tell her that. Instead, I keep my back to her like a coward.

"Was I wrong to keep it from Knox? Maybe. But the moment I took that test and found out I was pregnant, I knew I would protect my child with everything I am. That includes shielding him from his father, a man who made it clear he doesn't want kids and will never see him as more than an accident some woman used as a ploy to gain access to his fame and fortune. Knox and all that comes with him is the last thing I want. The last thing I've ever wanted. The only person I've ever wanted is you. I understand if this is too much for you to overcome, I do. I will accept my fate, as long as you know you are the only person I've ever wanted. You are the only man I've ever loved. It's always been you, Angus."

Her words fall silent, but the wooden board under her feet squeaks when she takes a step down the stairs toward me. But being the coward that I am, I take the last step from the porch and flee from the only woman *I've* ever loved.

I'm not in control of my emotions and I need the trek back to my truck to gain some semblance of sanity. I need space. Time to wrap my head around it all.

Around the fact that Mia and Sawyer aren't mine.

They never were.

And most shocking, that a woman like Mia loves me.

She fucking loves me.

Chapter Forty

Angus

Sitting in the cab of my truck, soaked to the bone after my walk back to the barn, I've started the engine, but can't seem to shift it into drive.

It killed me to leave Mia on my doorstep. The doorstep to the house I had hoped to share with her and Sawyer forever, not just while my loft was being worked on. My loft has been ready for me to move back into for the last two days, but I didn't tell anyone because that meant leaving *them*.

Now that they've become a part of my life, how am I supposed to live without them? To pretend like I haven't experienced the best life has to offer? Anything else will be second-rate. How do I not take care of them? Not have dinner waiting for her when she gets home. Not read Sawyer his bedtime stories or help Mia change the sheets in the middle of the night when his diaper leaks. I want their highs and lows. I want their everything.

My teeth are chattering, but I barely register the cold as I put my truck in drive to head home. Not home, but the loft. My truck knows better, though, and it steers me to Mom's place where the lights are on.

Felling like a zombie on autopilot, I knock on Mom's front door before letting myself in. The open cuts on my hands sting as I slip off my boots and weave through the house to find Mom sitting at the kitchen table with a cup of tea warming her hands, seemingly oblivious to my arrival.

"Hey, Mom. You okay?"

She startles and glances at me before dropping her gaze to the cup in her hands. "Hey, son. I'll be fine. It's just one of those nights."

What's left of my broken heart crumbles into pieces at the sight of the desolate woman before me.

"Care if I join you?"

"That would be nice." She pats the space to her left.

I take the seat, scooting the chair closer so I can I put my arm around her. She rests her head on my wet shoulder, not commenting on the state of my appearance.

"I miss him." Her voice is solemn. I've never heard her like this.

"Me too."

God, how I miss my dad.

"Your father was far from perfect, but he loved me something fierce. In the end, that's all that matters. Life without him is just so much less than it used to be."

"I can't imagine how hard this has been on you. I'm so sorry."

Lifting her head from my shoulder, she snaps out of her melancholy, transforming into mom mode.

"Child, you are drenched! What happened to you?"

"Got caught in the rain."

"Stay there. I'll be back," she says, springing to action.

"I'm fine," I lie.

I'm far from fine, but she doesn't need my shit right now.

In a flash, she's back with towels in her hands. "Up you go."

I stand, as instructed.

She throws one over my head, giving it a little rub, but as I have little hair to dry, she leaves it draped around my neck before handing me the other towel. Instructing me to dry myself, she heads into the kitchen. Cupboards open and close. The mixing bowl, whisk, and flour she sets out means she's about to make her famous remedy for shit nights like tonight.

"How about some pancakes?"

"You don't have to do that, Mom."

"Nah, let's have some pancakes."

There's a light in her eyes that wasn't there when I arrived. Maybe she needs this as much as I do.

"Sounds perfect."

Mom's pancakes have always helped heal everyone else's broken hearts. Maybe tonight they're for her broken heart.

She mixes the ingredients and pours the first glob of batter in the pan when the all-knowing woman that she is takes me by surprise. "It's Mia, isn't it?"

"What?" I don't know what else to say, too shocked to make sense of the conversation.

"You love her, don't you?"

"Mom... I..."

"She loves you, too. I can see how things have changed between the two of you."

"How? How do you know everything?"

"It's a gift."

"It's frightening."

She smiles. "So, if I'm right, what are you going to do about it, son?"

"There are complications we need to deal with before we can take things any further. It's complicated."

"Ah, so you know who his father is, then?"

What the? How? Does she have my house bugged? How is she so spot on?

"I do," I say, cautiously.

She plates three perfectly round pancakes. I don't know how she does it, but there's never a wonky one. She places them in front of me, followed by butter and syrup.

"Eat up. I want to show you something."

Once again, I do as instructed, because I don't know what else to say or do.

She cleans up the kitchen while I eat and when she finishes, she goes to the built-in bookshelf in the family room and pulls out a photo album. Taking a seat on the couch, she pats the spot beside her and I take it.

She flips through the album and stops on a page that says Knox's 2nd birthday at the top. And there it is. It's like looking at Sawyer's twin. He is the spitting image of my oldest brother and I've never seen it.

"You've always known?"

"As he got older, I couldn't deny the truth. But for the life of me, I can't figure out how or when this could have happened. She's always been head over heels for you."

Even Mom knew? I've spent years thinking my attraction to her was unreciprocated. So many wasted years.

"It's not my story to tell."

She smiles and pats my cheek affectionately. "I know. I raised you right."

"There's no way we can be together. She has to tell him."

"And once she does, what does that mean for the two of you?"

I sigh, frustration bubbling up once again. "What can it mean? I'm her son's uncle. As if her being Daisy's best friend and Chris's sister wasn't enough. I'm not sure we can get past this."

"Do you love her?"

"So much," I confess for the second time tonight. "But is love enough?"

"It's always enough."

I snort. "I wish I was as optimistic as you."

"It will all work out."

"Sure hope you're right, Mom."

"If you love each other, it will work out just as it should."

Mia's confession plays in my head and my heart rate picks up. Hope is still buried under all the anger brewing inside me, but the sound of Mia confidently telling me she loves me and my mom's certainty it will all work out manage to reactivate that strange flip of my stomach, a reaction my body has only ever had for Mia.

Unable to keep it in, I tell my mom the best thing anyone has ever said to me. "She told me tonight she loves me. She's *in love* with me. Can you believe that?"

"Of course I can." She takes my hand in hers. "I'm happy for you. If I know your brother, he won't stand in your way. You are going to get through this. As long as you love each other through the hard times, you'll get through this."

"From your lips, Mom... from your lips."

Chapter Forty-One

Angus

The exertion it takes to lift the rack of weights above my chest this morning is excruciating. Not surprising since I haven't been to sleep yet. It's eight in the morning. I've got a pot of coffee in my system, yet I have nothing in me. Physically, emotionally, or mentally.

Drained. I am completely drained.

Thank God, it's Tuesday. I only have to make it another hour until my appointment with Dr. Laughlin. I think even the doc is going to be shocked and bewildered at how to deal with the Knox situation.

When I left Mom last night, things didn't seem so insurmountable, feeling better than when I had arrived. Her pancakes have a funny way of doing that. But, once I was out of the comfort of Mom's presence, the visions of Mia and my brother together plagued my thoughts. Erasing any hope I might have had.

Doubt crept back in.

Sleep never found me.

The pathetic sound of my voice telling Callen I was in love with Mia and Sawyer, haunting me.

The nausea hasn't stopped swirling in my stomach as all the reasons we will never work overtake any bit of rational thought in my head.

But through all the negative thoughts, there is one thing louder than the rest of them. She loves me. She is *in* love with me.

I wish I could say the beauty in her words wiped away the bleak narrative consuming me, but that would be a lie. Because the negative is a hell of a lot easier to believe than the positive.

I'm not sure Mom is right this time.

Love may not be enough.

Chapter Forty-Two

Mia

Feeling like a shell of a human, I stand next to the bar faking a smile. Speaking when spoken to. Nodding when appropriate. Pretending my entire world isn't on the verge of implosion.

It's been two weeks since I blew up my world. I've barely eaten. My nerves are so frazzled I can barely do my job. Every time my phone rings or the ping of a text comes through, I panic, thinking, this is it. But I haven't heard a thing from any of the McKinnons outside of the norm. I've seen Daisy multiple times, if she knew, she would have said something. This I know for sure.

I've avoided Sunday dinner the last two weeks, but other than that, things are eerily normal. Too normal.

I'm so on edge that a couple of days ago our receptionist, Jane, tried to hand me a large legal-sized envelope and I wouldn't take it from her. I honestly thought I was being served. That Knox had filed legal papers asking for custody.

She looked at me like I was crazy and left it on the desk at the nurses' station. Thankfully, she's been kind enough not to bring it up again. Who knows what she must think of me?

The day after I came clean to Angus, I texted to tell him we would find another place to live, but he told me to stay. He was back in the loft and didn't need the house. I've stayed, selfishly not wanting to leave his space, and frankly, I have nowhere else to go.

The thing is, it doesn't feel like it did when he was living there with us. A piece of us is missing. Sawyer has asked for his Gus Gus more times than I can count, and it hurts my soul every time he does. I should have known better than to bring Angus into our lives like I did. Sawyer's heart was at risk too and now he's paying the price.

Keeping Sawyer's father's identity was a decision I made the minute I found out I was pregnant. I was so certain it was the right thing to do that I didn't think about it often. Until Angus kissed me at the stroke of midnight.

He changed everything.

Subconsciously, I knew the day would come when the truth would reveal itself. How could it not? But I never could have imagined the shame would be so all-consuming. Or that seeing the pain on Angus's face would shatter me the way it has.

Yet, here I am. Faking it until I make it, because all I have is Sawyer and there isn't anything I wouldn't do for him. Even if that means spending my Friday night at a loud country bar, when I would rather be anywhere else. No, I didn't have to come out tonight, but after the wake-up call I got yesterday, I knew it would be best if I were here.

Dr. Gibbons pulled me into her office yesterday to ask if I was okay. She said she was worried about me and asked if things were okay at home. Lying, I told her everything was great and told myself to snap out of it. If I can put on a brave face at home for Sawyer, I can do it at work, too.

Everything I do is for Sawyer.

I selfishly indulged, letting Angus into my arms and my heart. As a result, I lost him and will no doubt lose much more.

I'm lost in my head when someone says my name. I register Hailey's voice, but I missed her question.

"I'm sorry. What was that?"

She raises her voice, thinking the music was the reason I didn't hear her. "I asked where your husband was. Is he not going to make it?"

I'm surprised it took as long as it did for someone to ask, and hate that another lie has to leave my mouth.

"Oh. I. Uh..."

"Speak of the devil." Jane smiles.

A gasp escapes me when a familiar hand slides across my palm, his fingers lacing with mine.

"Hey, babe. Sorry, I'm late." He places a kiss on my cheek.

I don't look at him, afraid I'll fall apart in front of everyone. Tears burn my eyes, my body shaking from the shock of his presence.

Angus is here.

What does it mean?

Does he forgive me?

Or is he simply being true to his word, being the kind man that he is, showing up to continue the farce we've concocted for my employer?

He must feel me shaking because he wraps an arm around my shoulders, pulling me into his side. His lips brush against my temple as he whispers, "You're okay. I got you."

His words are my undoing.

"Excuse me. I'll be right back." I beam the biggest smile I can muster and make a beeline for the bathrooms without looking at him. I'm too terrified to see his face, because with one look I'll know if he's here out of the kindness of his heart or if he's here because he wants more.

Luckily, it's early enough in the night that there isn't a line, and I walk right into the bathroom and into an empty stall, locking the door behind me. I tip my head to the ceiling, coaxing my tears back inside where they belong as I take deep breaths in through my nose and out of my mouth. Two weeks of waiting for the other shoe to drop has every nerve of my body frayed and misfiring, but I haven't cried.

"He's here. That has to mean something," I whisper to myself just before the sounds of the bar fill the small room when the door opens, drifting away when it closes.

"Mia, you okay?"

Shit.

"All good." I leave the cocoon of my stall much sooner than I would have liked to find Jane leaning a hip against the counter, a concerned look on her face.

"You sure?"

Just keep lying Mia. You excel at it, after all.

"I'm sure. Thanks for asking." I wash my hands for something to do as she watches me in the mirror. "Sawyer hasn't been sleeping well this week, and I feel like a zombie. We'll probably have to make it an early night. I'm not as young as I once was, and a Friday night out after a week of no sleep isn't as easy these days."

"I can't imagine. I'm not a parent, but I've watched my sister with my niece and nephew, and she's been right where you are. She stays home with them and when they were tiny, she'd be lucky to get a shower every few days."

"It's tough as a—" I catch myself. Almost slipping and mentioning how tough it can be as a single parent. I'm such a terrible liar. "Well, it can be tough for any parent, but I'm pretty lucky. He's usually a great sleeper. I'm sure this is just a phase."

"Well, no one will think any less of you if you take off. We all get it."

"Thanks. I appreciate that."

Jane stays to use the facilities, and I venture back to the bar where Angus is holding court. When he sees me, he excuses himself, meeting me halfway.

Reaching for me, he wraps his arms around me in a giant bear hug that takes my breath away, clutching me to him so tightly it's almost painful. He holds me as though he thought he never would again. Or maybe he's saying good-bye. Maybe the other shoe *is* about to drop, and he's sorry for the shitstorm about to come, because he finally told Knox.

I don't know what's going on in his head, because I still haven't summoned the courage to look him in the eyes. I'm clueless about what comes next, but it doesn't stop me from taking advantage of being in his arms, inhaling the scent of him in case it's the last time.

Sooner than I'd like, he releases me, grabbing my hand. "Dance with me. We need to talk."

He isn't asking, and he doesn't wait for my reply. With his hand in mine, he leads me to the busy dance floor. What small semblance of calm I had found in the bathroom takes flight, leaving me a shaking mess once again.

We fall into a slow two-step. I keep my eyes on the floor, not ready to know what I'll find in the relentless stare I feel.

We take two silent trips around the floor before he finally speaks. "Mia, look at me."

My insides run cold from the authoritative tone of his voice, but I can't.

"Goof, please look at me."

The earnestness in his voice gives me the strength to face him. When I do, his expression is serious, focused on nothing but me.

"I can't do this anymore."

My beleaguered heart sinks and the tears I fought earlier beg to fall, but I can do anything for Sawyer and that includes not crying in front of my coworkers. I blink them back and drop my gaze once again.

Sliding his fingers through mine, he moves us off the dance floor to an empty corner of the bar. He drops my hand and reaches out to touch my face, but I take a step away. The touch that once brought me comfort and pleasure, is too much now. Each touch brands me, leaving me scarred. People move around us, but I don't see their faces. The music is nothing more than white noise. Our surroundings blur as I wait for him to tell me all the reasons he's done with me.

Closing the distance between us, he takes my hand in his once again, and I brace myself. "Mia, there's nothing fake about the way I feel about you and Sawyer. I want... no... I need this to be real."

"What?" I whisper, not sure I heard him correctly.

"The last two weeks have been fucking awful. I'm sorry for going quiet for so long, but I needed the time to sort through the mess in my head. I talked to Dr. Laughlin. I talked to Mom. And I missed you."

My body stills, fear consuming me.

"You told your mom?"

"Don't worry. I didn't tell her about Knox. It's not my story to tell. But she knows how I feel about you."

My body sags in relief but doubt still has a firm grip on my heart.

"And... You... You still want to be with me? Even though..."

I'm as confused as I'm sure I sound, because how could he still want me?

He lifts my chin with his forefinger and kisses me as though I'm precious to him.

"Of course I do," he says against my lips. Then, pulling back, his caramel eyes meet mine and he picks up the pieces of my heart, patching it back together with his words. "Loving you is like living on the sun. Trying to exist without you is like existing in the dark. And God, do I need to be blinded by your light. I need you like I need my next breath. My next heartbeat."

The tears I've been fighting for two weeks finally get their way as they stream down my face, dripping off my jaw. Someone must have spiked my beer, because none of this makes sense.

"Happy tears?"

I nod. My body shaking from the sobs overtaking my body.

Wrapping me in his arms, he turns me so I'm facing the corner, giving me privacy. "Deep breaths, baby. I got you."

Angus McKinnon loves me. This can't be my life.

His words, the warmth of his embrace, his manly citrus scent, everything about him settles me. My surroundings become clear again. The song playing is recognizable, but who knows what it is. My sobs subside.

"Is this real?" I ask, needing confirmation I heard him correctly.

His mouth lifts on one side, igniting the fire low in my belly that always roars to life when he aims his smile in my direction. Even though I'm drowning in a melting pot of emotions, he strokes the passion inside me.

"As a heart attack. I want to make this work between us. If you'll have me?"

All I can do is smile up at him.

"The thing is, we can't be an *us* until Knox knows."

And there it is. The other shoe has dropped. I knew this was coming, but still ice infiltrates my veins at the mere thought, diminishing the abundant joy from a moment ago. My tears dry instantly.

"Goof, we have to tell him. I'll be by your side every step of the way, but we can't do this if the truth isn't out there."

"I know."

He's right. I know he's right, but it's still my worst nightmare coming true.

"Babe, I need you to know it won't be easy for me either. I want nothing more than for Sawyer to be mine and I hope you know that Uncle or Dad, I couldn't love that kid more."

He loves me, and he loves my son. This should be the happiest moment of my life. Instead, every fear I've buried since I found out I was pregnant has come to fruition.

"What if he rejects him?"

"I know my brother, and beneath that egotistical persona he's a good man."

"You heard him that night. I refuse to be treated like some groupie who he thinks is after his fame and fortune."

"If he says anything disrespectful to you, I'll kick his rock star ass."

"He's your brother. I would never ask you to pick sides."

"Let me make one thing clear." His lips gently caress mine for the briefest moment before resting his forehead against mine. "Your heart is the only one that matters."

There have never been a more beautiful eight words spoken.

"Angus." Choked by emotion, it's all I can get out.

"This. Us." He moves his finger back and forth between us. "It feels right, doesn't it?"

I nod.

"I love you, Mia. And you love me. At least you did two weeks ago." His dark eyes beg for reassurance.

"I've loved you my entire life. I always will."

"Then it's settled."

"You're sure? Being with me means an instant family. Two for the price of one."

"I'd say I'm a pretty lucky guy then."

Before I can reply, I'm back in his arms, his lips against mine.

We stay tucked away in the corner a few more seconds

before the real-world smacks us upside the head with the sound of a familiar voice clearing her throat.

Why can't everyone just leave us alone?

Angus slips his fingers through mine, and we turn to face the last person I want to see right now.

"Hey, baby sister."

"Don't baby sister me. Outside now. Both of you."

She's just as pissed as I thought she would be.

Neither of us argue. There's really no point when Daisy is this upset. We follow her outside and once on the sidewalk, away from prying eyes, she lets loose. "How could you?" She directs the question at Angus, pointing her finger into his chest.

He doesn't react. He's as cool as a cucumber.

My cucumber.

This thought and the feel of his hand in mine send a giddy shiver through my body. I should be worried about my best friend's wrath, instead I'm preoccupied with the fact that Angus loves me. Is in love with me.

My giddiness is short-lived, because Daisy is just getting started.

"My best friend, Angus?" she shouts. "She's a mom! Not some random hook-up! What the hell?"

"Two things," he says calmly. "First, I know she's a mom and I love them both. Second, you don't have to tell me the difference between Mia and other women. There is no comparison."

She opens her mouth to continue, but her words die on her lips. Her eyes move from him to me, down to our joined hands, then back up to look her brother in the eyes. "You love her?" It comes out in a shocked whisper.

"Yes."

His answer is simple. It's everything.

Her attention moves to me. "And you love him?"

"I do," I answer honestly.

He squeezes my hand, and we wait for her to put the puzzle pieces together. When her brows furrow, I know what she's thinking.

"Is... Are you?"

"No," I interrupt. "He's not Sawyer's father."

"I don't understand." She's confused. I get it. I've kept this from her our whole lives. "I mean, I assumed you two hooked-up when you didn't come home after the party, but love.... How could I have missed that?"

"It's always been her. I just never had the balls to tell her."

She stares at her brother, dumbfounded.

A feeling of lightheadedness hits me at the sound of his words. There's no hesitation. No fear. To hear him speak of his feelings for me so freely eases my mind of all the concerns and worries I know I should feel right now.

"And you? Since when?"

It's time to tell my truth. If Angus can do it, so can I. "Always."

"What do you mean, *always*?"

"Well, I can't remember a time I didn't feel this way about him. If you need me to pinpoint it, I'd say fourth grade. Back then, it was a crush. Now it's the real deal."

"And by real deal, you're saying you are *in love* with my brother?"

"I am."

He lifts our joined hands and presses a kiss to the back of my hand. Daisy looks horrified at the display of affection.

"Why didn't you ever tell me?"

"He's your brother. I knew you wouldn't approve. And I never thought he would feel the same way, so why tell anyone? I was embarrassed. I kept it to myself."

"You could have told me."

Releasing his hand, I step toward Daisy. "I'm sorry, Dais."

She lifts her hand to stop me from getting closer. "No."

"Daisy," I plead.

"I can't. Not now."

She walks past us, leaving without another word.

"Well, that went well," Angus jokes.

"That was bad, wasn't it?"

"She'll be fine." He tugs on my hand, opening the door to the bar. "C'mon, I wanna dance with my wife."

Chapter Forty-Three

Mia

After we left the bar last night, Angus followed me to pick Sawyer up from the sitter and then all the way home. He walked us to the front door, sweetly kissed Sawyer on the head, and not quite as sweetly placed a kiss on my lips.

It wasn't long. It wasn't heated. It was perfect.

Did I ask him if he wanted to come inside? Of course I did. Unfortunately, he declined my offer. He'll be staying at the loft until we talk to Knox. But we both decided we would brave Sunday dinner. It's an excuse to see each other and to gauge how Daisy is taking our news. If she isn't over the two of us being together, she won't be ready to hear about Knox.

Baby steps.

She's been quiet all night, not sharing our secret with the rest of the family. But Daisy, being Daisy, doesn't hesitate to let her feelings be known. She may be quiet, but she's certainly not avoiding us. Her stare downs are unrelenting. When she isn't focused on me, she directs her attention toward her brother.

My best friend says what she thinks. She doesn't hold back. Not knowing what's going on in that head of hers is frightening.

Quietly, I wrap my sweater around me and, sneak outside to find the boys. Angus and Sawyer put on their coats and disappeared after sharing a piece of apple pie. I wander off the deck and head toward the pasture. Before long, I spot them in the distance hanging out with Bernadette.

Taking my time, I watch the two of them together. Sawyer is in Angus's arms as they pet the cow's head and carry on what appears to be a riveting conversation. When I'm about ten feet away, Sawyer spots me.

"Mama, look. Bernie."

"I see her, buddy." I walk to the opposite side of the beloved cow and smile at them over her wide body. "You two having fun over here?"

"Moooooo!" Sawyer replies. Angus and I both laugh.

A horse whinnies from the barn and Bernadette's tail swooshes as we sit in this moment. Angus is beaming at me. After everything we've shared, this new smile he shows only to me is new and beautiful, and it makes my cheeks heat.

He is beautiful.

"I love you so fucking much," he mouths. Then quietly adds, "I can't wait until this is over and we can end all the charades."

Angus continuing to so freely share his feelings for me is still new and sends me spinning with giddy, schoolgirl glee. If only there weren't so many other emotions attached to his declarations.

"Me too, but I'd be lying if I said I'm not scared."

"What worries you the most?"

"I can take whatever your brother, our families, the people in town dish out, but I will not accept any crap directed at my little boy. And what if Knox tries to take him or asks for split custody at some point? I don't know what I'd do if either of those things happened."

"Shit, I didn't even think of that."

"It's all I think about. That and what if the world finds out? What if he wants to make it legal and there is a public document out there? Sawyer didn't ask to be in the public eye, to have to deal with paparazzi. I don't want him bogged down with all the b.s. that comes with being Knox McKinnon's son."

He rests his head against Sawyers and takes his little hand in his. "Didn't think of that either."

"These thoughts have plagued me since the day I found out I was pregnant."

"Goof, I'm so sorry."

"It's okay. He has the right to know. It was wrong of me not to tell him before."

"You were protecting yourself and your son. I get it."

"The whole town is going to know," I sigh on a heavy breath.

"So?"

"Well, let's see, I'll be the slut," I mouth the last word so Sawyer doesn't pick up on it, "who got knocked up by one McKinnon brother and then fell in love with another."

"Anyone who has anything to say about it will have to

answer to me," he says sternly, but quietly so he doesn't startle Sawyer.

I force a smile but look away. He means well, but he has no clue. "That's sweet, but as the woman in this situation, everyone will look at me differently. It's just the way it is. I will forever carry this scandal. Knox will come out unscathed, and as long as I live in this town, I will be the woman with a scarlet letter on her chest."

The concern in his eyes says it all. The worries that are always in the back of my mind, never even crossed his.

"I'm sorry. I know everything in your world is about to change, but I'll be by your side every step of the way, if you'll still have me?"

"Do you think I would go through all of this if it weren't for a real chance with you?"

"Fancy seeing the three of you out here," Daisy says, joining us. I've been so focused on Angus, I have no idea how long she's been within earshot, and what she has overheard.

Angus doesn't seem worried though. He gives her a nod and keeps his attention on me when he acknowledges her. "Hey, sis."

"Hey, bro. Hey, bestie. What are you two whispering about over here?"

Shit. Shit. Shit.

Sawyer bounces with excitement in Angus's arms. "Daisy! Look! Bernie!"

As if she knows a battle royale is about to go down, Bernadette backs up, like she refused to do when she placed herself in the doorway of Gus's house the night I told him about Knox. I wish I could do the same when Daisy takes her place, standing between us.

"Say, bye," Angus says, waving to the bovine.

"Bye, Bernie!" Sawyer waves. He starts to put his hand in his mouth, but Angus stops him. "We have to wash our hands after petting the animals. No hands in the mouth."

Daisy watches her brother's interaction with Sawyer in complete surprise. "When did this happen? When did you become domesticated?"

He looks offended. "What? Didn't think it was possible?"

"I'm not sure what I think about anything anymore." The hurt in her tone floods me with guilt.

"Dais, I'm sorry we didn't tell you sooner."

"I'm not. It's our business," Angus cuts in. "We're allowed to keep it to ourselves until we're ready to share."

He's right, but this is Daisy. We need to tread lightly.

"I have one question." She pauses, staring across the pasture, not looking at either of us until she speaks again. Her eyes on her brother. "Is this it? Are you in this for the long haul? Are you ready to be a daddy?"

"That's three questions."

Ugh. Why is he messing with her right now? And why am I breaking out into a sweat in anticipation of his answer?

"They should all have the same answer if everything you said last night is true." She crosses her arms over her chest, waiting.

"Yes. Mia is it for me. There will never be anyone else. I'm in this for as long as she'll have me, and if given the honor, I will take care of this kid like he's my own. Till my dying day."

Daisy looks at me, her eyes glossy. She doesn't have to say anything. I know what she's asking and I nod in reply.

Yes, I feel the same. If we can get through the storm ahead, there will be no one else. Ever.

In an unexpected move, she throws her arms around me. My body sags with relief as her embrace holds me up. "Your place tonight. You put that kid to bed and then you are going to tell me everything."

"Everything?"

"Okay, maybe not *everything*, because ew." She gags. We giggle and hold each other. "I'm happy for you. He's a pretty great guy."

"He is," I say, smiling at him as he watches our friendship mend.

Releasing me, she turns to her brother. "Your only job in life is to make them happy."

He reaches out to her with his free arm and squeezes her to his side. "That's the plan."

"When are you going to tell everyone else?" Her question is more like a demand.

"Soon," Angus and I say in unison.

* * *

"What do you mean, you knew?"

"Sweetheart, Sharon and I have known since he was a baby who Sawyer's daddy was. Have you not seen Knox's baby photos? It's quite clear."

On my way to work this morning I called Mom. I'd been avoiding her since the incident with Rhen, but I'm spinning and I need her. As happy as I am that Angus and Daisy have my back, there is a firestorm ahead and not having Mom's shoulder to cry on has been hard.

This morning, I practiced what I would say to her when I called, agonizing over exactly how to break the news. I told her about my lifetime of loving Angus, to getting knocked up by his brother and now embarking on a life with Angus. And here she is, showing no signs of surprise whatsoever.

About any of it.

What in the world?

"If you knew about Knox, why didn't you ever say anything?"

"I asked you who the father was until I was blue in the face. You refused to tell me, so I let it go. Then one Sunday dinner at the McKinnon's, when Sawyer was about six months old, I was standing by the fireplace, showing him the pictures on the mantel when I saw it. There was a picture of Knox around the same age and for a moment, I thought I was looking at a picture of my grandson. Shocked, I swung around to find you and found Sharon had been watching me with tears in her eyes. We both knew right then and there."

I blow out a breath. All this time, they both knew.

"But you were so insistent on keeping it to yourself and we wanted to respect your wishes. We put our heads together a hundred times, trying to figure out how in the world it could have happened. Now it all makes sense."

"And you don't think less of me for behaving so foolishly?"

"Of course not! There isn't a single person who hasn't acted impulsively and done something regrettable. But like you've said many times, there is no way anyone can regret the outcome of what might have been your biggest mistake. Because look at that beautiful little boy you get to be a mama to."

The shame over how I've felt about her the last few weeks washes over me. I've been casting stones without even knowing if the rumors are true. And she has, unbeknownst to me, known my truth for two years and hasn't judged me for a second. She loves me unconditionally.

"Thanks, Mom. That means more than you could know."

Despondent, she replies. "I have no business throwing stones. None of us do."

My heart plummets as I read between the meaning of her words, but she doesn't elaborate and because I'm not sure I have the bandwidth for more, I don't question her.

Pulling into an open parking spot, I shift the car into park and take a peek at Sawyer in the back seat, where he happily plays with a dinosaur. "And Angus. What do you think? Is it too strange to be with the brother of the father of my child?"

"Well, nobody is going to call it typical, but you've been in love with that man your whole life. Who cares?"

"What about Sawyer? Is it all too confusing to grow up with that kind of controversy surrounding his existence? If the world finds out he's Knox McKinnon's son and his mom is in a relationship with his brother, what could that do to him? It's like I'm knowingly setting him up for scrutiny and ridicule. Is it worth it?"

"Does Angus love Sawyer?"

"Yes."

"Well, with your love, Angus's love, both of your families' love, we will make sure that boy knows his worth. What I hear is you questioning whether your happiness is as important as your child's. The answer is yes, Mia. Always put on your oxygen mask first so you can help those you love when they're in need. In this case, I think Angus may be the oxygen in your mask."

"I miss you so much, Mom."

"We miss you too, sweetheart."

"Are you and Dad okay? Are you happy there?"

"It's a big change, but as long as we're together, your father and I will be just fine."

What she's saying is things aren't perfect, but they love each other enough to push through the hard times.

"You know, I'm always here for you, too, right? If you ever need to talk. About anything."

"Oh, my sweet girl. Of course, I do. But you don't need to worry about little old me. We are living our best life down here in the sunshine."

"But I do worry."

"I know you do, but we're fine, Mia. We're fine."

"It's okay if you aren't."

"I know."

I gasp when I see the time on my dash. "Shoot, I have two minutes to get him checked into day care and get logged in for work. I have to go."

"Go, honey. We'll talk soon."

"Love you."

"Love you, too. Kiss that boy for me."

Turning off the car and my phone, I grab Sawyer and rush into the clinic.

Half my heart is relieved after hearing Mom's comforting words, the other half reeling from the insinuation of the other part of our conversation. There has definitely been trouble in paradise, and I have a sinking suspicion my father's heart may have broken along the way.

Chapter Forty-Four

Mia

"Four minutes. Fuck." Angus rubs his hands over the scruff on his face.

We've been dreading today. We're both nervous. Scared. Ready, yet never less ready for anything. You name the emotion and we've likely felt it over the last two days.

"I think I'm going to be sick," I say, wrapping my arms around my middle.

This is it. The day I've been hoping would never come, even though I knew it would eventually.

"I've got you, Goof." He takes my face in his hands, placing a kiss on my forehead. "I got you. C'mon, it's time."

Sitting on the couch, he opens the laptop and dials. There's no turning back now. My heart is in my throat, my stomach is in knots, and the moment Knox's face comes on the screen, I want to slam the laptop shut.

"Bro, it's good to see your face, and who do we have here?"

I hold my hand up and wiggle my fingers in reply, a weak smile on my face.

"I fucking knew it! I saw you sneak in from somewhere at the wedding, looking a little disheveled. Good for you. You two are perfect together."

Knox's smile is wide. He means it. He really is happy for us.

"Thanks, man, but we aren't calling to announce our relationship."

"What's up then? Mom, okay?" he asks, concerned.

"Mom's fine. Uh, actually Mia needs to talk to you about something and I'm here because as much as we want to be together, this conversation needs to happen first."

His brows knit, and I can't tell if he's putting two and two together.

"What the hell do I have to do with your relationship?"

Nope.

I take a deep breath and just say it. "Knox. Sawyer is your son."

"Excuse me?"

"That night after the Grammy's at Nicolette Gwen's...."

"Shut the fuck up."

"Watch it, brother."

"Why are you just telling me now? Isn't the kid like two or three already?"

My cheeks heat, but I use my anger to his reaction to steel myself and sit up straighter. Standing my ground. "Well, that same night you made it pretty clear you never wanted to be a dad and any woman who claimed to be pregnant with your child was only after your money."

"I didn't say that."

"She's being kind. You said all that and a lot more. Made a total ass of yourself. The entire family was there."

"You said it shortly after we... well, you know."

Gus's knee bounces in irritation.

"Okay, so don't you think I should have known from the start, regardless?"

"Yes, I see that now and I'm sorry, but I didn't want you to accuse me of being after your money. After everything you said, when I realized I was pregnant two months later, all I wanted to do was protect my child."

"So, that's what this is? A way for you to clear your conscience so you can be with my brother?"

"I've always loved your brother from afar and if it weren't for Sawyer, I would regret our drunken two minutes, but how can I when it gave me my beautiful boy?"

"So, what do you want from me?"

"Nothing. You have a right to know and now you do. I want nothing from you."

"You don't want child support?"

I shake my head.

"No money of any kind?"

"No, Knox. I have a good job, with insurance and day care paid for. I won't keep him from you if you want to see him, but I will *always* be his primary guardian. I will fight you with everything I have if you ever try to take him away from me."

"Honey, you don't have to worry about that. Besides, it looks like he's already got a father figure."

Angus's jaw tics. "Don't be like that. We stopped everything between us once she told me."

"Well, you have my blessing. Now, is that all? I have to get to soundcheck."

"Knox, come on. Let's talk about this."

"Listen, I really have to go, but I have one question."

"What's that?" I ask, and even I can hear the nervous shake in my voice.

"Does the rest of the family, or all of Goose Hollow, for that matter, already know?"

"Nobody knows, but Mom has a feeling. She says he looks just like you."

"Well, I assume the family will know soon. Please send me a text when that happens, so I'm prepared for the onslaught of calls and texts that will follow."

"Of course. Not a problem."

"Do you have questions about him or anything?" I ask.

"Nope. All good. Gotta go. Talk to you later."

The screen goes blank, and Angus and I sit in silence for a beat before he pulls me into his arms. I'm numb from the inside out. Maybe I'm in shock. He lays us down on the couch and he holds me until Sawyer wakes up from his nap with crazy bedhead and no clue that the wheels are now in motion.

Sawyer's life has changed forever.

Chapter Forty-Five

Angus

Mia and I have kept the Knox news to ourselves for the past few days, figuring family dinner would be the best time to tell everyone. Today is the day Mia's secret is no longer hers. After today, everything will change for her.

Sure, my life is about to change, but only for the better. I'm getting Mia and Sawyer out of all of this. Mia will get a label. A reputation.

Will the family judge her? Treat her differently? Accept us together? Will they judge me for being with her instead of Knox?

Those are the questions I ask myself as I watch each of my siblings, waiting for their reactions. We've just shared that not only is Knox Sawyer's father, but that we're in love and moving in together. Mia explained her reasons for keeping the information to herself, reminding them of the conversation that took place that night. I've shared the timeline of our relationship.

Now, the house is silent as the news sets in. It's a lot.

Even Owen, who always has something to say, seems dumbstruck. We didn't plan on him being here tonight, but he's family and his presence changed nothing.

"Who wants pie?" Mom asks, breaking the silence, then dashing into the kitchen before anyone answers.

"Whoa," Cal says as soon as she's out of earshot.

But it's Daisy who sounds more than shocked. Narrowing her eyes at Mia, she says, "I can't believe you didn't tell me."

"I'm sorry. I shouldn't have kept this from everyone."

"No, you shouldn't have kept it from *me!* Or Knox! How could you?" She throws her napkin on her plate.

"Daisy, come on. We were all there that night. I heard what he said. It makes sense." Cal turns his attention from my sister to the love of my life. "I just hate that you've had to go through this on your own. You've always been like family, but now, well, shit. There's no getting rid of us."

He takes Sawyer from Charlotte's arms. Cal's taking this in stride. He already knew I was in love with her. I guess Mom did too. Heck, Mom knew Knox was Sawyer's father. So, there was less to share than we might have thought, but my brother will never know how much his acceptance means to me.

"I always knew you were special," he says, rubbing noses with his nephew.

Daisy isn't ready to let it go. "I still can't believe you didn't tell me. How did I not see it?"

Mia scoffs. "Who would have ever thought I would be

with Knox? Pretty sure this was the one and only time I was ever alone with him."

My dinner nearly comes up at the repulsive thought of the two of them together.

"I should have told you, but for more reasons than you'll ever know, I couldn't."

Mom is back with pie. Clearly, she didn't miss a word while she was in the kitchen. "What reasons, other than my oldest son and his blathering on like a fool, about not wanting a family?"

Mia clears her throat and I take her shaking hand under the table, so she knows she's not alone.

"I was afraid he and the world would think I was just some groupie who got knocked up for his fame and money. I don't want to be famous, and I certainly don't want Sawyer to grow up in the public eye. I don't want his privacy compromised. You rarely hear good things about the children of famous people? Forget about the rest of the world. I didn't want to have to walk around Goose Hollow with a scarlet letter on my chest. I don't want anyone to look at Sawyer as anything other than the loved child he is. He deserves better than just being seen as Knox McKinnon's son."

She takes a big breath, and then, speaking to everyone, looks at me. "The day I found out, the thought of Angus knowing broke my heart."

"What?" My question quiet. Just for her.

"I was so ashamed. I didn't want you to know. I'm so sorry."

Tears fill her eyes and my soul fractures. I've dried too many tears from her cheeks and seeing them on the verge of falling kills me.

"You never have to feel ashamed, Mia," Mom says, taking her other hand. "Never. I wish you had told us, I do. But luckily, you didn't keep him from us, and we've been a part of his life since the day he was born. But it would sure mean a lot for him to know me as grandma."

Mia covers her face with her hands as her sobs break free. Mom stands and approaches Mia, bringing her to her feet so she can take her in her arms. Mia cries in Mom's arms and the rest of us watch on with tears in our eyes.

"What did Knox say when you told him?" Callen asks.

I step in and answer for her. "Um... he was shocked. He didn't show any interest in Sawyer, and he gave us his blessing."

Whispered curses float around the table.

"But a couple days later, he emailed Mia and said he was sorry for his reaction and offered to be in Sawyer's life as much as she wants him to be. He offered money and said if she refuses, he'll open a trust for him. The only thing he asked was to be the one to teach Sawyer to ride a horse."

As I take in the shocked faces of my family, I wonder if I've overestimated how cool they would be about the two of us being together. Daisy's mouth is still hanging open. Owen is staring at Daisy as if she's a bomb he's afraid is about to detonate. Charlotte is all smiles while Callen furrows his brow. Mom is still holding Mia with tears in her eyes. She loves us all unconditionally and is going to support me no matter what. That's enough for now.

We're gonna be okay.

"So, like we said. I'm moving back into the house, and Mia and I are gonna make a real go of this. Not that it matters, but do any of you have anything to say about that?"

"Of course, not. We're happy for the both of you," my mom says.

"What she said," Owen declares. "Let me know if you need any help with the move."

"Thanks, Owen. I appreciate it."

But I don't need any help. She's living in my house, and I've already got my things packed and in the back of my truck, ready to go home with them tonight after dinner.

"Daisy, are we okay?" I ask my sister.

"I really don't know. It feels like I'm in an alternate universe. I need some time. It's one thing to keep your crush on Angus from me, but to keep the fact that Sawyer is my nephew from me, from my entire family, I'm sorry, but I can't just forgive you with open arms this time."

After aiming all her vitriol at Mia my little sister gets up and leaves the room. When the front door slams shut, Mia gasps, another small sob escaping. My heart twists for her.

Owen rushes after Daisy and Mom wraps Mia up again. "She'll come around, honey. She'll come around."

Chapter Forty-Six

Mia

Sharon was wrong.

Daisy hasn't come around.

She hasn't replied to any of my calls or texts because she's blocked me. I've gone to her house, but she won't answer the door. Her car was in the driveway both times, so I know she was home. She just didn't want to see me.

She'll speak to Angus, but she won't speak to him about me. He's tried, but Daisy can be stubborn when she wants to be. And when she's angry, there is no getting through to her without a fight. Even then, she rarely caves.

It's been weeks with no contact. Daisy and I usually talk every day. Not being able to share what's going on in my life with her sucks. I'm done being ignored.

I'm taking control of the situation.

If there is one thing Daisy is, it's professional. So, today, I will confront her at work. Is it a low-down, dirty way of forcing her to talk to me? Sure is. Do I care? Nope. Desperate times call for desperate measures.

Thanks to Charlotte's meddling, I know she and Daisy will be at Goose Hollow Park this afternoon. The town has commissioned them to revamp the playground and picnic area of the park and they're meeting with citizens to talk about the new plans and get their input.

"You two gonna be okay over here?" I ask Angus, as I run my fingers through Sawyer's hair.

It's a beautiful late spring day and we've stopped at The Shack to get the boys a sweet treat before I leave them to infiltrate Daisy's day.

"We've got our ice cream and once we're done, we'll go for a little stroll. We'll be more than okay."

"Thank you," I say to the man I get to call mine. No more hiding. No more secrets.

The last two weeks of falling asleep in his arms has been a dream come true. A dream marred by the loss of Daisy in my day-to-day life.

"Go get her."

For the last thirty minutes, I've been sitting on the small amphitheater steps with close to fifty of my neighbors, beaming with pride. Daisy and Charlotte are kicking ass. This project is completely pro-bono, but I don't think they've ever worked on anything that means more to them.

They gave a quick presentation outlining their plans and, for the most part, have been fielding questions from those in attendance. Daisy hasn't acknowledged my existence, but Charlie gave me a wink when I first sat down. She seems confident this will work. I sure hope she's right, because I'm far from certain.

"Thank you all so much for coming today. We promise to take all your concerns into consideration. Your input and your children's happiness and safety are what's most important to us," Daisy says to the crowd, wrapping things up.

I've been too chicken to raise my hand to speak, but Charlie remedies that, not letting me squander the reason I'm here. "One sec, Daisy. It looks like we have one more question. You in the blue shirt. Did you have something you wanted to say?"

It's now or never.

Standing, I breathe deeply and even though she refuses to look at me, I address my best friend. "Um, yes. I just wanted to say, I think what you're doing here is wonderful. I especially love how you're putting the safety and well-being of the children of Goose Hollow first. Because, as any parent will tell you, those things are all that matter."

Her emotions get the best of her, and she finally looks in my direction. But the moment is fleeting, and she quickly looks away.

"Becoming a parent is one of the scariest things a person can do. When you bring a life into the world, it's up to you to keep them safe. And that can take on many forms. Physically, of course, but we also have to shelter them from those who might do them mental harm. That might make them feel unwanted or who may bring chaos and scrutiny into their lives."

A few people have turned around to watch me, confusion in their eyes. Everyone knows Daisy and I are as close as sisters, and this conversation is strange indeed.

"A child's emotional and mental health is equally important, as is their confidence and happiness. The world is tough enough to navigate these days with the internet and those who hide behind keyboards spewing hate. It's hard for adults to manage, and as parents, it's our job to make sure we do everything we can to protect our children from that kind of hate, no matter the lengths we have to go to. No matter the sacrifice. I know I would do anything for my little boy. Even if my actions seem extreme to some, in the end all that matters, all that has ever mattered is his well-being. There is nothing I wouldn't do to keep him safe."

Daisy's eyes meet mine, but her walls are still up, and I can't tell what she's thinking.

"Anyway, I just wanted to say thank you to both of you for keeping the children of Goose Hollow safe and for sacrificing your time and energy to make the park a better place for the people in our community."

There's a smattering of perplexed applause. Folks are likely wondering what my tangent was all about but feel obliged to clap at the sentiment.

"Thank you, Mia. Daisy and I are happy to work on this project, and as you said, the children of Goose Hollow are our number one priority." Daisy doesn't add to her comments and Charlie closes the meeting.

People mill about and speak to Daisy and Charlie one on one, but staying right where I am, I wait until the last person walks away before I approach the girls. Just as I open my mouth to speak, Daisy picks up her things and walks away.

"She'll come around. I know she will," Charlie says, sounding certain.

That's what everyone keeps saying, but I'm not so sure.

Chapter Forty-Seven

Mia

"Buddy, let go of your truck so we can get you in this thing. Help your mama out."

Sawyer hands me his truck and puts his arm through the strap of his car seat. I snap him in and return his truck. "Thank you."

My phone pings just as my butt hits the driver's seat. My chest tightens, hoping it's Daisy. As happy as I always am when his name appears on my phone, I sag in my seat when Angus's name pops up and not his sister's. It's been two days since I pleaded my case during the park meeting.

ANGUS

Meet me at Knox's place. I'll grill and we'll take the boat out after dinner. Sound good?

. . .

Oh, this man and his heart. He has been doing his very best to keep me distracted while I wait for Daisy to *come around*, as everyone likes to tell me she will. I would rather lock myself up at home and pout and worry, but Angus isn't having any of that. He's making sure I don't have time to dwell in my misery.

MIA

Sure, I'll run home and change.

ANGUS

No need. I grabbed your favorite sweats, your sexy slides, and a change of clothes for Tater. Just get that booty of yours over here.

Tater appears to be sticking. I'm not sure when it happened, but this is his new nickname for Sawyer. He and his Gus Gus are two peas in a pod.

Angus has immersed himself in our daily lives. He's changed his hours at the bar, leaving the weekday evenings to his staff. If the bar is slow on Fridays and Saturdays, he comes home as early as possible. He helps get Sawyer ready in the morning and helps with our nighttime routine. He's had genius ideas for potty training, and they could play for hours if I let them. But he also respects my rules and doesn't cave and break them, even when I know he wants to.

Then, after Sawyer's in bed, he's all mine. We talk and we laugh, and we make love.

To think myself and pretty much everyone in Goose Hollow doubted Angus McKinnon ever wanted a life like the one he's currently living is almost funny now. He was born to be a loving partner and father-figure. To those of us in his life, it shouldn't have come as a surprise. Now and then, I wonder if he'll tire of the monotony that comes with taking on a ready-made family. But in my heart, I know him, and I know he's in this for the long haul. He's thoughtful and kind, but Angus doesn't do anything Angus doesn't want to do.

MIA

Thank you. We'll head that way right now.

ANGUS

Love you, Goof.

My heart skips a beat, like it does every time he tells me he loves me. I'm like a walking smiley face with heart eyes emoji, thanks to the love of this man.

MIA

Love you.

I double check my phone for any missed calls or texts from Daisy before starting the engine, but there's nothing.

She'll come around.

She'll come around.

Everyone is sure of it.

But what if she doesn't?

Putting the car in drive, I point us toward the lake. The lake I haven't been to since my parents sold our family home and moved away. It should feel odd to be going to Knox's place, but friends and family make more use of his lake house than he does.

I think he had it built, so when he came home to visit, he had a place to hide. So he wouldn't have to stay with anyone. He's always been a loner. He loves his family, but he's always needed his space. Always wanted more than what Goose Hollow could give him. It's a shame, because his family misses him.

The McKinnon siblings are close, but Knox keeps himself just on the periphery of their tight-knit circle. Although, I have no idea what the four of them get up to on their annual birthday week trips. Being that they were all born in August, every year the four of them go on vacation together. They escape somewhere the paparazzi can't find them and spend a week together. It's just them, no other family members. No friends.

The only exception they ever made was last year, when all the chaos happened with Charlie's stalker on day one of their trip. There was no way Callen could leave her behind. And since the two of them share a birthday, she finished the rest of the trip with the siblings.

What happens this summer? Will Knox still take part? I

knew when I revealed the truth, it could damage relationships. I expected Daisy's reaction. After keeping it to myself this long, it was one of the many repercussions I feared. But I had no intention of coming between brothers. Things have been strained since Knox found out about Sawyer. He replies to Angus when he reaches out to ask how he's doing, but he insists that he's fine and too busy to talk. Gus worries about him, but I don't know what to think. He's shown no interest in getting to know his son, other than to teach him to ride a horse. He's asked no questions about him or his life for the last two and a half years.

Knox has only reached out twice. Once, shortly after our video call, to tell me he wouldn't seek custody, but he would start a trust for Sawyer if I refuse to accept child support. When he said he wanted to teach Sawyer to ride, hope for some kind of relationship between the two took root. It's not a lot, but it's something. But the only other time I've heard from him was a text to get my email address and Sawyer's social security number so he could get documents drawn up for the trust and so *his people* had my contact info.

When my tires hit the dirt road leading to Knox's house, my mind snaps to attention. The road isn't too rough, but it's still best to have my wits about me in case a rock jumps out of nowhere and attacks the vehicle.

A few minutes later, I'm pulling a sleeping Sawyer out of his car seat. This happens every time we hit the road to the lake house. Where my body moans and groans from the movement, it soothes him to sleep. But as soon as he hears Angus yell, "I'm in the kitchen!" he wakes right up.

"Gus Gus," Sawyer says under his breath as he squirms to get out of my arms.

"Incoming!" I yell, releasing my boy who takes off running to see his bestie.

"Tater! How was your day?" I hear as I round the corner to the kitchen to find Sawyer already in his arms. When he sees me, Gus's face lights up. "Hey, baby."

"Hey, baby," I reply, placing a kiss on his lips. Sweetly, Sawyer leans in and places a kiss on my cheek and I giggle. "Thank you, buddy."

"Go change. I've got him."

"You sure? I can wait until you're done."

"All the prep work is finished. I'll start grilling when you're back. I'll take him outside to run around." His lips press against the top of my head. "Take your time."

"Cool, be right back."

A few months ago, I would have pushed back, feeling guilty. But now I know he wants to hang out with Sawyer as much as my little boy wants to hang out with Angus, so I let him help. It's something I'm slowly getting used to. It's nice.

Sure enough, my favorite sweatshirt and sweatpants are in a duffle bag. The sweatshirt is a grey sweatshirt with The House logo on the front. On the back there's a fireman holding a hose that's shooting beer into a pint glass and the words, *"I got hosed at The House."* It's my go to comfort item. He also packed my brush and favorite hand lotion, because after wearing gloves and washing my hands a hundred times a day at work, my skin takes a beating. He's thought of everything.

After I'm changed, my skin is moisturized and smells like vanilla, I slip into my pillow slides. Angus thinks they're hideous, but I love them. I shuffle out back, but as soon as I open the sliding back door, I'm frozen to the spot. Sawyer is perched on the top of the picnic table and Daisy is sitting on the bench in front of him.

She's here.

"Hey, babe. We've got company," Angus says from my left where he's prepping the grill.

Stepping outside, I close the door behind me and cautiously make my way toward my son and his aunt. Rounding the table so I can see her face, I manage a, "Hi."

"Hey," is all she says.

"Mind if I sit?"

She shakes her head, and I plant myself beside her.

My instinct is to apologize again, but I'm not going to, because I was doing what was best for me and my son and for that I'm not sorry. Instead, I wait and let her take the lead.

Daisy pats the tabletop. "It's really a magnificent table, isn't it?"

I smile at the thought of what this table means to Charlie, Callen, and Daisy. "The table that started it all."

She chuckles but doesn't elaborate.

Close to a year ago, Charlie ended up in McKinnon's Hardware store to buy the supplies she needed to make this table. There she ran into Callen, who she hadn't seen in over two years. This table was also what prompted Daisy to ask her to build more for a wedding and from there, they went into business together. It holds a special place in all our hearts.

Sawyer turns so he can see me. "Mama, Aunt Dais here."

She's always been Aunt Daisy to him, even before she knew the truth. "She is."

He turns back to face her as he pushes his truck across the table.

"Mia, I'm sorry. I may have overreacted. To be honest, I'm not sure. Part of me is still hurt that you didn't trust me, while another part of me understands you were protecting our boy here."

"It's not that I didn't trust you. I knew if you knew, you would insist I tell Knox and that wasn't in the best interest of my son."

"So, why now?"

"Because I am in love with Angus and there was no way I could be with him if he didn't know. If Angus hadn't returned my feelings, I may have never said a word." I see a flash of anger in her eyes. "I'm sorry, it's the truth. My child's emotional well-being and distance from paparazzi and internet vultures is too important."

"As it should be." She ruffles his hair. "I heard everything you said at the park. It just took me a minute."

"I get it, too. First Angus and then Knox. It's a lot."

"There isn't anything about Cal I need to know, is there?" She winks.

Burying my face in my hands, I peek up at her. "Well..."

Her eyes bulge and behind her, Angus whips around, a horrified expression mirroring his sister's.

"Haha! You should see your faces. No! C'mon, you deserved a scare just for asking."

Pointing a spatula in my direction, Angus yells from the BBQ, "Not funny, Goof."

"He's right. That was mean."

"If I can't find humor in some of this, I'll go crazy."

"Your mama thinks she's funny." She tickles Sawyer, and he giggles with pure abandon.

His laugher is far and away the sweetest sound there is. It's impossible not to smile when you hear it.

"Hey, Daisy?" Her eyes look up at me. "You have a nephew."

Her smile is bright. "So, I do." Lowering her voice so her eavesdropping brother doesn't hear, she whispers, "And if things go the way I think they're going, I may have another sister soon."

She gets up from the table, bringing Sawyer with her. I join them, wrapping them up in a hug. "I love you both so much, Mia."

"I love you too, Dais."

She pulls back to look at me. "No more secrets? Unless it's for the safety of your child, of course."

"No more secrets."

"Good." Raising her voice to be sure Angus hears her next question, she asks, "So, is Angus as gross to live with as he was as a teenager?"

She finally came around.

Chapter Forty-Eight

Mia

"Boys! Where are you? Grandma is waiting for us to stop by before we head into town," I yell outside the locked bedroom door.

"We're almost done. We'll meet you in the living room," Angus replies.

I'm not sure what I was thinking when I agreed to give Angus control over Sawyer's Halloween costume this year. I didn't expect them to be locked away in our bedroom for so long. I'm a little worried.

My little boy is almost three, and this is the first year he really knows what's going on. We've practiced his Trick or Treat and he's been walking around with his pumpkin bucket for the last several days singing, "Trick or Treat. Smell my feet. Give me something good to eat." Angus taught him that *after* I agreed to letting him surprise me with his costume. My only requirement was that I didn't want a mask covering his face, because, well, he's just too cute to cover up.

Finally, I hear steps in the hallway. One is Sawyer's usual patter along with a loud smacking sound. When they come into view, I cover my mouth as I burst out into laughter.

"Twick o Tweet, Mama! We Goof's!"

"Yes, you sure are," I say to the toddler sized Goofy in front of me. He is absolutely adorable, with his enormous head and long ears, but it's Angus, in his matching costume, that includes giant feet that has me doubling over. He didn't skimp on a cheap costume either. His look is top tier. He's ridiculous in the best possible way.

"Happy Halloween, Goof," Angus says proudly. "Do you approve?"

Wrapping my arms around his neck, I place an approving kiss on his lips. "As long as I get to take it off you later, you have my seal of approval."

"Don't make promises you don't intend to keep, little lady." He tries to grab my butt, but his giant three fingered hand makes it impossible. "These damn gloves," he whispers.

"Mama, we go to Gamma's." Sawyer reminds us.

"You're right, buddy. Grandma Sharon is waiting to see you. We better get going."

Chapter Forty-Nine

Sawyer

Eight and a half years later.

"Hey, kiddo, how you doin'?" Mom asks from the doorway of my room.

"A little nervous, but I'm good."

"You know you don't have to do this?"

"I'm not nervous like that. I'm excited nervous."

"As long as you're sure?"

"Mom, it was my idea. Stop worrying."

"Okay, okay." She holds her hands up in surrender. "Let's get going then. Everyone's waiting."

It *was* my idea. After years of making wishes when I blew out my birthday candles, I decided to grant my own wish.

Since I'm the only one who could really grant it anyway. One day, a few weeks back, Dad and I were in the barn when I finally got the guts to talk to him.

"I know what I want for my birthday this year."

"What's that, buddy?"

Oh, man. Why am I so shaky? I've wanted to ask him this for so long. I just hope I'm not too late. Maybe he's changed his mind. Maybe Grace and Aidan are enough, and he doesn't need me to be his anymore.

"Sawyer?" he says, his head tilted to the side like he does when he's wants to know more.

"Well, you've been asking me for a really long time and I've always wanted to say yes, but I was too chicken. I don't know why."

"Bud, are you saying what I think you're saying?"

"Only if it's what you still want?"

"Of course it is!"

He drops the brush he was using on his horse and walks over to me. He picks me up in a great big bear hug and then sets me down on my boots.

"Have you talked to your mom and dad about this yet?"

It always makes me feel icky when he calls Knox my dad, but I know what he means. Knox is my father, but I call him papa. He has a say in the things I do, not just Mom and Angus. But it makes me feel bad for dad, because I've always lived with him.

"No, I wanted to make sure you were okay with it first."

"Bud, I know you have a father, but I hope you know I love you as much as I love your brother and sister. There is no

difference to me. You are my son, in here," he says, pointing to his chest.

I try not to feel embarrassed when tears sting my eyes, but I tell him what I've always felt to be true.

"Gus, you're my dad. I know Knox made me, and I do love him, he's a great papa, but you're my dad. I want to have the same last name as you and mom and Aidan and Grace."

He hugs me again. "I love you so much, Tater."

Finally ready and dressed in my wedding clothes, as I like to refer to my khaki pants and long-sleeved button-down shirt. It's because of all the buttons that it took me so long to get ready. I'm surprised to see Dad dressed up in a suit and tie. Mom, Gracie, and Aidan are also wearing their fancy wedding clothes. But it's Dad and his big smile that makes me so happy. I knew this was a big deal to him, but it makes me feel all weird inside to see how excited he is. It's more than happiness, but I'm not sure what you'd call it.

Angus can't adopt me, because Papa Knox is my actual dad. He's always around and we go riding at least once a week unless he's out of town. I know he loves me, and I love him too, but Gus has been my dad for as long as I can remember.

When I was born, Mom gave me her last name. Then she married Angus, and they had my brother and sister. They're all McKinnon's. Technically, I am too, but at school I'm still Sawyer Powell, because that's what my birth certificate says. When I turned ten, Mom asked me if changing my last name to McKinnon was something I wanted to do. It had been brought up before, but she said since I was double digits now, they would leave it up to me. When I said no, she said if I ever changed my mind to let her know. I wanted to say yes, but not for the reason I should have wanted to.

I was proud to be related to Knox McKinnon, but I wanted the McKinnon name mostly so I could be like Angus, and I felt bad about that. It's nothing against Knox, he's just not Angus.

Now, seeing the person who has always been my dad all dressed up and grinning for a silly name change at the courthouse, I'm so glad I finally said yes.

"You look nice," I say to him, pulling on his tie.

"Thanks. You clean up nice, too, Tater."

"You didn't all have to get dressed up for the judge to sign a piece of paper."

"Buddy, this is a big day for all of us. Even if it is just a piece of paper," Dad assures me.

"C'mon, we're running late. Everyone in the truck," Mom commands and, of course, we all do as she says. There is nothing Mom hates more than being late.

It doesn't take us long to get to town and once we park the truck and all climb out, my tummy feels nervous. Mom holds my hand on the way in, while Dad carries Gracie and holds Aidan's hand. Goose Hollow is small and so is the courthouse. My parents know the lady at the front desk, and she tell us to go on in through the big brown doors to the left.

When the double doors open, I can't believe it. Grandma and Grandpa are here all the way from Florida! Papa Knox and my stepmom Ryan are here, and so is Grandma Sharon, Uncle Cal, Aunt Charlie, and all my cousins. Aunt Daisy is blowing one of those things we make noise with on New

Year's and Uncle Owen is holding his camera up, recording us as we walk in. Everyone is clapping and cheering.

All the attention makes my cheeks hot.

Dad hands Gracie to Grandma Sharon. Grandpa Powell takes Aidan because Mom, Dad, and I need to take our paper up to the judge's table. Papa comes with us because he and Mom need to sign the paper before the lady can stamp it.

They each sign and when the ladies' stamp clunks on the table, it makes me jump, but Dad and Papa each put a hand on my shoulders. My nervous nerves go away because I feel safe with both of my dads and my whole family around me.

We watch the judge sign the paper and then he says, "Young man, by the state of Oregon and the town of Goose Hollow, you are officially a McKinnon."

Everyone goes crazy. They clap and yell and Dad picks me up in the best bear hug he's ever given me. When he sets me on my feet, he bends down so he can look at me in my eyes. "I love you, kiddo."

I feel too much to say anything, so I just throw my arms around his neck and hug him again. When I release him, Mom is waiting for her hug and after her is Papa.

"Come here, kid," he says in his way that sounds serious, but I know means he's trying hard not to get mushy. He's taller than Dad and has to bend way down, but he gives me a good hug, too. While I'm in his arms, he says, "I'm prouder of you than you will ever know. It's an honor for you to carry on the McKinnon name. I hope you know how much we all love you. How much *I* love you."

He's still holding me when I nod my reply, but I don't let go of him just yet. I feel so much my eyes sting. And I don't want him to see me crying.

Because I do know I'm loved. All the people here today love me, and I feel lucky. And Mom's right, having two dads is kinda awesome.

I've always wanted the world to know I'm a McKinnon and now I am.

"Hey, Sawyer," Gracie calls out.

I turn around, and as soon as I do, my family starts singing, and a cake with candles appears out of nowhere.

Today I turned eleven and became a McKinnon.

Best birthday ever!

Want to take another trip to Goose Hollow or fall in love with another sweet and sexy Lisa Shelby romance?

Join Lisa's reader group, Lisa Shelby's Love Geeks over on Facebook and follow her everywhere @lisashelbybooks to stay up to date.

Don't forget to sign up for Lisa's newsletter for your FREE copy of We Are Tonight!
Sign up at www.lisashelbybooks.com

Also by Lisa Shelby

Standalone Novels

Disregarded Heart
Blackbird

Series

The Only in Goose Hollow Series
Only Wanna Dance With You
The Only Heart That Matters
The Only Thing That's Real
It Could Only Be You

The Between the Pines Series
Raised On It
Bottle It Up
Get your FREE copy of We Are Tonight when you signup
for my newsletter at www.lisashelbybooks.com

Lisa Shelby is a USA Today bestselling contemporary romance author, a self-proclaimed love geek and cake-pop addict. Born and raised in the Pacific Northwest, this is still where Lisa calls home with her husband and their dogs. When she isn't sitting in a coffee shop writing her next happily ever after, you can find Lisa with her husband likely eating tacos, traveling, listening to live music, or binging way too many TV shows.

Join Lisa's Reader Group: Lisa Shelby's Love Geeks